* * * * * * *

Turning my attention to the bag in front of my car, I quickly discovered that it was one of those very large black plastic lawn bags that people use to put leaves in. The bag appeared to be full. The bumper of my car was almost touching it. I had come within an inch of hitting it.

As I reached down to pick up the bag and move it out of the street, I sort of grumbled under my breath something about how people should be more careful when they are hauling trash. It wasn't until I tried to pick it up that I found it to be very heavy. It was much heavier than I expected a bag of leaves to weigh, even wet leaves.

Although it looked like a lawn bag full of leaves, there had to be something else in it to be so heavy. I tried to pick it up again. When I did, the bag split open at one of the bottom corners exposing a human foot. I let go of the bag immediately and took a quick step back as I looked at the foot.

Seeing a foot sticking out of the lawn bag was the last thing I had expected to see. However, after a couple of seconds, the surprise of seeing a human foot wore off. It was then that I realized that the toenails appeared to be painted. That was enough to make me think there might be a woman inside the bag, although in this day and age it didn't necessarily mean it was a woman.

* * * * * * *

Other titles by J.E. Terrall

Western Short Stories	Western Novels
The Old West	Conflict in Elkhorn Valley
The Frontier	Lazy A Ranch
Untamed Land	(A Modern Western)

Romance Novels	Mystery/Suspense/Thriller
Balboa Rendezvous	I Can See Clearly
Sing for Me	The Return Home
Return to Me	The Inheritance
Forever Yours	

Nick McCord Mysteries
Vol – 1 Murder at Gill's Point
Vol – 2 Death of a Flower
Vol – 3 A Dead Man's Treasure
Vol – 4 Blackjack, A Game to Die For
Vol – 5 Death on the Lakes

Peter Blackstone Mysteries	Frank Tidsdale Mysteries
Murder in the Foothills	Death by Design
Murder on the Crystal Blue	

MURDER OF MY LOVE

A PETER BLACKSTONE MYSTERY

by

J.E. Terrall

ISBN: 978-0-9844591-1-7

This is a work of fiction. Names, characters, and incidents are either a product of the author's imagination or are used fictitiously, and any resemblance to actual persons, living or dead, is purely coincidental.

Printed in the United States of America
First printing / 2012   www.lulu.com
Second printing / 2013   www.creatspace.com

Cover: Front cover was done by author, J.E Terrall

Book Layout/
Formating: J.E. Terrall
                    Custer, South Dakota

MURDER OF MY LOVE

To
Dannette, a good friend and supporter.
Thanks, Danny

CHAPTER ONE

IT HAD BEEN RAINING off and on in the Denver area for the past few days and today was no exception. The cold September rain splattered against my windshield as I drove my girlfriend, Jennifer, back to her apartment. The windshield wipers seemed to be keeping time to the music on the radio which was soft and slow. Jennifer was sitting beside me with her hand resting lightly on my leg. We were feeling very close to each other.

We had spent the evening enjoying an excellent dinner and some dancing at one of our favorite nightclubs. Although the weather was less than ideal, it had not dampened our enjoyment of our night out together.

It was late when we arrived at Jennifer's apartment. I took her hand as I walked her to the door. After sharing several goodnight kisses and saying goodnight several times, I reluctantly returned to my car and headed across town to my apartment. It would have been the end of a perfect evening if I could have stayed the night with her, but I had a meeting with a potential client in the morning.

Jennifer had to go to work early, too. New computers were being installed in her office, and she had to be there early to transfer information from the old system to the new one. She also had to train the office personnel in the use of the new system.

As I drove back to my apartment, I could not help but think of Jennifer. Jennifer and I had been friends and occasionally lovers for a good many years. Over the past few months I had been seeing no one else. As far as I knew, she had not been seeing anyone else, either. Our relationship seemed to be getting a bit more serious with each passing week, not that I minded.

My mind was filled with pleasant thoughts of Jennifer. My thoughts were mostly about the evening we had just shared together and where our relationship might be headed. She had worn her sexy black dress that I liked to see her in, and I had on my best suit. The memory of her warm breath on my neck, the feel of her arms around me and her body moving slowly against me when we danced seemed to consume my thoughts as I drove along the rain covered streets of Denver.

Jennifer was one of the sexiest women I have ever known. She had a body that any eighteen-year-old girl would kill for. She was also a warm and caring person, although she could stand up for herself when it was necessary. She was smart, too.

Needless to say, I didn't really have my mind on what I was doing when I turned the corner off Kentucky Avenue onto Downing Street. That part of Downing Street ran along the west side of Washington Park.

As I turned the corner, the headlights of my car suddenly lit up something large, black and shiny lying in the street. I slammed on the brakes. The tires slid a little on the wet pavement. The last thing I wanted was to find out when it was too late that there was something in the bag that could damage my car.

I was still holding my breath when the car came to a complete stop. It took a minute or so for my heart to start beating again. Once I was able to breathe normally, I looked out over the hood, but could not see the bag. I was sure that I had not run over it, but I might have hit it. I had not felt any kind of a bump; so I was reasonably sure that I had not hit the bag very hard, if at all. If I had hit it, it had not been hard enough to do any damage. I let out a sigh of relief at the thought that I had managed to avoid doing any damage to the car.

After turning on my four-way flashers in the hope that no one else would come around the corner and run smack into me, I checked for traffic. When I didn't see any, I got out to see what it was that I had come very close to running over.

I took a quick look around as I walked toward the front of the car. At first the street appeared to be deserted, probably due to the lateness of the hour. However, before I could move around in front of the car, my attention was drawn to the sudden sound of the rapid beat of footsteps running down the street. I looked up and saw the dark figure of a man running down the street next to the curb. He jumped into the passenger's side of a car that was parked about halfway down the block. The car quickly sped away without turning on the headlights. With the quickness of the man's departure, it was obvious that someone had been waiting in the car with the engine running.

When the car got to the corner, the brake lights came on as it slowed only slightly to make the turn. The car skidded on the wet pavement and slammed into the curb, then quickly disappeared around the corner. The car apparently had not hit the curb hard enough to make it come to a stop, but I was sure that there would be enough damage to the tires or wheels that it would probably require some attention at a repair shop very soon. The collision with the curb certainly would have left some kind of marks on the curb as well.

Everything happened so fast that I was unable to get a good look at the guy or at the car. Other than the fact that it was a dark colored late model sports sedan with fancy chrome wheel rims, I couldn't be sure about much of anything else. It was too far away and too dark for me to see what make of car it was, or to get even a part of the license plate number. The only thing I could be sure of was the license plate was a Colorado plate.

I had no idea what was going on. I wasn't even sure that whoever was in the car that sped away had anything to do with the bag. However, I couldn't think of one logical reason for the fast getaway if they had nothing to do with the bag in the street.

Turning my attention to the bag in front of my car, I quickly discovered that it was one of those very large black plastic lawn bags that people use to put leaves in. The bag appeared to be full, and the bumper of my car was almost touching it. I had come within an inch of hitting it.

As I reached down to pick up the bag and move it out of the street, I sort of grumbled under my breath something about how people should be more careful when they are hauling trash. It wasn't until I tried to pick it up that I found it to be very heavy. It was much heavier than I expected a bag of leaves to weigh, even wet leaves.

Although it looked like a lawn bag full of leaves, there had to be something else in it to be so heavy. I tried to pick it up again. When I did, the bag split open at one of the bottom corners exposing a human foot. I let go of the bag immediately and took a quick step back as I looked at the foot.

Seeing a foot sticking out of the lawn bag was the last thing I expected to see at that moment. However, after a couple of seconds, when the surprise of seeing a human foot wore off, I took another look at the foot. I realized that the toenails appeared to be painted a deep dark red and the foot was fairly small. That was enough to make me think there might be a woman inside the bag. Although in this day and age, painted toenails didn't necessarily mean it was a woman.

Grabbing the bag at the top, I tried to get the plastic closer off the bag so I could open it. Any other time it would have popped right open, especially if I didn't want it to open. But when I do want those things to open, it becomes very stubborn and difficult. It took a couple of hard pulls to get it to open.

Once I finally got it opened enough to see what was inside, I found the face of what appeared to be a young woman. She was staring back at me. The woman's face was covered with small bits of leaves and twigs. Pulling the bag open a little further, it became clear that she was surrounded by leaves and other lawn debris. Someone had obviously gone to a lot of trouble to stuff the woman in the bag.

The woman had what looked like black or very dark brown hair and possibly brown eyes, though it was hard to tell in the dim light of a streetlight that was several yards down the street. The headlights of my car did little to help me see because of the black bag.

As I looked at the woman, it seemed that she was looking up at me as if pleading for help. I had seen enough bodies in my life to know that she was dead. It was obvious that there was nothing I could do for her. However, if I had to guess, I would say that she had been dead for several hours, maybe longer, but then I'm no expert on the subject. Right then, I needed to call the police.

I returned to my car, sat down on the front seat and placed a 9-1-1 call on my cell phone. After I identified myself and explained where I was located, I told the 9-1-1 dispatcher what I had found. She asked me to stay on the line, not to touch anything and to please remain at the scene until the police arrived. I assured her that I would stay at the scene, but I could see no reason for me to stay on the line until a police unit arrived so I hung up. It wasn't as if things were going to change before the police arrived.

I got back out of my car and walked around to the front of it. The rain had stopped, at least for the moment, but the pavement was still wet and so was the plastic bag. As I looked at the bag, I wondered what had really happened.

Looking down at the body, I wondered why she had been stuffed into a plastic lawn bag with a bunch of leaves and other lawn debris. The fact that the leaves were wet indicated to me that they had been stuffed in the bag at the same time as the woman, which would have been sometime after it started raining. If I remember correctly, it started to rain off and on several days ago.

I turned and looked down the street toward where the sport sedan had sped around the corner and disappeared. I wondered if the guy that ran down the street to the waiting car had dumped the bag in the street. Maybe he had come back to move the bag from the street so no one would hit it, but that didn't seem to be a very likely scenario.

As I thought about it, it was unlikely that he was coming back to move the bag out of the street. If he had been, why did he run away? After all, why would he need to run away so fast that the driver almost wrecked the car trying to get out of there if they had done nothing wrong?

Had the person driving the car run over the woman? A quick look at the bag told me that it didn't look like it had been run over. That kind of a low slung car would have ripped the bag open and strewn most of the contents all over the street. It would have probably damaged the under-carriage of the car as well. The bag showed no marks on it to indicate it had been run over.

I began to think that whoever was in the car may have killed the woman and dumped her body in the street for someone like me to run over. If that were the case, the fact that they ran might indicate that they had not expected someone to come around the corner so quickly. After all, the hour was late and traffic was very light around the park.

Maybe they thought if someone ran over her, it would be harder for the police to identify her, determine how long she had been dead, or figure out what had happened to her. Not very smart thinking with all the high tech lab tests they can do now days. But criminals often don't think, which is why they get caught.

The next question that came to mind was why? What reason did anyone have for killing the young woman, if in fact she had been murdered? It occurred to me that there was always the possibility that she had not been killed by those in the car, but that they had simply dumped the body for the person who had. That still left the question of who had killed her - an open question.

The woman looked to be young enough to have been a college student. Maybe it was an accident which scared whoever was with her. She wouldn't be the first young woman to die at some frat party and then be dumped somewhere else in an effort to protect the fraternity. I knew that didn't happen very often, but it had happened.

I had done a lot of speculating while I waited for the police, but I still didn't have anything that would tell me why the woman was dead, and why her body had been dumped in the street. I looked around then knelt down to take a closer look at the woman.

Since I had already ripped the lawn bag open, my fingerprints would be on the outside of the bag near the top. I was very careful not to touch anything inside the bag. It would be easy to explain my fingerprints on the outside of the bag where I had held the bag while I ripped it open, but not so easy to explain fingerprints anywhere else, especially inside the bag.

Using my pen, I put it in the hole I had made in the bag and lifted it open for a better look inside. The young woman didn't appear to be wearing any jewelry, at least none that I could see. In fact, she didn't appear to have any clothes on, although it was hard to tell with all the leaves in the bag, the way her body was curled up, and with so little light. From what little I could see of her in my headlights, the woman had probably been killed, stripped of her clothes and anything else that might help identify her, and then stuffed in the bag with the leaves.

A lot of thoughts ran through my brain while I waited for the police. Was it a crime of passion? Maybe she had been raped and then killed. Then again maybe it was something entirely different. I tended to lean toward something different for several reasons.

A crime of passion doesn't usually have so much care taken to make it hard to identify the victim. It would take time to get a bag, rake up some leaves, put the body in the bag and stuff leaves around her, and then transport the body all the way to the park to dispose of it.

If she had been raped then killed, someone might have gone to the trouble of putting her in a lawn bag, but why? Maybe it was an attempt to contaminate any evidence by stuffing the bag full of leaves. It was unlikely that she would have been dropped off where she was so quickly found if she had been raped.

In the final analysis of the situation, it was my guess that it wouldn't take the police lab very long to figure out what had happened to the woman and what the cause of death was. It might, however, take longer to figure out who she was.

I began to hear the sounds of a siren in the distance and decided that it might be best if I wasn't leaning over the body when the police arrived. It has been my experience that there are some policemen who do not like private investigators. I returned to the side of my car and leaned back against the front fender with my arms crossed and waited.

IT TOOK A FEW MINUTES for the first police car to arrive at the scene. I had no idea how far away he had been when he got the call, but I could hear the siren for sometime before I saw the red and blue flashing lights of the black-and-white unit coming toward me from the other side of Washington Park.

When the black-and-white came around the corner, I watched and waited for it to come to a stop. The police car pulled up behind my car. A tall and rather athletic looking young policeman got out of the car. From where he had parked, it would have been almost impossible for him to see the lawn bag.

"Are you Peter Blackstone?" he asked as he walked toward me.

"Yes."

"Did you call 9-1-1 and report that you found a body in a plastic bag?"

"Yes, I did."

"Where is it?"

"In front of my car."

"Did you hit it?" the officer asked as he started walking around to the front of my car.

"No, but it was close. My car is right where it stopped. I haven't moved it," I replied without moving away from the fender of my car.

As he stepped around in front of my car, I heard his breath catch. I could also see the look on his face in the light from my headlights. The fact that he knew what he would find still didn't stop him from being a little shocked at the sight.

I continued to watch him as he knelt down and looked at the woman. After a few seconds, he looked over the lawn bag and the front of my car, not touching anything. I could tell by the expression on his face that he knew that I had not hit the bag.

He stood up and walked back toward me. As he did, I could hear him talking on his radio. He was asking for an ambulance and a homicide detective. When he had finished on the radio, he looked at me.

"While we wait for the homicide detective, I have a few questions to ask you," he said as he stood looking at me.

"No problem."

He asked the usual questions like my name and address, and what I was doing at the location. I showed him my Driver's License, my Private Investigator's License, and my concealed weapons permit. After he took a bunch of notes for his report, I answered his questions. Other than questions that would identify me, most of his questions had to do with what I was doing there, and what had happened. I had no reason not to tell how I happened to be in that area, or about what I saw.

I had just finished answering his questions when I heard the sounds of another siren. The ambulance arrived first. The officer talked briefly to the EMT personnel. I watched as they made sure that the woman was dead. They called in for the Coroner, then walked over and stood on the curb to make sure that no one disturbed the body.

WITHIN ABOUT TEN MINUTES a dark colored car came around the corner with a flashing red light on the dash. It was followed only seconds later by a dark blue van with the word "Coroner" printed in bright yellow on the side.

There was no doubt in my mind that the homicide detective was in the car. As he got out of his car, I was pleased to see that it was Captain MacDonald.

Mac and I have known each other for over fifteen years, but I wouldn't say we are friends. However, we do have a healthy respect for each other, and that goes a long way with me. We have helped each other from time to time, and we have gotten in each other's way from time to time; but we get along pretty well for the most part.

When he saw me standing next to my car, he simply nodded then walked on by. He stood over the bag looking down at the body while he slipped on rubber gloves. He knelt down next to the bag. I couldn't see what he was doing, but my guess was that he was looking at the woman and seeing the same things I had seen.

After a couple of minutes, he stood up, nodded at the Coroner and talked to one of the EMTs for a couple of minutes.

It was clear to me that he was giving him instructions. He then came over to talk to me.

"What's your part in all this, Pete?"

"Nothing more than I almost ran over her."

"You want to fill me in on everything you know?"

"Sure."

I spent the next five to ten minutes telling him what I heard, what I had seen and what I knew, which wasn't very much. I even suggested that he check out the curb for trace evidence where the car had slid into it. I was pretty sure that he would find traces of rubber from the tires as well as metal and chrome from the wheels.

"That's about it. I didn't get a good look at the car. I would not be able to identify it except for the damaged right side wheels. As for the person who drove the car, I couldn't tell if it was a man or a woman. I didn't get a real good look at the guy that ran off and got in the car except to tell you that he looked like he was in pretty good shape.

"As for a description of him, he was maybe six-one or six-two and probably weighed somewhere around a hundred and eighty to two hundred pounds. He was wearing a dark colored rain coat, probably black, and no hat. His hair was dark brown or black. I'm pretty sure he was a white guy. Like I said, he seemed to be in good shape because he moved pretty well. I only saw him from behind. That's about all I can tell you. Sorry."

"Can you think of anything else that might help us find this guy?"

"I'm afraid not," I said after thinking about it for a moment.

"Thanks. I don't think that will be much help, but it's better than nothing."

"Sorry. If I think of anything else, I'll give you a call."

"Do that. Thanks, Pete. I'll call you if I have any more questions."

"Sure," I said, than walked back to my car.

As I was getting in, I could see a woman in the window of a house across the street. I had noticed her earlier, but decided not to mention it to Mac. Besides, if I knew him, he would be knocking on every door in the neighborhood and questioning everyone to find out if anyone had seen anything.

AS I STARTED TO PULL AWAY from the scene, I glanced over toward the house again. This time I caught a glimpse of something moving in the bushes at the end of the porch. I wasn't sure what it was, but I got the impression that there was someone hiding there. It could have been a neighbor that didn't want to be seen for some reason, but I didn't think so.

I turned the corner at the next street and drove to the alley that ran down the block behind the houses. I stopped and shut off my headlights, but didn't turn in. The alley was dark and there was very little light. I waited.

It wasn't long before I saw a shadowy figure run across the alley. Since I didn't see any cars parked in the alley, I guessed that he was just passing through, probably headed for the next street over. I wondered if he had a car parked on Corona Street, or if he was just some guy who was curious about what was going on.

I pulled up to the corner of Corona Street and Ohio Ave and stopped. It wasn't but a few seconds before I saw the same shadowy figure come out from between the houses, run across the street and jump into a car. From his size and the way he moved, I was pretty sure that it was the same guy that I had seen running away from the scene. He got in on the passenger's side of a black sports sedan parked at the curb. The car didn't pull away from the curb right away. I could make out two people sitting in the car, they appeared to be talking.

I turned on my headlights then turned the corner. The driver had probably seen my headlights as I turned the corner because the car pulled away from the curb in a hurry. It sped down the street at a high rate of speed. There was no doubt that the driver wanted to leave the area as quickly as possible.

The car sped down the street for a couple of blocks before it turned a corner. By the time I got to the corner it had disappeared down one of the alleys. The way the driver was driving, I figured that I would have little chance of catching up to him. I seriously doubted that I would be able to get close enough to get a license plate number, anyway. I did, however, see the car as it passed under a couple of street lights before it got too far away. It looked like a BMW or Lexus. I couldn't be sure which, but it was a black sports sedan for sure.

Since I had no real interest in the case, I could see no reason to risk my neck, and my new car, giving him chase. The case was in the hands of the police. I decided that it was time to head for home and try to get some sleep since I had an appointment in the morning. I could call Mac first thing in the morning and tell him what I saw, and give him a little better description of the car.

THE DRIVE BACK TO MY APARTMENT was uneventful. It had started to drizzle again and was turning a little colder. If it got much colder there was a chance of getting a little snow. I doubted that any snow we got would stick to the pavement as it had been fairly warm over the past week or so. Some of it might stick on the lawns for a little while.

I turned into the apartment complex and drove around back to where my garage was located. After putting my car in the garage, I went directly to the backdoor of my apartment and went inside.

It was getting pretty late and I needed to get some rest. Once in bed, I laid there staring up at the ceiling. My thoughts turned to the events that had occurred at Washington Park. My mind was full of questions, but none that I could answer with any hope of knowing if I had the right answers.

I wondered if I was supposed to have run over the body. That hardly seemed likely. How would anyone know that I would be coming around that corner at that very moment? The only answer I could come up with was that nobody would know I would be at that place, at that time. The body had to have been dropped off for just anyone coming around the corner to run over, or to simply find it. I just happened to be the lucky one. Lucky, indeed. Lucky I didn't run over her.

The one thing that didn't make any sense to me was why drop off a body in the middle of a city street in a residential neighborhood? There could only be two possible answers. One was that it accidentally fell out of the trunk of the car, but that seemed very unlikely. The second was so it would be found quickly, but why? If whoever killed the girl didn't want anyone to know she was dead, there were dozens of places in the area I could think of where a body could be dumped and not be found for God knows how long.

Why was that beautiful young woman killed in the first place? She had been a very pretty girl from what little I saw of her. She was probably in her early-to-mid twenties. She couldn't have been a very large girl and still fit in that bag with all the leaves. What did she get into that got her killed? Maybe she was just in the wrong place at the wrong time.

It was getting very late and none of my questions were going to get answered tonight. I had other things that I should be thinking about, and one of them was getting some sleep.

It helped to put my mind to rest a little when I decided that I would have a talk with Mac in the morning and find out what he knew about the woman's death. I would also tell him about the car.

I reached over and shut off the bedside lamp, turned on my side, closed my eyes and tried to shut down my mind for what was left of the night. It took awhile, but I finally drifted off to sleep.

CHAPTER TWO

WHEN MORNING CAME, I found myself waking up to the irritating sound of my alarm clock. I could still see in my mind the face of the young woman staring up at me from the plastic lawn bag. The first thought that came into my head was, had she been identified yet. I seriously doubted that the police would have found out who she was so quickly, but a call to Mac would answer that question. It would also give me a chance to tell him what else I saw in the area last night.

It came to mind that I had a meeting with a couple from Kansas in my office this morning. From our phone conversation, I knew they wanted to talk to me about their missing daughter. The idea flashed through my mind that the two girls, the one in the plastic lawn bag and the one missing, could be one-in-the-same person. I quickly set that thought aside as highly unlikely. The odds of the woman in the bag and the missing girl being the same person were way off the charts.

My first order of business was to take a shower. I have always liked a shower in the morning as it tended to wake up not only my body, but my mind as well. I needed a clear head.

After my shower, I dressed and made my breakfast. It was my usual practice not to listen to the news before I finished breakfast. Even though it ran against my grain, I still had an urge to turn on the radio to find out if there was any news on the body that was in the street last night. In spite of the urge, I was able to resist it and keep my few minutes of ignorant bliss, which I had always treasured, while I ate breakfast.

Once breakfast was over and I had cleared the table, I grabbed my coat and headed for the car. During the twenty minutes or so it normally took me to get to my office, I listened to the news. There was nothing on the local news other than a short reference to a woman found in a plastic lawn bag near

Washington Park. There were no other details, which was what I had expected since it happened late last night.

It was my guess that the newspeople had gotten most, if not all, of their information by listening in on the police radio. I doubted that they had had a chance to interview the detective involved in the investigation. Without interviewing the lead investigator, they were not likely to get any additional information that might provide some details by news time.

I would be willing to bet that there were newspeople crawling all over the police station this morning trying to get details. I doubted that they would get anything since it was the practice of the Police Department not to give out any information without first talking to the lead investigator regarding what they could release to the media.

I was sure the police were not saying anything. But then there was a strong possibility they didn't know anything, yet. With nothing to go on, it would probably take several days, maybe more, to figure out the name of the victim. To figure out the cause of death would take the medical examiner and the lab at least two to four days to complete the tests. It would probably take a bit longer to figure out why she was dumped in the street by the park. There was no telling how long it would take to discover where she had been killed, since it was pretty obvious that she had not been killed where she was found.

I ARRIVED AT MY OFFICE a few minutes before eight-thirty. My appointment with Mr. and Mrs. Dwight Sutherland wasn't until nine. While I waited for them, I thought it would be a good idea to give Mac a call to tell him about the guy I had seen in the alley. I would also tell him about the car that was in such a hurry to leave the area.

I placed a call to the First Precinct. The phone was answered by Sergeant Russell.

"Denver Police Department, Sergeant Russell. Is this an emergency?"

"No."

"How may I help you?"

"Hi, Russell. It's Peter Blackstone."

"How are yah, Pete?"

"Pretty good. Is Captain MacDonald in?"

"Yeah. I'll put you through to him. Hang on."

"Thanks."

It didn't take but a minute or so for Mac to get on the phone.

"Hi, Pete. You got something else for me because I've got nothing?"

"Maybe. Last night, right after I left you at the scene, I saw some guy run across the alley between Downing and Corona Streets. He cut through the yards over to Corona Street and jumped into a car. I tried to get a license number for you, but he wasted no time in getting out of there. I followed him for a little ways, but lost him," I explained.

"Did you get a chance to see what kind of a car it was?"

"As it passed under a couple of street lights, I was able to determine that it was a black sports sedan. It was either a BMW or a Lexus, probably a Lexus. It was definitely a black sports sedan with what looked like very expensive custom chrome rims. I can't say for sure, but they looked like they might have been the same kind of rims I saw on the car that sped away from the scene. They were certainly not your run-of-the-mill chrome rims. They were custom rims. I'm sure of that."

"That covers half the sports sedans in Denver. I'm afraid that won't help very much," he said with a disappointed tone in his voice.

"Sorry, but that's the best I can do. I think I could pick out the chrome rims if I saw them again. The ones on the right side of the car had to have suffered some severe damage hitting that curb."

"There are a lot of places to get them around here."

"Maybe not. These had to be special. Maybe even special order rims."

"If he damaged the rims as much as you say, he may try to get new ones," Mac said as he began to think about it. "I'll check out all the shops that sell chrome wheels in the metro area, especially the ones that sell high-end or custom chrome rims."

"Good. I'll talk to you later. Let me know what you find out."

"Okay. Thanks, and call me if you think of anything else."

"Will do," I said then hung up.

I HAD NO MORE THAN HUNG UP the phone when there was a knock on the door to my office. I turned to see two people standing there looking at me. The look on their faces gave me a clue as to how concerned they were, but about what I had only a hint. I stood up and motioned for them to come in.

"I take it you are Mr. and Mrs. Sutherland?"

"That is correct," Mr. Sutherland replied. "I'm sorry about being a little early."

"No problem. Come in and sit down, please."

I motioned them to chairs at a conference table near the window. Before we sat down Mr. Sutherland reached out to shake my hand. As we shook hands, I noticed that he had a strong grip and that his hands were rough. It was obvious that he worked with his hands.

They sat down in the chairs at the table while I sat down across the table from them. I took a minute to look them over while I sat down.

Mr. Sutherland was wearing a dark blue suit and a tie that didn't seem to go very well with the suit. He didn't look like he felt very comfortable in a suit. From the fit of it, I would have guessed that he probably had had it for sometime and didn't wear it very often, probably only to weddings and funerals. He struck me as the jeans and work shirt type of guy.

He was rather tall and appeared to be in good physical shape. The dark tan of his hands and face gave me the impression that he probably worked outside most of the time, either in construction or maybe farming. The tan on his face stopped at his forehead which indicated that he wore some kind of a hat most of the time. He wasn't wearing a hat now.

Mrs. Sutherland was a rather plain looking woman, yet rather nice looking. The coat and dress she wore were simple and practical, nothing very fancy or flashy. She used very little makeup, but she didn't really need it. She probably did her own hair. Her eyes were dark brown as was her hair. There was something familiar about her, but at the moment I couldn't figure out what it was, or why I thought so.

"I understand that you drove all the way in from Kansas to see me. From your phone call yesterday afternoon, I understand that your daughter is missing. Is that correct?" I asked.

"Yes, Mr. Blackstone. We heard that you are the best investigator in the Denver area," Mr. Sutherland said getting right to the point.

"I take it she went missing here in the Denver area?"

"Yes."

"What is your daughter's name?"

"Emily. Emily Sutherland," Mrs. Sutherland replied.

"Have you reported her as missing to the Denver police?"

"Yes, sir, but they didn't give us a lot of hope that they could find her," Mr. Sutherland said.

"What makes you think that I can find her?" I asked.

"Well," he said, then glanced toward his wife before looking at me again. "The police have a lot of other things to do. We understand that. We figured that if we hired you to find our daughter, you would be able to devote all your time to finding her. Is that right?"

Finding a missing person is hard work especially if they don't wish to be found. As for putting all my time into finding their daughter, it showed me that he didn't think I had anything else to do. Luckily for them, that just happened to be the case. I didn't have any other clients at the moment.

"How long has she been missing?" I asked, ignoring his question.

"We're not sure."

"Would you explain that for me, please?"

"You see, Emily always calls home on Wednesday evening. A week ago last Wednesday we didn't get a call from her. We didn't get a call from her this past Wednesday, either."

"Emily always calls at seven o'clock on Wednesdays," Mrs. Sutherland added.

"That's seven o'clock our time," Mr. Sutherland said. "We live in the Central time zone."

"Are you sure that she wasn't out on a date or maybe out with friends? Maybe she just got busy and forgot to call?"

"She has always called at the same time every Wednesday for over a year. Yesterday and last week were the first times that she didn't call," Mrs. Sutherland said.

I was beginning to understand their concern. Most parents get concerned when there is a sudden change in their children's routine or behavior. This was certainly a change that would worry most parents.

"Did you try to call her?"

"Yes, of course. All we got was her answering machine," Mrs. Sutherland said. "We left messages for her to call us back, but she never returned our calls."

"We even called the police and ask them to stop by and see if she was okay. They called back and told us that she wasn't at her apartment. That's when we filed a missing person report with the Denver Police," Mr. Sutherland added.

"If what you are saying is correct, she could be missing anywhere from eight days to almost two weeks."

"That would be right, Mr. Blackstone."

"What was Emily doing here in Denver?"

"She's attending school. Emily goes to the art school here in Denver."

"Would that be the Denver School for Artists?"

"Yes. Have you heard of it?"

"Yes, I have. Is she doing well?"

"Yes," Mrs. Sutherland replied with the look of a proud mother. "Emily has been doing very well. You should see some of her work."

"Mary," Mr. Sutherland said to cut her off.

Mary looked at her husband, then looked down at her lap. It was clear that Mr. Sutherland wanted to keep things focused on their missing daughter. That was easy for me to understand, but the more I knew about their daughter the easier it would make things for me.

"It's all right, Dwight. You don't mind if I call you Dwight, do you?"

"No, of course not."

"Good. You can call me Peter. It's important that I know as much about Emily as possible. The more I know about her, the better my chances are of finding her."

"Oh," he said, looking a little embarrassed.

"The last time you talked to your daughter, what was the conversation about?"

"Mary, you were the last to talk to her. You tell him."

"We talked about money mostly. It is very expensive at that art school."

"Was she worried about her expenses?"

"Yes, but that was nothing unusual. We don't have a lot of money, but we manage," Dwight said.

"So money was a problem for her?"

"No. Well, yes. She was always a little worried about what it was costing us to let her go to that school. But I told Emily we would send her some money to help her."

"Do you know if she had any kind of job?"

"Yes. She said that she was going to start a part-time job the next week. She would be able to make a little money doing some modeling at the school. Emily said that it would help pay some of her expenses."

"When was she to start this new job?"

"It would have been the Monday before her next call to us. We were hoping to find out more about her job the next week, but she didn't call."

"Did she say what kind of modeling she would be doing?"

"She said it would be modeling in one of the art classes. Ah – figure drawing – or something like that, I think she said. Emily assured us that it was okay and that it would not interfere with her regular classes," Mrs. Sutherland said.

If my limited knowledge of "figure drawing" class was correct, it meant that she would be posing in the nude or partially nude while other students in the class drew her. It was a fairly common practice to have live models in many art schools. I wondered if there was more to it than simply posing for students so that they could practice drawing the human form.

"Mr. Blackstone, do you think you can help us?" Dwight asked.

Dwight looked at me with eyes that were pleading for help. If it was a straight missing person case, it would not take me very long to figure out what happened to her. The thing was that there were few straight missing person cases. The problem with missing person cases is that they often turned out to be so much more.

About the only thing I could do for the Sutherlands was to take a few days to look into it. I would not be able to assure them that I would be able to find her. I felt I needed to explain that to them as well as give them some idea of what it might cost them.

"These types of cases often tend to get very expensive because it takes a lot of time and effort to find the person missing, especially if they don't want to be found."

"Do you think that she doesn't want to be found?" Mr. Sutherland asked, the expression on his face showing me that he didn't think his daughter would simply choose to disappear.

"I'm not saying that, Dwight. I'm just saying that a missing person case can be hard to resolve."

"Oh. Well, we don't have a lot of money, but we can pay you some."

I felt a little sorry for them. Their daughter was missing, and they had no idea how to find her. They didn't even have a clue where to start looking.

"I'll tell you what, you give me a deposit, and I'll get started. I will send you a bill at the end of every week with my expenses. As long as you pay me, I'll continue to work on your case. I don't usually do it that way, but I'll make an exception this time."

"How much would you need to get started?" Dwight asked with a worried look on his face.

I explained my fees and expenses in detail. I told him that I would set aside the usual up-front retainer if he agreed to the weekly payment plan.

"If you need a moment to think about it, I'll step into the outer office so that you can discuss it between yourselves. If you would prefer to check around and talk to other private investigators, that will be fine. I'll leave my offer open to you."

Dwight looked at Mary. It was clear that they thought I was expensive, but actually I was no higher than most other private investigators in the area that did the same kind of work. It just seemed high to them.

"We'll take your offer, Mr. Blackstone," Dwight said.

"Okay. What I need from you is a picture of your daughter. The most recent one you have of her would be best."

"I have one here. It is her graduation picture from high school," Mrs. Sutherland said as she took a photo out of her purse. "It's two years old."

"I will return it to you when I'm finished," I assured her as I took it from her.

"Thank you."

"I also need to know where she is living."

"Emily rents an apartment about three or four blocks from the art school. We'll be staying there while we're in town."

"I'll need the address."

Mrs. Sutherland took a pen from her purse and wrote out the address on a small piece of paper.

"Emily lives alone at that address," she said as she handed the paper to me. "We stopped by just in case she was there on our way over here, but didn't get an answer when we rang her buzzer in the entrance. The manager wasn't there, either, so there was no one to let us in."

"I see. I'll check it out and let you know what I find. I would like it if you didn't go back there until I've had a chance to look around her apartment."

"Why is that?" Dwight asked.

"There might be something there that will tell me where she is, or where I might find her. I don't want you to help her by cleaning up her apartment or moving anything that might help me find her."

"Oh," Dwight said.

"Have you been in her apartment since she stopped calling?"

"No. We don't have a key. We were hoping that the manager would let us in, but he wasn't there. We met him when Emily first got the apartment. He knows who we are."

"Do you know who any of her friends are here in Denver?"

"I'm afraid we don't," Dwight said.

"Does she have a boyfriend?"

"She did casually mention a boy she had classes with once. I don't think there was anything to it other than that they were just friends and classmates," Mrs. Sutherland said.

"Do you know his name?"

"I think she called him Preston, but I don't know if that was his first or last name. Emily only mentioned him as being in one of her classes, but I don't know which class."

"That might be of some help to me. Give me a couple of days to do a little looking around, then I'll call you. By that time I might have a better idea of how things should go. Will that be okay?"

"Yes, that would be good," Dwight said as he looked at his wife to make sure that she agreed.

"I guess that's about all I'll need for now."

"When will you be ready to start?" Dwight asked.

"I will be starting this morning," I assured him.

Dwight looked at his wife and smiled. He seemed relieved that someone was going to look for their daughter.

"Thank you very much," Dwight said as he stood up and reached out a hand to me.

"You're welcome," I replied as I shook his hand. "Remember, I don't want you going to her apartment."

"Yes. I guess there is nothing else we can do here now that you are looking for her. Maybe it would be best if we returned home. We can't afford to spend money for a motel room. Besides, I have a lot of work to do on the farm," Mr. Sutherland said.

"I think that would be a good idea. I will call you as soon as I have any information."

"Thank you," Mrs. Sutherland said.

After shaking Mrs. Sutherland's hand, I watched them as they left my office. I wondered what I had gotten myself into. I got the impression that these folks could hardly pay for the trip from Kansas to Denver, let alone pay me. I don't usually take cases without a sizeable retainer, and here I was taking it on a weekly payment plan.

After the Sutherlands left the office, I sat back down and looked at the picture of Emily that they had left with me. It was a high school picture of Emily in her cheerleader's uniform that was taken less than two years ago, the year she graduated from high school. The girl in the picture was a very lovely looking girl. Emily wasn't very tall, but she had a nice figure. The smile on her face gave the impression that she had her whole life ahead of her. She looked like a younger version of her mother. She had brown almost black hair and brown eyes. She looked happy. I wondered if things might have changed for her.

Since I had little else to do, I decided that I might as well get started. The first place to start would be at Emily's apartment. I wanted to get there and look around before her parents tried to get in again. I had a feeling that Mrs. Sutherland would insist on going by Emily's apartment one more time to see if their daughter might have returned.

I LEFT MY OFFICE AND DROVE over to Emily's apartment. I had no problem finding the building where her apartment was located. However, it was hard to find a parking place. Once I found one, I parked then walked up to the apartment building.

As I entered the outside door of Emily's apartment building, I found another door inside. It was a security door that required someone to either buzz you in, or you had to have a key. There was a bank of buttons on the wall to the left, one for each apartment. I pressed the one to Emily's apartment, but didn't get an answer. I tried the one for the manager, but didn't get an answer there, either.

On the wall to the right was a block of mailboxes. There was the apartment number and the last name of the resident of that apartment. Emily's apartment was number 23. It was on the second floor.

I looked around in the hope that someone would come by and let me in. It took about ten minutes or so before someone showed up. It was a young woman who was heading out of the building. When she opened the door to leave the building, I smiled and nodded at her as I held the door open for her. She was carrying a large portfolio and an art box for paints, brushes and other things for artwork. She seemed pleased that I held the door for her.

As soon as she was out the door, I slipped into the building before the security door had a chance to close. I took the stairs up to the second floor. It didn't take me long to find Emily's apartment. A quick look around showed that the hall was empty.

Since I didn't have a key to her apartment, I tried the door. It was locked. I looked around and saw no one in the hall; so I picked the lock and quickly stepped into the apartment, closing and locking the door behind me. I looked around the room as I slipped on a pair of rubber gloves. The last thing I wanted to do was to leave fingerprints all over the place for the police to find if Emily's disappearance turned out to be the result of foul play.

The apartment was fairly small. It had a living room which was maybe ten by twelve feet in size. The furniture looked like it was old and not in very good shape. There was an overstuffed chair and a sofa in an outdated orange material. In front of the sofa was a coffee table that had seen better days. The tables at the end of the sofa were of different styles and outdated like the rest of the furniture in the room. The table lamps didn't match, either. The carpet was old and worn.

Along one wall were bookshelves made from cement blocks with boards laid across them. Most of the books had to do with art. I did notice that there was no television. However, there was a cheap radio on one of the end tables.

Off to one side of the living room near a door was a small kitchen table. There were two metal chairs with plastic covered seats and backs, one on each side of the table. The table was rather small. On the table was a half empty box of cereal, salt and pepper shakers and an empty sugar bowl.

A door led to a very small kitchen with hardly enough room to turn around. There was very little counter space. The stove had only two burners and an oven that was very small.

A quick check in the small refrigerator led me to believe that she didn't eat in the apartment very often, if at all. It contained only a few things, none of them would make much of a meal. There was a bottle of orange juice that was over half empty, four or five bottles of water, and a variety of condiments from a couple of fast food restaurants located in the area.

The only other door off the living room led to a bedroom. There was a single bed, an old dresser, and a small bedside table in the bedroom. There was an alarm clock and a small table lamp on the bedside table. The bed had a very nice looking quilt on it. If I had to guess, it had probably been made for her by her mother or grandmother. On the dresser were a number of pictures, most of them of her family.

There was one picture that didn't seem to fit with the rest. It was a picture of a young man. From the background, it was obvious that it had been taken in the living room of Emily's apartment. The young man didn't look anything like Mr. or Mrs. Sutherland, so I doubted that it was a son. None of the other family pictures indicated that the Sutherlands had a son. If I had to guess, it was probably a picture of Emily's boyfriend.

I pulled back the curtain to the closet. It wasn't a very big closet and there were not very many clothes. Most of the clothes in the closet were the kind of clothes that would be found at places like K-mart or Walmart, certainly not from any high-end clothing store. But that is what I would have expected after meeting Emily's parents.

As I continued to look through the closet, I got a bit of a surprise. I found some rather expensive clothes pushed way in the back out of sight. I began to think that something was very wrong here. I found two very expensive dresses with labels from a very elite and very high-priced women's store. The dresses were the kind that most conservative people, like Emily's parents, would consider too revealing. They were not the kind of dresses that her parents would probably approve of her wearing.

When I looked in the bottom of the closet, I found two pair of very expensive and very sexy high heeled shoes that would go well with the dresses. I was beginning to think that their little girl might not be such a little girl anymore.

A search through the dresser drawers left me wondering. I found no jewelry and no makeup. There were none of the things that a young single woman was likely to have had either in or on her dresser. The things I found, and the things I didn't find that I had expected to find, made me wonder if Emily was actually living there. If she didn't really live there, then where did she live?

The bathroom was very small with just a shower and no tub. The sink had almost no space to put anything on it. There was a small medicine cabinet above the sink, but it was empty. There was no storage space in the bathroom for even a spare towel.

I continued to search the apartment looking for anything that might give me some idea of what was going on. I did find an address book, but it didn't seem to be of much help. There was very little in it. It seemed to be names and addresses of fellow students from high school, high school teachers and some family members. I found nothing in the address book that would point to anything out of character for her. There were no addresses or phone numbers for the Denver area. They were all from her hometown area. I didn't figure that it would be of much help.

I began to think that she must have a portfolio of her artwork and some art supplies if she was an art student. I searched the apartment from top to bottom, including under the bed, but my search did not produce any such items. In fact, I found nothing to indicate that she was or had been an art student, except for the art books on the bookshelves. Even the pictures on the walls were not anything she had done.

When I finished my search of the apartment, I stood in the middle of the living room and looked around. I wasn't looking for anything. I was just taking a moment to let my mind go over everything I had found while my eyes just sort of took in the room.

As my eyes scanned the room, it suddenly registered in my mind that there was something on the floor under the sofa. It looked like a piece of paper that might have fallen off one of the end tables. I walked over to the sofa, bent down and picked up the paper.

It was a piece of paper that had been torn out of a small ringed notebook. On the paper was a date and what looked like it might have been part of a phone number. The problem with the phone number was that it was missing the exchange numbers, the first three numbers of a telephone number. Without those numbers, it would be very difficult to find out who the number belonged to. There was a slim chance that I might be able to find out who the number belonged to by checking phone numbers using each exchange in the Denver Metro area. It would probably give me a lot of numbers, but I might get lucky. But I would try the reverse phone number in the telephone book first. There was little chance that either of these methods would produce any kind of usable result. Either way it was a long shot at best, as well as time consuming. There was also the possibility that it was a cell phone number which wouldn't be listed in the phone book.

The date on the piece of paper had no significance to me. The date was two weeks ago. It could be just about anything from a date with her boyfriend, to a birthday, to God only knows what. It was becoming clear that I had not found very much that would help me find Emily. However, I found a great deal to make me wonder what was going on.

My next move was to go to the Denver School for Artists. Maybe I would have better luck there.

I slipped the piece of paper into my pocket as I took another quick look around to make sure that I had not missed anything, and to make sure I had not left any sign that I had been in her apartment.

Before leaving her apartment, I decided to take the picture of the boy from her dresser. I slipped it under my sport coat, then made sure there was no one in the hall who might see me leaving her apartment. The hall was clear. I wiped off the door knob before I left the apartment building without being seen, and returned to my car. I drove to the Denver School for Artist.

CHAPTER THREE

IT DID'T TAKE ME VERY LONG to get to the Denver School for Artists as it was not far from Emily's apartment. The hard part was finding a place to park near the school. Once I parked my car, I walked to the Administration Offices.

As I approached the front of the building where the Administration Offices were located, I noticed a lot of young people hanging around on the front steps of the building. Some of them had large black portfolios while others had just small boxes. One of the small boxes I saw setting on the steps had a label that read "ArtBin". I was sure that it held a budding young artist's art supplies that he or she would need in his or her classes.

Once inside the building, the first thing I noticed was the halls were full of people scurrying from one place to another. I must have arrived during a break between classes. I managed to make my way through the kids.

I worked my way into the Administration Office then headed toward the long counter. It took me a few minutes to work my way up to the counter. I had to wait for a few minutes to get to talk to someone who might be able to help me.

The woman that came to talk to me was in her upper forties to her early fifties. She looked like she had just about had enough of the one student she had been talking with. It seemed that he had a lot of questions. When he finally got some papers from the woman, he turned and started to leave. He had a disgusted look on his face. He apparently had not gotten the answers he had wanted, but probably got the answers he needed.

I moved closer to the counter where the woman was standing. I smiled at her, but she didn't smile back. She looked like it had been a long day and it wasn't over yet.

"Can I help you," she asked without any sign of emotion or interest in what I wanted.

"I would like some information on one of your students, an Emily Sutherland."

"Who are you?"

"I'm Peter Blackstone and I am representing Mr. and Mrs. Sutherland. It seems that their daughter is missing. I would like to know when she last attended class here, what classes she had and who her instructors were while attending your school."

"I can't give you that information," she said flatly and started to turn away.

"Then who can?" I asked to her back.

She turned back and looked me right in the eye and said sharply, "No one."

"You said 'no one', is that correct?"

"That's what I said."

"I see that it is your intention to be uncooperative."

"You are very clever. You got it right the first time. Congratulations."

She said it sarcastically with a grin of satisfaction on her face. It was clear that she was feeling very superior and in control at the moment, or she was just having a very lousy day. I decided that she was having a bad day, but she was not going to put me off so easily.

"One more thing," I said as she started to turn away again. "Since you have chosen to be that way, how would you like it if this place was crawling with uniformed police officers for a couple of days?" I asked.

Now that caught her attention very fast. She turned back and looked at me. The expression on her face was one that made me think that she was wondering if I could really do what I said.

"I can assure you that they would be interrupting every single class, and talking to every single instructor and student until they got the information they needed," I said without giving her a chance to respond. "By the way, that might take a couple of days. And who knows, maybe more. Are you ready for that?"

I could tell by the look on her face that she didn't want to be responsible for such a disruption of the entire school. She looked down for a moment before she looked up at me again for a minute or so. I got the impression that she was wondering if I could really pull off my threat.

In order to make my point and convince her that I meant business, I reached for my cell phone and opened it up.

"If that's the way you want it," I said rather casually as I pushed the first number to make a phone call.

"Wait. I'll get you the information you want."

"Thank you," I said as I closed my phone and put it away.

The woman typed something into a computer that was setting on a nearby desk. I watched her as she looked at the computer screen, then began to write down something on a piece of paper. As soon as she was finished, she looked at me for a moment before she handed me the piece of paper.

I took the piece of paper and looked at it. It showed me that the last class Emily attended was on a Wednesday, nine days ago. The class was her one to five o'clock "Figure Drawing" class. It was also her last class of the day. The piece of paper showed me that Emily had that same class three times a week, Monday, Wednesday and Friday. It also showed me that her instructor for that class was Franklin Steuben.

"I would like to have the rest of her schedule, please."

"That's all the classes she was taking this semester. She dropped her other three classes just before she started the current semester."

"You're telling me that she was only taking the one class?"

"Yes."

"Do you have any idea why she dropped the other classes?"

"I don't know why," she said as she looked at the computer screen. "It shows here that she was getting good grades in all her classes the semester before. It also looks like the 'Figure Drawing' class was all she needed to graduate."

"Based on that, she was a good student with a good degree of talent?"

"Yes. The only other thing I see here is that her last grade in her 'Figure Drawing' class was down."

"How much was it down?"

"It looks like it went from a four point to a two point," she said as she looked up at me.

The look on her face gave me the impression that she was surprised to see such a drastic drop in Emily's grade.

"When did she get that grade?"

"Just last week. It would have been at the last Monday class she attended."

"Is this a new class for her?" I asked.

"Oh, my, no. This was her fourth and final semester in that class."

"Did she have a different instructor?"

"No. It was the same instructor that she had last semester when she was doing so well."

It seemed a little strange that her grade point would drop so quickly unless there was some outside reason for it. My next move was to have a talk with her "Figure Drawing" instructor, Mr. Steuben. I didn't bother to ask her for Emily's past schedule. I could get that and anything else I might need later.

"Where would I find Franklin Steuben now?" I asked as I looked up at her.

She pressed a few keys on the computer and took a minute to look at something on the screen before she answered.

"Mr. Steuben is on break right now. You would probably be able to find him in the instructors' lounge."

"Where might that be?"

She was much more cooperative now. She gave me directions to the lounge.

AFTER THANKING HER for her help, I followed her instructions and found myself in front of the instructors' lounge door. I pushed open the door and stepped inside. I looked around the room and noticed there were three men sitting at a table in the corner. Since I had no idea what Mr. Steuben looked like, I walked over to the table.

"Excuse me. Would one of you gentlemen be Mr. Steuben?"

A voice from behind me said, "I'm Mr. Steuben."

I turned around to find a rather nice looking man sitting on a sofa. He had a notebook in one hand and a pen in the other. Beside him was a stack of papers. It looked as if he was grading the papers, but I couldn't be sure.

Mr. Steuben appeared to be in his early thirties. He had dark brown hair and brown eyes. He had a beard that was well trimmed and actually looked good on him. He was wearing tan slacks and a red polo shirt.

I walked over to him and sat down on a chair across a coffee table from him. He looked up at me, but didn't say anything.

"My name is Peter Blackstone."

"Franklin Steuben. What is it you want?" he asked rather sharply.

He didn't look like he was at all interested in what I wanted. In fact, he looked rather bored and acted as if I was the one bothering him. He was right in that assumption.

"I'm looking into the disappearance of Emily Sutherland."

"I didn't know that she had disappeared," he said without any emotion as he continued to make notes in his notebook.

"She has. Can you tell me the last time that you saw her?"

He stopped writing and looked up at me before he responded to my question.

"I think it was a week ago last Wednesday. She was in my Wednesday afternoon class."

"Her class schedule shows that she had your Figure Drawing class on Monday, Wednesday and Friday. So from what you're saying, she was not in your Friday class last week and any of your classes this week. Is that correct?"

"That was very clever of you to have figured that out so quickly, and all by yourself, too," he said with an arrogant grin.

I thought about the response I got and wondered what his problem was. It was apparent that he felt he was superior to just about anyone.

"I do have my moments," I said, not wanting to get into a pissing match with him. One that I was sure he would not win.

"I'm glad to hear that."

"How was she doing in your class?"

"She was an average student as far as her artwork went, but she was much better as a model for the rest of the class."

"Would you be so kind as to explain that to me?"

"What is it you don't understand? She had a very nice body with smooth lines and nice curves. I suppose some would say that she was even sexy looking. However, her ability to draw was childish at best," he said with a note of superiority. "Does that answer your question?"

I ignored his question. After all he didn't really expect me to answer it anyway.

"Was she modeling or drawing in the last class she attended?"

"She was attempting to draw in the first half of the class, but posed for the rest of the class during the last half."

"What time did she leave?"

"The class was over at five that afternoon."

"That's not what I asked. I know what time the class was supposed to end. I want to know what time she left your classroom."

"As far as I know, she left with the others at five o'clock," he said after taking a moment to think about his answer.

He didn't seem to like my last question very much. He hesitated before he answered. The look on his face gave me the impression that Emily might not have left his classroom at the end of the class, and he knew it. After all, she would have had to get dressed. It seemed to me that I had caught him a little off guard. It was the first of my questions that he seemed to have to think about before answering. He was hiding something and I wanted to know what it was.

"Did she leave with anyone?"

"I wouldn't know. I left the classroom first. I had an appointment," he said.

I got the feeling that he responded to my question with more information than he really wanted me to know. It was clear that I had shaken him up a little, but why. I decided to press him a bit more.

"May I ask who your appointment was with?"

"I don't think that is any of your business," he replied sharply.

I noticed that he glanced over at the instructors that were sitting at the table. It was beginning to look like I would have to get him away from the other instructors in order to find out anything more. It would have to wait for another time. I would catch up with Steuben later.

I stood up and looked down at him. He was looking up at me. His eyes told me that he was worried about something. It might have been something I said, or just the fact that I was there questioning him. I had not told him anything about myself. He might have thought that I was a cop. Whatever the reason for him to suddenly become a little nervous, I would let him stew about it for awhile. I would catch him someplace private where we could have a real heart to heart talk, and find out why he dropped Emily's grade.

"I'll be talking to you again," I said just to assure him that I wasn't finished with him.

I didn't wait for him to respond to my last comment. I simply turned around and left him in the room watching me leave. I wondered what the other instructors in the room thought about our conversation. I was sure that they had heard at least some of it.

I WALKED OUT OF THE BUILDING and down the street to my car. I got in and sat there for a few minutes watching the front of the building. I had no idea what I was waiting for, or why I was looking at the building. Maybe it was just to think for a few minutes about what I had been told.

I wasn't looking at anything special when, to my surprise, I saw Steuben come out of the building. It was a surprise because I knew he had another class in less than an hour. I knew there was a store nearby. Maybe he was going to get something before class.

Steuben started down the steps of the building, but was stopped by a young man who looked like he might be a student. Steuben said something as he sort of pushed the young man aside and continued down the steps. I didn't hear what Steuben said, but the young man looked at the back of Steuben as he walked away, then flipped him the finger. He was obviously pissed off with Steuben for pushing him out of the way and not talking to him.

At the bottom of the steps in front of the building, Steuben stopped for a moment. He looked around as if he was looking for someone then hurried across the street. He got into a bright red Porsche 911 and quickly sped away. It looked like he was in a hurry to get out of there.

I wondered what burr I had put under his saddle to get him to move so quickly. If it wasn't clear before, it was very clear now. He knew a lot more than he was telling me. I had scared him, but I had no idea what it was that I had said that frightened him. That left me with more questions that needed to be answered.

I thought about following him, but I really didn't think it was important for me to follow him at this time. I could spend a little time tailing Steuben some other time. I started my car and headed back to my office.

WHEN I ARRIVED AT THE OFFICE, I sat down to regroup. There were a few things that didn't seem to add up. I looked at the picture I had taken from Emily's apartment. I was almost one hundred percent sure it was her boyfriend. I took the picture out of the frame and turned it over. There was a name on the back of the picture. The name was Jeffery Slocomb. I immediately recognized the last name. However, I was not sure if the picture was of the son of the man that I knew, but that didn't seem important now.

I began to think about what my next step would be. What I really needed to do was find out who Emily's friends were and talk to them. The picture of Jeffery Slocomb gave me the idea that he might be just the place to start.

The first thing I needed to find out was if Jeffery Slocomb was the son of Ralph Slocomb. I decided that the easiest way to find that out was to call Ralph Slocomb's club and ask.

As I reached out to pick up the phone, it began to ring. I hesitated for a second before I picked it up.

"Peter Blackstone Investigations."

"Is this Mr. Blackstone?"

The voice on the line had the sound of a young male. With just those few words, I got the impression that he might be a little nervous about talking to me, but I had no idea why.

"Yes, it is. How may I help you?"

"My name is – ah – Jeffery Slocomb. My father is Ralph Slocomb."

I had to admit that it was a bit of a surprise to be hearing from Jeffery Slocomb. However, the call had cleared up one of my questions, so far, but I didn't comment on it. He was the son of the Slocomb that I knew.

I waited for him to say something, but all I could hear was him breathing. I didn't know if he was waiting for me to say something, or if he was thinking about what he should say to me. I was about to say something to him when he spoke again.

"Mr. Blackstone, I need some help."

"What kind of help do you need?"

"I would rather wait until we have a chance to meet, if you don't mind."

"I don't mind. Where would you like to meet?"

"Can we meet at your office?"

"That can easily be arranged. Did you have a time when you would like to meet?"

"Could we meet at – say – two-thirty this afternoon?" he asked.

"Sure. I'll see you at two-thirty in my office. Can you give me some idea what it is you wish to talk about?"

"I'd rather wait until we meet in person."

"All right. I'll see you at two-thirty at my office."

"Okay," he said, then the phone went dead.

I sat there for several minutes thinking about the phone call. I had no idea how I could help Jeffery since he gave me no clue why he wanted to talk to me. It did intrigue me a bit, though.

I didn't know Jeffery, but I knew his father. That is to say, I knew of him. I had never had any direct dealings with him, but I had read about him a number of times in the local newspapers.

Ralph Slocomb was well known by the police. He was into gambling and prostitution, mostly. There may have been drugs involved, but it was never proven and there apparently was no evidence of it. He was considered to be a small-time operator by some, at least as far as crooks go, along the Front Range and in other large cities. Even as a small-time operator, he had obviously made a lot of money. He owned a large house in Cherry Creek. Cherry Creek was a well-to-do suburb in the Denver area where many of the houses were in or very close to the one million dollar price range. Some of the homes were well over a million.

It seemed that Mr. Slocomb, the old man, had managed to keep a very low profile as far as his illegal activities were concerned. His prostitution operation had been well hidden under the guise of an escort service for businessmen who often came to town to do business and wanted a little company in the evenings when their work was done. The police had never been able to pin anything on him that would hold up in court, but that didn't mean he was squeaky clean, either.

As for the gambling part of Mr. Slocomb's operations, he kept that pretty low key, also. He had private parties at different locations around the city. Most of them were held in private homes, and many of them in the foothills just outside the city limits. Since they were held in various locations, and at different times, it had been very hard for the police to actually catch him at it. There was also the fact that most of his "clients" were well known in their communities back home and didn't want anyone to know what they were doing while they were in Denver. That tended to make it hard to find witnesses that would come forward.

By keeping a very low profile, he had managed to avoid scrutiny by the police, as well as avoid trouble from the bigger mobsters in the Denver metro area. Since Mr. Slocomb kept his gambling parties limited to just a few invited guests, the bigger mobsters didn't consider him much of a threat to their operations. As a result, they didn't bother him.

There had been rumors within the police department that Ralph Slocomb had a couple of high ranking police officers, and a couple of local politicians as regular customers to both his escort service and his gambling houses. It was also hinted that there were some high ranking police officers on his payroll allowing him to stay in business. No one had made any kind of open accusation because it would be very hard to prove, and could end up getting the accuser in a world of hurt. Cops tend to protect cops, especially in the higher ranks.

If there were high ranking police officers involved, it could make it difficult for the honest cops to plan a raid on any of Slocomb's gambling places. The high ranking officers would know where the raids were going to be, thus being able to inform Slocomb well in advance of the raid.

Now I'm not saying that there were any cops involved in Slocomb's operations. However, with so many rumors floating around about it, and so few raids made that were effective, it seemed a likely possibility.

After a quick look at my watch, I realized that I had sometime before my visit with Jeffery Slocomb; I decided that I would go get something to eat. I left for a café that was located just a few blocks from my office.

I ARRIVED BACK at my office in plenty of time to get there before Jeffrey Slocomb was to arrive. As I got off the elevator and began walking toward my office, I saw a young man sitting on the floor next to the office door. He had a worried look on his face. I recognized the kid immediately. It was Jeffrey Slocomb. He looked just like his dad.

"I'm sorry if I'm late," I said as I took my keys out of my pocket.

As I unlocked my office door, he stood up.

"You're not late. I got here early."

"Well, come on in," I said as I opened the door.

Jeffrey walked into my office while I walked around to my desk.

"Have a seat, Jeff. Is it all right if I call you Jeff?"

"Sure. Everyone calls me Jeff, except my mother."

I didn't reply to him. I simply smiled and looked across my desk at him. It was the look on his face that bothered me. He looked like a young man that had the weight of the world on his shoulders.

"Okay, Jeff, what is it I can do for you?"

"Do you know who my father is?" he asked.

"Yes, but I don't know him personally."

"I want your assurance that what we say here will remain between us. I don't even want my father to know that I talked to you. Is that clear?"

"Your father will never hear that we even met from me. And what we talk about will remain between us as it does with all my clients. What is it you want to talk about?"

"I would like to hire you to find my girlfriend."

Under any other circumstances that would have been a normal request from someone looking for another person. But coming from him, it seemed to me to be a strange request. His father had a lot of connections in the Denver area. He could have dozens of people looking for his girlfriend in a heartbeat.

"What is the girl's name?"

"Em. Em Sutherland."

"Em Sutherland?"

"Yeah. I've tried to get her to tell me what Em is short for, but she just laughed," he said with a grin.

"How long has she been missing?"

"A little over a week."

"Do you happen to have a picture of her? It might make it easier for me to find her if you do."

"Yes," he said. "But you can't show it to anyone."

"Okay."

I watched him as he reached into his pocket and pulled out a photograph. He held the photo out to me and I took it. It was no surprise to find that the photo was of Emily Sutherland. However, it was a real surprise that the picture was a lot different from the one I had gotten from Mr. and Mrs. Sutherland.

The picture of Em that Jeff gave me was a picture of a rather stunning young woman who looked like she was a woman of the world. She was wearing a black dinner dress that was not only rather short, but had a deep cut front that almost went to her waist. She had a good amount of cleavage showing. Her makeup looked as if it had been done by a professional. Her hair was styled to show off her beautiful face. She was also wearing high heeled sandals that looked like they had close to five inch heels. I had to admit that she was one beautiful woman, even very sexy.

I looked at Jeff. He didn't seem to be old enough to be going out with a woman like the one in the picture. I knew that they were probably about the same age, give or take a year or two at the most.

"This is a very good looking woman. Where did you meet her?" I asked.

"I met her at my father's nightclub."

I knew what he meant by his "father's nightclub". His father owned a club in the downtown area. It was a very nice dinner club and upscale bar in the downtown district. It was a place where a lot of well-to-do business types would gather for business lunches and for a drink after work. Later in the evening, it was a club that was one of the most fashionable and expensive nightclubs in the Denver area. It was probably the only legitimate business that his father owned.

The fact that he had met Em at the downtown club gave me reason to believe that she was earning some money keeping the customers of the club happy. I didn't know what duties she would perform there, but her good looks had something to do with it. It could have been nothing more than looking pretty and being a good hostess to people in the club. It would also explain the expensive clothes I found in her apartment. In fact, her dress looked very much like one I had seen in her apartment.

I wondered if she might work in some of Mr. Slocomb's less legal operations. I also wondered if she was being paid for services like those performed by a call girl.

"What do you know about this woman?"

"She's fun, and we enjoy some of the simple things in life. We get along very well. When she's with me, she's like no one I have ever met. She doesn't always dress like that. She only looks like that when she's working. Most of the time she wears hardly any makeup, and she likes to wear jeans and sweatshirts."

"What does she do for a living? Is she a cocktail waitress?

"She serves drinks to the clients in my father's nightclub," he said. "She also works as a hostess at the club."

I wondered if she did more than that, but I wasn't going to suggest anything else to him. From what he had told me about her, he sounded very much like a young man who was in love with her.

"I will see if I can find her for you. There is one thing that might help me find her. Do you know any of her girlfriends?"

"Yes. June Parker is her best friend."

"Where might I find her?" I asked as I wrote her name down.

"I think she works as a model at the Denver School for Artists. She might be a student there. I'm not sure."

It was beginning to look like another trip to the school was going to be in order. I wasn't sure that I would find anyone there by the name of June Parker, but I would have to find out.

"Okay. I guess I can get started."

"Ah - - can you give me some idea of what this is going to cost me?"

I thought about what he asked. Since I wasn't getting paid what I should from Mr. and Mrs. Sutherland to find their daughter, and since he was asking me to find the same person, I might as well make a little something out it. I explained what my fees were and how much of a retainer I would need.

"That sounds fair," he said as he reached into his pocket and took out a checkbook.

Jeff wrote out a check for the amount of the retainer I had requested. As soon as he signed the check, he handed it to me. I looked at it then looked at him.

"It's good, Mr. Blackstone."

"I'm sure it is. There is just one thing."

"What's that?"

"If you don't want your father to know about us talking, maybe it would be better if you cashed a check and paid me with cash."

"Oh, that's okay. That is written on a checking account that my father doesn't know about. But if you prefer, I can get you cash," he said as he looked at me.

"No. Your check will be fine as long as you're fine with it."

"I'm fine with it," he said as he stood up.

"Okay," I said as I stood up and reached out to shake his hand.

"Where can I get in touch with you when I have something to report?"

"Oh. Call me at this number at any time."

He wrote his cell phone number on a piece of paper and gave it to me. I glanced at it, then looked up and smiled.

"I look forward to hearing from you," he said, then turned and left my office.

I SAT AT MY DESK for a little while thinking about what was going on. It struck me as strange that Jeff Slocomb had come to me for help in finding the girl he knew as Em. He undoubtedly knew that his father had a network of people working for him who could probably find her faster than I could by myself.

Another thing that struck me as strange was why didn't Jeff want his father to know that he had been dating Emily. It seemed clear that Jeff had probably been discouraged from dating any of the girls that worked at his father's nightclub. The only reason I could think of for his father not wanting Jeff to date the girls working for him was because they probably worked at his other businesses, too. One wrong word from one of them, and Jeff might find out how his father really made his living. Was it possible that Jeff didn't know that his father had a few illegal businesses on the side and didn't want him to find out? I couldn't help but think that may have been the reason. It certainly made sense to me.

My thoughts turned to the actions of one Franklin Steuben. After I talked with him, he left the school as if his tail was on fire. What had I said to him to make him leave in such a hurry? I couldn't think of anything that would make him so nervous. I knew that he had a class in less than an hour from the time he left the school. I wondered if he had gotten back to the school in time to teach the class. That might be something to check out even if I had no idea what it would prove either way.

CHAPTER FOUR

ONCE AGAIN MY THOUGHTS turned to the young woman I had found in the lawn bag. There was something familiar about her, but I couldn't put my finger on it. I thought that it might be a good idea if I contacted Mac to see if he had come up with an ID on the woman in the lawn bag.

I decided to give him a call. I placed a call to Mac's office but found that he was at the Coroner's Office. I asked to have the call transferred to him. The phone rang only a couple of times before it was answered.

"Coroner's Office, how may I help you?" a young woman's voice asked.

"I understand that Captain MacDonald is there. Is that right?"

"Yes. Hold on and I'll get him. Can I tell him who is calling?"

"Peter Blackstone."

I only had to wait for a minute or so before Mac came on the line.

"What's up, Pete?"

"I was wondering if you might have figured out who the woman in the lawn bag was."

"Not yet. She had nothing on, no clothes, no jewelry, no tattoos, no scares, no nothing. They haven't found anything in the lawn bag that was any help to us, so far. What's your interest in her?"

"I'm working on a missing girl case right now. It came to me this morning that she looked like someone I had seen before, but I can't think of where."

"You think the girl we have might be your missing girl?"

"No, but then I'm not sure."

"Do you have a picture of your missing girl?"

"Yeah. Could I come down to the Coroner's Office and check it out? It might help us both out, but then again, it might not," I said.

"Get on down here. I'll wait for you."

"I'm on my way," I said then hung up.

I immediately got up and started out the door to my car. I left the parking garage and drove to the Coroner's Office. It only took about thirty minutes to get there.

I ENTERED THE CORONER'S OFFICE and found Mac waiting for me. He wasted no time.

"The Coroner has our victim on the table," he said as he led the way into the lab.

As I entered the lab behind Mac, I could see the young woman lying on the hard, cold, stainless steel table. She no longer had pieces of leaves and twigs on her face or in her hair. She had been cleaned up. She looked so young, and so dead. I walked over to the table and looked down at the face of the young woman.

"Damn," I said half under my breath. "I was hoping to find her alive."

"Is this the girl you are looking for?" Mac asked as he looked at me.

"Yeah."

"You got a name?"

"Her name is Emily Sutherland. She's from Kansas. She was going to school at the Denver School for Artists. I have a witness that claims the last time he saw her was a week ago last Wednesday at around five o'clock in the afternoon."

"What's this witness's name?"

"Franklin Steuben. He is an instructor at the art school. She had his class on Monday, Wednesday and Friday. He said she didn't show up for class last Friday afternoon."

"I guess I'll go have a talk with him."

"Any idea what the cause of death might be?" I asked the Medical Examiner.

"It looks like she was strangled to death. There is an indication that she was on some kind of drug. We don't know what kind yet. We should know by tomorrow at the latest. But if I had to guess, it was probably cocaine," the Medical Examiner said.

"Did you find anything else?"

"This might be a little strange. I only found one injection sight, but from the location it could be where she had a flu shot. It's on her arm, not a common place to shoot up cocaine. I have found nothing to indicate that she was a regular user. In fact, I found nothing to indicate that she had ever used it or anything else before," the Medical Examiner explained.

"Were there any signs of a struggle? Maybe she was given it by force."

"No. Nothing, but I'm not anywhere near finished with my examination of her. One thing I do know is that the injection sight was there before she was strangled. That much I'm sure of."

I had to think about what I had just been told. It just didn't add up to me. What had Emily gotten into that led to her death? My thoughts were interrupted by Mac.

"Pete, have you talked to this Steuben guy?"

"Yeah."

"What's your opinion of him?"

"He's arrogant and has a superiority complex. Plus, he's an ass."

"Did you get anything out of him?"

"Nothing that would help."

There was more that I could have told Mac about Steuben, but I had already made Steuben nervous. I wanted to know what it was that I said that made him so jumpy. The one thing that came to mind while I was talking to Mac was that Steuben could have been the man that ran from the scene where I found Emily's body. It made me angry to think that her instructor might have had something to do with her death.

It also came to me that not only did Steuben fit the description of the man I saw at the scene, but so did a lot of other men. It didn't matter that much that I didn't say anything to Mac about him. I couldn't identify him as the man with any degree of confidence.

I wanted to have another talk with Steuben, only this time I wouldn't be so easy on him. I wanted him alone, preferably in some dark alley. I knew my feelings at the moment were not very logical. Well, maybe logical, but not very helpful. If I went off and beat the hell out of Steuben, I could end up in jail for assault. I wouldn't be any help to anyone sitting in jail.

What I really wanted was to know more about Steuben and his relation to Emily before I talked to him again. My gut feeling told me that he was involved with Emily's death in some way. The only thing I didn't know was how. If he wasn't involved, then why was he so nervous about talking to me?

I took one last look at Emily, before I turned to leave the lab. As I headed for the door, I stopped when Mac spoke to me. I slowly turned around and looked at him.

"Where are you going?" Mac asked.

"I'm going to tell Emily's parents where their daughter is. They have worried long enough."

Mac didn't say anything, he just looked at me. I turned and left the lab. Once I was out of the building and in my car, I sat behind the wheel to think. It didn't seem right that a beautiful young country girl like Emily should end up on a slab in the Coroner's Office in a big city.

There was no doubt that Mr. and Mrs. Sutherland would be devastated by the loss of their daughter. There was nothing I could do about her death, but I could find out who had killed her and why. It might bring some small measure of consolation to her parents, but it would not make me feel better. It was often said that finding the killer of a victim, and bringing the killer to justice, would bring closure for the family. I had my doubts. As far as I was concerned, closure was way overrated.

I REACHED DOWN and started my car, then headed back to my office. It didn't take me long to get there. As I opened the door to my office, the phone started to ring. I picked it up.

"Peter Blackstone Investigations, how may I help you?"

"I think it would be a damn good idea if you kept your nose out of other people's business. You have found Emily for the Sutherlands. Now drop it. Consider this your one and only warning," the deep male voice said, then the phone went dead before I could say anything.

I set the receiver on the cradle and looked at the little box sitting next to the phone. The Caller ID simply read "Unknown caller". It was probably made on a "no contract" cell phone, which meant that whoever had called me didn't want me to know his name. I could understand that.

It suddenly occurred to me that I had heard the phone when it started to ring. How did the caller know that I had just entered my office? The answer was obvious. Whoever had called me had to be somewhere close by, and had seen me return to my office.

I went to the window and looked down at the street below, not that I expected to see anyone. I couldn't make out anything unusual. Nine stories up makes everyone look like little ants running around on the sidewalk. As I looked down at the street, I tried to think if I had ever heard that voice before. It didn't sound familiar.

I wondered what I had gotten myself into. I had apparently stepped on someone's toes and he didn't like it. The only problem I had at the moment was that I had no idea whose toes they might have been. Giving it some thought, I could think of a couple of people.

The first one to come to mind was Franklin Steuben. I had scared him with something I said, but what was it? There was little doubt that he knew more than he was telling me, but did it have anything to do with Emily's death? He was probably not the one that called. He was more the type to get someone else to make the call, but I still couldn't rule him out.

The second one was Ralph Slocomb. His son had come to see me about Emily, but Jeff had made it clear he didn't want his father to know anything about his relationship with her. It crossed my mind that Jeff had been followed to my office, or that his father had found out about Emily and Jeff some other way. It would be just like Ralph Slocomb to have one of his goons call me and try to intimidate me. The only question was why? Did he have something to do with the death of Emily? I seriously doubted that Jeff had anything to do with it. It came to mind that maybe Jeff might think that his father had something to do with Emily's disappearance in an effort to keep him from seeing her.

It suddenly occurred to me that Jeff might not know that Emily had been murdered. I reached over and picked up the phone. I placed a call to the number Jeff had given me. The phone rang several times, but I got no answer or voice mail so I couldn't leave a message for him to call me.

I still thought that a trip to the Denver School for Artists to find out if Steuben had returned to his scheduled class after my visit was in order. The only question I had was what would it prove?

I LEFT MY OFFICE and headed over to the school. When I walked into the Administration Office, the same lady I had talked to earlier saw me coming toward her. It didn't look like she was going to be very willing to talk to me. I smiled as I approached the counter.

"Good afternoon."

"What is it you want this time?" she said bluntly.

"I have two questions for you. The first is did Mr. Franklin Steuben teach his afternoon class yesterday?"

"No. He got called away on a family emergency."

"I see. And would you be so kind as to give me the names of the students that took Mr. Steuben's afternoon class? I would like names and addresses, please."

"I don't think I should give you that information," she said, but not with the same conviction that she had earlier in the day.

"Would it help if I were to tell you that this is no longer a missing person investigation, but a murder investigation?" I said softly so no one else in the office could hear me.

"Oh, my God," she said, the look on her face was one of shock.

She slowly turned away from me and looked at her computer for a couple of minutes. I wasn't sure if she was going to help me or not. She then began typing something into the computer. When she was done typing, she pressed a key off to the side. She then turned and looked at me. I wasn't sure what she was doing, but I could see that she was having a little trouble dealing with what I had told her.

"I would appreciate it if you said nothing about this to anyone. You see, her parents have not been notified yet. We wouldn't want it to get out before they are notified. I'm sure you can understand that."

"Yes. I understand," she replied softly.

It wasn't but a minute or so before she turned and walked over to a printer. She picked up a couple of sheets of paper from the tray and brought them over to me.

"I hope this will be of help," she said as she handed me the papers.

I took a look at the papers. It had the names of fourteen students on them, along with their addresses and phone numbers. The heading read "Figure Drawing – Franklin Steuben's class". I looked up and smiled at her.

"Is this the only figure drawing class Steuben has?"

"Yes. All his other classes are design classes that deal with using computers to design things."

"Is this the only class he had that Emily Sutherland was in?"

"Yes."

I took the papers she gave me and neatly folded them up. I put them in my coat pocket then turned away from the counter. I stopped and turned back toward the counter. I looked at her again. I wondered if she would answer another question for me. There was only one way to find out.

"Can I ask you another question, please?" I asked quietly.

"Yes," she replied as she leaned closer to me.

"What do you think of Mr. Steuben? You know, what are your feelings about him?"

She looked around to make sure there was no one close that could hear her, then said, "He's an ass. I don't trust him. He thinks he's God's gift to women. I think he's an arrogant, self-centered, pompous ass," she said without a moment's hesitation.

I couldn't help but smile. I was in total agreement with her. The only question that I wanted answered was, is he also a murderer? I doubted that she would have the answer to that one, but she might have the answer to another question that came to mind.

"Has he ever been accused of sexual advances toward any of his students?"

"No, I don't think so," she said in a whisper. "But I've overheard talk around the lounge that he flirts with the young pretty girls in his figure drawing class. Rumor has it that he gives better grades to the prettier girls in his classes, especially the girls that respond to him."

"Thanks for your help. Let's keep this our little secret."

She smiled and nodded her head in agreement.

"Oh, one other question. Could you give me Steuben's home address?"

She didn't hesitate one second. She looked up his address and copied it down on a small piece of paper. She folded the paper, looked around the room then gave it to me. I slipped it into my pocket before I left the office.

As I walked out of the building, I got to thinking about what the woman in the Administration Office had told me. I wondered if the reason that Emily had suddenly started getting mediocre grades after doing so well in the figure drawing class was because she wouldn't play his games. It was clear from my talk with Steuben that he thought Emily was a very pretty girl, even sexy, but not much of an artist.

My next stop was my office again. I wanted to go over the list to see if I could figure out who I might like to start with. I also had to make a call to Emily's parents. There was no sense in putting it off any longer.

AS SOON AS I ARRIVED back at my office, I sat down at my desk and began looking over the list of students. I was particularly interested in the names of the girls in the class. I felt they were the ones that could tell me more about Steuben than the boys in the class. However, I was not about to overlook the boys. If anyone had felt that Steuben was giving better grades to the pretty girls in the class, they would know.

As I skimmed through the list of names, two names caught my eye. The first was the name Preston. Emily's parents had mentioned the name Preston as someone who might be a friend of Emily's. The name on the list was D. Preston Nielsen. I had no idea what the D stood for, or if this was the Preston that Emily had mentioned.

The second was June P. Cullens. I don't know why I had the feeling that the P stood for Parker. Maybe I was just looking for anything that would help me. It was the only P in all the names, except for Preston. There was no Parker listed anywhere. I knew I was reaching, but I had little else to go on. If Emily and June worked at Slocomb's nightclub, how many other students might work there.

There were no other names on the list that seemed to jump out at me. That's not to say that I wouldn't find a name or two later. The one thing I was sure of was that I would be talking to everyone on the list, sooner or later. Someone knew what kind of relationships Emily had had and with whom.

I leaned back in my chair and took a little while to think about the list of students and what I knew up to know, which was very little. I also thought about the call I had received telling me to drop the case. When I finally glanced at my watch, I realized that it was a little past supper time. I needed to contact Mr. and Mrs. Sutherland before it got much later as I was sure they would probably turn in early.

I placed a call to Mr. and Mrs. Sutherland. I didn't want to tell them that their daughter was dead over the phone, but it was a long drive to their farm in Kansas. There was also the fact that I didn't know where the farm was located.

The phone rang only a couple of times before it was answered. I gave them the bad news as gently as I could, but it never seemed to be easy. It certainly wasn't easy for them to receive that kind of news.

After I hung up, I sat staring at the wall. I wanted to know why such a nice young woman had been murdered. I decided that I was not ready to give it up. In the morning, I would start my search for Emily's killer or killers.

Since I had gotten a warning to leave the investigation alone, I decided that it might be best if I didn't leave anything around that someone might find if they broke into my office. I put the list in my pocket and made sure that everything I had on the case was secure. I then locked up my office and went to the parking garage to get my car. I was ready to go home.

AS I ENTERED THE PARKING GARAGE, I looked around. I had no idea if whoever warned me to drop the case might already know that I had not dropped my investigation. I wasn't about to take any chances and get caught off guard.

I didn't see anything unusual in the parking garage. There were no cars there that I didn't recognize, and no one standing around watching what was going on. Most of the cars were gone for the night. It wasn't that it was all that late, but it was late enough that most of the offices in the building would be closed.

I got in my car and headed for home. I had no more than turned out onto the street when I noticed a dark sedan pull away from the curb. It looked like it might have a pretty fancy set of wheels. I got to thinking that it may have been the same one that sped away from the scene by the park. As I drove along the street, the car stayed about the same distance behind me all the time. I drove through an area of town that had a lot of street lights in the hope of getting a better look at the car. I was able to make out two people in it.

I wanted to get the license plate number off the car, but it never got close enough for me to see it. In fact, I got the impression that whoever was in the car wanted me to know that they were following me. It dawned on me that they might be there to remind me of the phone call I received earlier to drop the case. I decided to let them follow me to my home.

When I got to my apartment, I pulled into the parking area and stopped. I immediately got out of my car and waved at them as they drove on by. I had hoped to get a license number, but no such luck. The license plate was covered with mud, probably on purpose.

After they drove by, I got back in my car and drove around behind my apartment building and parked my car in the garage. I made sure there was no one around before I crossed the parking lot to the backdoor to my apartment building and went inside to my apartment.

Everything in my apartment looked to be in order. I couldn't find anything that had been disturbed. After I grabbed a bite to eat, I took a shower and got ready for bed. Sleep did not come easily. It was well past midnight before I finally got to sleep.

CHAPTER FIVE

I WAS AWAKE EARLY, earlier than usual. I had gone to bed thinking about Emily's murder, and woke up with it on my mind. I could still think of no reason for her to have been murdered. There had to be a reason. People don't kill for no reason. Someone knew what that reason was. I wanted to know, too.

Unable to go back to sleep, I got up and took a long shower. It was more to wake up my brain than anything else. I had often found a shower in the morning helped me think better. The only other thing that would help was a good breakfast.

As soon as I finished my breakfast, I headed to my office. I parked in the parking garage and looked around before I got out of my car. It was a habit of mine which had proven in the past to be a good one. I took the elevator to the ninth floor and got off.

As I approached the door to my office, I noticed that it was open. I wasn't sure if someone had broken in last night, or if I had company I might not want to see. With the threat that I had received yesterday, I felt it was important that I be ready for anything.

I reached under my coat and put my hand on my 9mm automatic. Stepping as lightly as possible, I moved closer to the door. I could hear a chair squeaking as if someone was rocking back and forth in a chair that needed oiling. I knew that my desk chair would squeak like that when I rocked in it. I normally found it soothing when I wanted to try to think, but this time it was a warning. Someone was sitting in my chair waiting for me. I got the impression that whoever it was; they had been waiting a long time and might be getting a little tired of waiting.

Stepping up close to the door, I took a quick look into my office. Sitting in my chair was a big man that I knew was one of Ralph Slocomb's goons, but I didn't know his name. I wondered what he wanted with me. There were only two possibilities that I could think of quickly. The first was that Ralph had found out that his son had paid me a visit and wanted to know what it was about. And second, it was one of Ralph's hired hands who had called me yesterday with a warning and figured that I had not taken the warning seriously enough.

A third possibility suddenly crossed my mind. It was possible that Ralph wanted to know what I knew about the death of Emily. That one made at least a little sense. Emily had worked for him in his nightclub.

I decided that the only way I was going to find out why Ralph's goon was sitting in my chair was to confront him. I drew my gun from under my coat and slipped it into my pocket. Leaving my hand on it, I casually walked into my office.

"Well, I see you found a way in," I said as I walked up to the side of my desk.

"Yeah, I did. You know, you have a nice comfortable chair," he said smiling up at me, but not bothering to get up.

"I'm glad you like it," I said.

I quickly stepped close to him and reached out with my free hand. Putting all my weight in it, I pushed him and the chair over backward. The big ape tried desperately to keep from going over backward, but it didn't work. He went crashing to the floor with his feet flying up in the air while his head bounced hard on the carpeted floor. While he was trying to regain his balance, I pulled my gun out of my pocket and stuck it in his face. He immediately stopped fighting to get up and just looked at it.

"I don't like people breaking into my office, and I don't like people sitting in my chair. What the hell do you want, besides getting yourself shot for breaking into my office?"

He didn't say anything as he looked down the barrel of my gun. He then turned his eyes toward me.

"I just want to talk to you," he said.

His voice showed how nervous he was with my gun pointed at him.

"I have a phone. You could have called and made an appointment, or did you call me already?"

"I've never called you," he said with a curious look on his face.

I got the impression from the way he looked at me that he didn't understand what I meant. It was possible that he was not the one who had called and threatened me. It was also possible that he didn't know who did call.

"Well, then, what did you want to talk to me about?"

"Can I get up?" he asked very politely.

"No. I think I prefer you right where you are. If I don't get the answers I want to hear, I'll just call the cops to come and get you. I will charge you with breaking and entering. That should put you out of circulation for three to five years."

"Okay."

"Okay, what?" I asked when he didn't start talking.

"I'll talk."

"Good idea. What did you want to talk to me about? I think that would be a good place to start."

"Mr. Slocomb asked me to talk to you about Emily Sutherland."

I wondered why he wanted to talk to me about Emily. Did he know his son was dating her? Did he know that his son had come to see me?

"What about her?"

"He wants to know if you are investigating her death."

Now, that came as a bit of a surprise. I wondered why he would think that I was investigating Emily's death. Was he hoping to find out what the cops knew? It was no secret that I was friendly with one of the city's best detectives, namely Mac, and that I had several friends on the force. He probably already knew that Mac was heading up the investigation.

"Now why would he want to know that?"

"Emily worked for him. He thinks that if you can find out who killed Emily before the cops do, it might save him a lot of trouble and some embarrassment."

"Why is that?"

"He didn't say, but I think it's because he doesn't want the cops snooping around his nightclub asking a lot of questions. It wouldn't do his business any good."

"There's nothing I can do about that. I have no control over who the police talk to, or what questions they ask. Let me ask you a question. Say that I am investigating her death, what would happen if I find out that he, or one of his hired goons, was involved in the death of Emily?" I asked.

"He wouldn't have sent me over here just to talk to you if he was involved. What he wants is not to be involved."

"What makes him think that I could keep the cops from talking to him and his people?"

"He's not afraid to talk to the cops. He's afraid that they will focus their investigation on him and no one else. That might not be good for him or his business. He told me to tell you that he had nothing to do with the death of Emily, and he wants you to prove it."

Now that was a big surprise. I had to think about that for a minute. Ralph Slocomb wants me to prove he had nothing to do with Emily's death. It felt a little strange; but after I thought about it for a moment, it seemed to make a lot of sense. Slocomb may be into prostitution and illegal gambling, and maybe into a little drug dealing, but I had never heard of anything that would make me believe that he was into murder.

"What you're saying is Slocomb wants to hire me to find him innocent of murdering Emily?"

"Yeah, but not really."

"What? Explain that to me."

"He wants you to do more than that. He wants you to find out who killed Emily and why. He said if you could do that, it would prove he had nothing to do with it. He also said that I was to agree to whatever price you wanted to charge, and to find out how much of a retainer you would need to get started right away."

"Before we get into what it will cost him, I have to know that I will have access to Mr. Slocomb. I may want to ask him a few questions during my investigation. Secondly, he must know that I will tell the police the name of the killer, should I find out who killed her, regardless of who did it. Third, I want access to any or all of his thugs and employees, should I feel the need to talk to them. Fourth, if he or any of his people lie to me, or give me a hard time, or give me the runaround, I will turn over everything I find out to the police. And he is to leave me alone to investigate in my own way. If he agrees to my demands, I will do what I can to find out who killed Emily. Is that clear?"

"Yes."

I then told him what I would need for a retainer before I would even start. It was quite a bit higher than I usually charge, but Slocomb could afford it. I wasn't sure if Slocomb's henchman had the authority to okay my demands, but it would get Slocomb thinking.

"I'll talk to Mr. Slocomb and give him your conditions. I think he will agree with your demands. Once I get his answer, I'll be in touch with you. If he agrees, I will bring the retainer you want so that you can get started. Where will I be able to get in touch with you, say this afternoon?"

"I'll be right here from one to two this afternoon. If I don't hear from you, or Ralph, by then, I'll assume he didn't agree to my demands; and I will go about my business. Is that fair?"

"That's fair enough. Now can I get up?"

"Sure." I said with a smile.

I tucked my gun back in my holster, then reached down and took his hand. After I helped him to his feet, he turned and walked out the door without further comment. I wondered what Slocomb would think of my offer. If he took my offer, I had to think that he might not have had anything to do with Emily's death.

As soon as Slocomb's goon left, I set my chair back up and sat down at my desk. I wondered if Slocomb would accept my offer. Since it wasn't likely that I would get a response until after lunch, I could spend my time looking into other leads. I sat down at my desk and picked up the list of students I had gotten from the school.

I BEGAN TO LOOK OVER the list of students that I had gotten yesterday from the Administration Office of the school. Of all the students on the list, the one I wanted to talk to first was June P. Cullen. If she was the June who had worked with Emily at Slocomb's nightclub, she might know something about what Emily was into that got her killed. I decided that it would be best if I talked to her at her home, away from Slocomb and his henchmen. I checked her address before I left my office for the building's parking garage.

When I got to the parking garage, I noticed the car that I had seen following me last night. The only difference was that the car was parked in the parking garage near the entrance. It was not the car that was usually parked there.

I watched the car out of the corner of my eye as I walked to my car. As I got in, I pulled my gun out from under my coat and put it on the seat next to me. I then started my car and drove out of the parking garage. Once out of the parking garage, I turned out onto the street and headed toward the downtown area.

After two cars passed by the entrance to the parking garage, the car pulled out and began following me. It stayed behind me for several blocks. It took me a few blocks before I found a place where I could pull over to the curb and stop. It happened to be in front of a book store, but I was more interested in the fact that it provided the driver with no place to go except to drive by me. That gave me the opportunity to get a license plate number.

As the black Lexus sport sedan drove by, I tried to see who was driving it. With the glare on the windshield and the heavy tinted side windows, I couldn't get a good look at the driver. The only thing I was sure of was that it was a man driving, and he was the only one I could see in the car. However, I did get the license number before he managed to get around the corner.

As soon as he was out of sight, I headed on down the street. When I got to the corner, I turned then turned again at the next corner. At that point I was pretty sure that I had lost him. I then turned into the parking lot of a busy restaurant and parked in the back corner as far away from the street as possible. I found a parking space between a large pickup truck and an equally large SUV which made it almost impossible to see my car from the street. I then picked up my phone and called my good friend in the Department of Motor Vehicles. The phone was answered after only a couple of rings.

"Department of Motor Vehicles, how may I direct your call?"

"Jennifer Taylor in licensing, please."

"One moment."

I knew that when calling any governmental agency a moment could turn into a half an hour or more. If Jennifer was busy, I could have to wait awhile to talk to her, but I needed information and would be willing to wait.

Thinking about Jennifer while waiting for her to answer the phone, was not at all unpleasant. Jennifer was one of the most beautiful and the sexiest women that I have had the pleasure of knowing. Her reddish brown hair and green eyes had always amazed me. We had dated off and on for years, but only recently had it seemed to be getting serious. When thinking of her it was easy to remember that she had been my first love, and I hers.

Suddenly, my thoughts of her were interrupted by her pleasant voice coming over my phone.

"Licensing, Jennifer speaking."

"Hi, Jennifer."

"Hi, Peter. What's up?"

"I need a little help. Could you run a license plate for me?"

"Sure."

I gave her the license plate number and listened as she typed it into her computer.

"Am I going to see you tonight?" she asked as she waited for the results to come up on her computer.

"I'm not sure. A lot depends on how things go this afternoon. Can I call you later?"

"Sure. Oh, here we go. I've got it for you."

"Okay. I'm ready."

"The car is a new Lexus four door sports sedan. It is black in color. The registered owner is a Mildred A. Dunberger. She has an address in Cherry Creek," she said then gave me the address.

I wrote down the address and thought about it. The name didn't ring any bells with me. I couldn't remember ever hearing it before. It would require a little research to find out who she was. But one thing was probably a good bet; she probably had money, given the type of car she owned and the address where she lived.

"Thanks, Honey. I'll give you a call later."

"Okay. Love you."

"Love you, too," I said, then hung up.

I sat in my car while I thought about the information that I had gotten from Jennifer. A thought came to mind that I should spend a little time in the library to find out just who Mildred A. Dunberger was, but for now I would pay a visit to the address. I didn't know what I would learn, but it was worth a visit.

I BACKED OUT OF THE PARKING SPACE and headed for Cherry Creek. I kept an eye out for someone tailing me, but I saw no one following me. It didn't take me long to find the home of Mrs. Dunberger. It turned out to be a rather large house. The front was of stone and brick with large arched windows on the main floor, and a Spanish styled tile roof.

It had a circular driveway that made a large sweeping loop in front of a fancy front door and entryway. It had the appearance of a very expensive home, something very close to a million dollars, probably more. Off to one side was a three car garage with servant quarters above it. In the drive sat a white Lincoln Town Car, a red Cadillac sedan and a green Jaguar sedan, but no Lexus. Since the garage doors were closed, there was no telling what kind of cars might be found there.

I had no idea if the three cars in the drive belonged to anyone living in the house. It looked almost like there was some sort of meeting going on at the house. I couldn't see why the owners of the house would have their cars parked out in front of their own house so early in the morning. I doubted that the cars belonged to anyone actually living there. It was more apt to be a meeting of a women's breakfast club, or of a morning Bridge club get together.

I didn't take the time to try to get license plate numbers from the three cars. I would have to drive up the driveway to see them. I didn't want to draw any attention to myself, so I drove on down the block. Jennifer would be able to find out how many cars and what kind they were that belonged at that address. Since I didn't feel it was all that important right now, I decided to head back toward the downtown area and find June P. Cullen's home.

After driving around the block, I headed back toward the downtown area. Ms Cullen's address showed that she lived not very far from where Emily had had her apartment.

IT DIDN'T TAKE ME LONG to get to the apartment building where Ms Cullen lived. I found a parking place and walked up to the apartment's front door. Beside the door was a bank of names with call buttons next to them. It didn't take but a minute to find the one with Ms Cullen's name beside it. I pressed the button.

While I waited for a reply, I looked around. The apartment building looked like it was a bit nicer than the one Emily had lived in. Although the building didn't appear to be any newer, it did appear to have had much better care. The trim on the outside of the building had been painted within the last couple of years. It looked as if windows had been replaced with windows that were probably more efficient and energy saving, as well as more secure.

From what I could see of the hallway through the door, it was bright and cheery. The entrance door was a fairly new security door that had the latest in electronic locks available for apartment buildings. Even the door looked as if it was very solid and would keep almost any intruder out. My thoughts were interrupted by an answer to the call button.

"Who is it," the female voice asked from inside.

"My name is Peter Blackstone. I would like to talk to you about Emily Sutherland. I understand that you attended the same art school and had at least one class together."

"I don't think I have anything to say to you."

"I also know that the two of you worked together at Mr. Slocomb's nightclub."

There was a lot of quiet for a moment or two. I was beginning to think that I would have to wait outside until she left the building to get a chance to talk to her.

"Jeffery Slocomb hired me to find her," I said, hoping that would get her to let me in so I could talk to her.

I waited. It took a moment or two before the door buzzed. I quickly pulled open the door and stepped inside. Since the call button didn't have an apartment number on it, and she didn't tell me what her apartment number was, I stood in the hall and listened for a door to open. I could see most of the apartment doors on the first floor, and only one at the top of the stairs.

Finally, a young woman leaned over the upstairs railing and looked down at me. I looked up and smiled at her, but she didn't smile back.

"Ms Cullen?"

"Yes," she replied as she looked down at me.

She didn't invite me up. I got the feeling that she was scared, but I wasn't sure why. I made no move to start up the stairs because I didn't know what her reaction might be. Instead, I waited a moment to let her decide if she wanted me to come any closer.

"I was wondering if I might come up and talk with you."

"I guess that would be all right," she said, but didn't sound too sure.

I went up the stairs, but not too fast. There was something about the way she looked at me that made me want to be very careful in my movements. She looked as if she might break and run back to her apartment at any moment. I didn't want that to happen.

When I got to the top of the stairs, I got a better look at her. Her eyes appeared to be bloodshot and red as if she had been crying. There were dark circles under her eyes. It was clear that she had had a bad night, but I had no idea why.

"I'm sorry to disturb you, but I would like to ask you a few questions about Emily. Would it be okay with you if we go into your apartment to talk? I don't think it's necessary that your neighbors hear our conversation," I asked, hoping that she would consent to my request.

"Are you a policeman?"

"No. I'm a private investigator. I was hired to find Emily by Jeffery."

"Does his father know?"

"Not unless Jeffery told him."

"Come in," she said as she turned and went back into her apartment.

I followed her into her apartment. As I entered, I took a moment to look around. Her apartment was much nicer than Emily's. Her furnishings were much newer and up-to-date. It was clear there had been a good deal of money spent to furnish and decorate the apartment. I wondered where she got the money to have such a nice apartment.

"What is it that I can help you with?"

"Please excuse me for asking, but why have you been crying?"

She looked at me as if I had asked the unthinkable, but also looked like she needed to talk to someone. I got the impression that she already knew that Emily was dead.

"You have already found Emily, haven't you?" she asked.

"Yes, I have."

"She is dead, isn't she?"

"Yes, but my guess would be that you already know that."

"Yes. So Jeffery didn't really hire you, did he?"

"Yes. He did hire me. He hired me before we knew that Emily had died. I have not had a chance to tell him. Emily's parents also hired me to find her. They do know that she is dead. Since she is dead, I have changed the direction of my investigation. I'm now trying to find out who killed her, and why."

"Are the police looking into it?"

"Yes. I still plan to find out who killed her and see that justice is done. I'm hoping that you might be able to help me in that quest."

"How can I help?"

"First of all, I would like to know how it is that you know that Emily is dead?"

"Jeff told me a little while ago. His father told him. I think his father knows someone that works in the Coroner's Office."

"I see. What was your relationship with Emily like?"

She hesitated for a moment or two before she started to talk.

"Emily and I met in the art school. She was shy and – I don't know – sort of quiet. She was a farm girl from rural Kansas who didn't have a lot of experience with boys. She was a darn good student and an excellent artist," she said while I sat quietly and listened to her.

"We became friends right away. We spent a lot of time together. I sort of helped her get used to what it was like to live in the big city."

"Did you introduce her to Jeffery?"

"Not right away. It wasn't until after she started modeling for figure drawing classes."

"I would like to talk about her time in school. Did she have any problems at the art school?"

"Not at first. She was real refreshing. She was so innocent. She used almost no makeup, but she didn't need it. She had that hometown girl look. You know, the girl next door type. She wasn't a drop-dead beauty, but she had a very nice figure and a killer smile. She could have had any boy in the school, but she was so shy that she wouldn't date any of them."

"She dated Jeffery," I reminded her.

"Yeah, but she didn't date him until after she started working for his father at his nightclub."

"You didn't answer my question. Did she have any trouble or problems at the art school?"

"Not at first. It was just in the last semester," she said, but didn't continue.

I got the impression that she didn't want to talk about it. I wondered why. What was it that she didn't want to tell me?

"Tell me about her last semester."

She hesitated for a moment or two just looking at the floor in front of her. I had a feeling that she was trying to gather her thoughts while getting her emotions under control. I simply waited until she was ready to talk again.

"She had been doing a great job in her figure drawing class. She got very good grades. If you ever saw any of her figure drawings, you'd know just how good she really was. She didn't really need a class in figure drawing, she was that good."

"Why did she take it?"

"She needed it to get her degree. It's one of those school things. You have to take the class even if you're better at it than the instructor."

"Was she better?"

"Yes. A lot better."

"What happened in her last semester?"

"Her teacher put some moves on her. She didn't like him. I think she was afraid of him. From what she told me, he wanted her to go to his apartment for some private lessons, if you know what I mean."

"I think I get the picture."

"When she told me about it, I told her what his private lessons were all about."

"Did she go?"

"No. You have to remember that she didn't have very much money. I got her a job at Mr. Slocomb's nightclub with the agreement that she was to work only as a hostess, nothing else. She didn't make a lot of money. Certainly not as much as the girls that worked in the escort service, but she made enough to get by on."

"Back to what happened when she refused to have the private lessons?"

"Steuben knew that she was one of his best students, but it made him mad when she wouldn't play his stupid games. He was nice enough looking that he could have gotten a woman his own age, but he liked them younger. Anyway, he threatened her with dropping her grades, which would have prevented her from getting her degree if she didn't go along with him."

"Why did she model for the class? I assumed she modeled in the nude?"

"Yes, she did. She had been modeling for his class for about three months before he started putting moves on her. She only modeled because she needed the money. Emily had never had a problem with him until lately.

"She had told me that he had started watching her closely during the last couple of months, even when she wasn't modeling, but never hit on her until about two, maybe three weeks ago. She said that it made her nervous. I told her to be careful around him. He was the kind of guy that would do almost anything to get what he wanted."

"Were you there on the day that Emily attended her last class?"

"No. I was not feeling very well that day and didn't go to class. Emily called me at home earlier that day. She wanted to talk to me, but she didn't want to talk on the phone. She was supposed to meet me at my apartment after dinner that evening, but she never showed up. I tried to call her a couple of times, but never got an answer."

"Do you know if Steuben had ever made passes at any of the other girls that modeled in any of his classes?"

"Not for sure, but I have heard rumors that a couple of the girls that modeled in his classes got better grades than they deserved. When you hear enough rumors like that, you start to think that there might be some truth to them."

"I'm afraid that isn't proof, but it might be of some help," I said. "Please don't take this wrong, but you are a very nice looking young woman with a very nice figure. Have you ever modeled for Steuben?"

"No. A friend of mine that had the class before I even went to the school warned me about him."

"Did he ever try to get you to model for him?"

"Yes. After class one day, he came up to me and put his hand on my shoulder. He told me how nice I looked and wanted me to model for him. I told him to take his hand off me, or I would report him to the president of the school. I also told him that if any of my grades were not what they should be, I would report him for that as well as his conduct," June said with a hint of anger in her voice.

"What happened after that?"

"I got the grades that I deserved, and he hardly talked to me the rest of the time I was in his class."

"Good for you. I want to thank you for talking with me."

"Are you going after that ass?"

"An ass, he is. But a murderer, I'm not sure. I can tell you this much, if I find he did murder Emily, he will pay dearly for it. Other than that, I can make no promises. The school might find out what kind of games he is playing as a result of my investigation, however," I said with a grin.

"That would be nice," she said with a hint of a smile.

"I best be going. I would appreciate it if you said nothing about our conversation."

"I won't."

As I got up, June stood. She walked me to her apartment door. As soon as I was out of the apartment, she closed the door. I could hear the door being locked as I walked down the hall to the stairs. I left the building thinking about what she had told me.

From what I had been told, Emily had apparently been modeling for several months before she told her folks. I wondered how long she had worked for Slocomb. I was pretty sure that she had not told her folks about that either.

It had become clear that the next people I should talk with were some of the students that attended the last class Emily had attended. I especially wanted to talk to the last one out of the classroom. The last one out of the classroom was the one most likely to have heard or seen something that might help.

When I got to my car, I stood and looked at the apartment building. It had been obvious that June had lost a dear friend. It was also obvious to me that she expected me to do something about it. I only hoped that I could. I got into my car and headed back to my office.

CHAPTER SIX

WHEN I GOT BACK to my office after stopping for lunch, I noticed the flashing light on my answering machine. I sat down and got a pen and paper so I was ready to write down any information before I pressed the button. There were two messages on the answering machine. I pressed the button for the first message.

"Who the hell do you think you are putting conditions on my hiring you? If I'm paying you, you do as I say. Call me back," the voice on the machine demanded, then gave me a number to call.

Not once did the person calling me give his name, but I didn't need one. I had gotten the message I had expected to get from Ralph Slocomb. He was a man with a temper that could be nasty at times, and he didn't like people telling him what to do. When I had laid down the conditions of my employment to his goon, I didn't really expect him to accept them. The fact that he didn't accept my conditions helped keep him on my list of prime suspects.

I thought about calling him back, but figured I might call him back after he stewed for a little while longer. I had another call on the machine that I needed to check out anyway. I pressed the button for the next call.

"This is Mac. I've got a little more information on the lab tests. Give me a call," he said, then the message ended.

It wasn't necessary for Mac to give me his number. I already had it, and he knew it. In fact, I knew it by heart. I picked up the receiver and placed a call to Mac. Any information he had might be of immediate value to me.

At this point I had only two suspects I could put a name to, Franklin Steuben and Ralph Slocomb. I believed that there might be someone else who committed the murder, but I didn't have a name. My unknown suspect was either the one I had seen at Washington Park where I had almost hit the lawn bag, or the person who had hired him to dispose of the body at the park.

There was still this thought running through the back of my mind that the man that ran from the scene could have been Steuben. He fit the description of the man, but my description was so vague that it could fit a lot of men in the Denver area, literally hundreds of them.

I placed a call to Mac. The phone was answered by the duty officer and quickly transferred to Captain MacDonald.

"Captain MacDonald."

"Peter. I got your message."

"Yeah. The lab report shows that our victim was forced to take the drug. It was cocaine just as the M.E. suspected. There were bruises on her arms and shoulders that were first thought to have occurred when she was put in the lawn bag, but the M.E. doesn't think so now. The M.E. said that some of the bruises indicate that she had been held down on a firm but smooth surface. Possibly on some kind of firm mattress with a smooth surface while she was forced to inhale the stuff. From the amount and severity of the bruises, she must have put up a good fight.

"He also said that she was probably naked when she was forced to take the drug. There were no marks on her body from the seams of clothes or from a bra strap that he would have expected to see even if she had on just a bra or panties while lying down."

"Does he have any idea where she might have been when she died?"

"No, but wherever it was, she had been forcibly held down on something that had to be fairly smooth, but with a sheet or light weight blanket over it. She had bruises that showed folds like you might find from lying on a wrinkled sheet, but only a couple of them. Not a lot of help, I'm afraid," Mac said.

"Any idea when she was murdered?"

"The lab said that it was really hard to determine without knowing where she was killed. The M.E. said that the best he could come up with was sometime between Wednesday and Friday of last week."

"You mean that she has been dead for a week or more?"

"That's what the M.E. thinks. He also thinks that she was kept somewhere cold from the time she was killed until you found her. He based that on the condition of the body."

"Was she kept in a freezer?"

"He doesn't think so. An examination of some of her cells and tissue didn't indicate she had been frozen at anytime. He thinks that she had been kept in a place that was cold, like a refrigerator. You got any ideas as to where our crime scene might be?"

"Not at the moment," I said with a hint of frustration. "Have you been to her apartment yet?"

"Yeah. I already have the crime scene people going over the place. They're still there and still looking. I talked to them a few minutes ago and they still don't have anything that will help. The only thing they said was that they seriously doubted that she was killed in her apartment. They're pretty sure that her apartment is not our primary crime scene."

"That would have been my first thought."

"Mine, too. You got any ideas as to who might have killed her?" Mac asked, frustration showing in the sound of his voice.

"Not yet, but I'm working on it."

"You wouldn't keep anything you have from me, would you?"

"Right now, I have nothing. I don't even have a hint as to who killed her or why. It would probably help if I knew where she had been killed. Did anything in the bag give you a clue?"

"No. Almost every yard in the city has the kind of leaves and branches that we found in the bag. The lab is still going through the bag for anything abnormal. They're hoping to find something that will get us closer to finding out where she was murdered."

"I hope they find something," I said.

"Me, too. I'll talk to you later. Keep in touch," Mac said.

"I will," I said, then hung up the phone.

After hanging up the phone, I tipped back in my chair and thought about what Mac had told me. She had been dead for at least a week, yet her body was just found. Why? Why had they waited to dispose of the body where it could be found quickly? Was it possible that whoever had killed her was getting scared that she might be found and believed it was necessary to get rid of her quickly? Where had her body been kept for that week?

Where was there a cold place big enough to keep a body other than in a morgue or in a freezer? Nothing seemed to make any sense.

At first it seemed a little strange that she had been put in a bag of leaves. But when I got to thinking about it, the leaves had apparently accomplished what was probably expected. The leaves had made it hard for the police to figure out where the primary crime scene was located. It also made it difficult to pin down the time of death.

Finding the person who had killed Emily was not going to be easy. It was looking like I wasn't going to get much help from the crime lab, either.

That thought brought back to mind the list of students. It was all I had to go on for the moment. The next one on the list that I was planning to contact was D. Preston Nielsen. Emily's mother had mentioned the name Preston as a friend of Emily's, but I had no idea how much of a friend. She had indicated that he might be a boyfriend, but had said that Emily referred to him as just a friend. I wondered if he was her boyfriend, and did Jeff know about him. I decided that Nielsen was probably my best shot at the moment. It was time to find him and see what he had to say.

I looked up his address, then went to my car in the parking garage. I left for the area near the school.

AS I DROVE DOWN THE STREET, I glanced in my rearview mirror. Not to my surprise was that same Lexus sport sedan that had followed me earlier. I smiled to myself. Whoever was following me was persistent, even if he wasn't any good at tailing someone. The only person I could think of that might want me followed was Ralph Slocomb. However, I would have thought that one of Ralph's henchmen would be better at it. That thought made me wonder if it was one of Ralph's henchmen. I had my doubts.

As I drove, I began to think about the car behind me. It looked like the same car that had followed me earlier, but I wasn't a hundred percent sure. If it was the same car, it belonged to Mrs. Dunberger, according to Jennifer. I had no idea why she would want me followed. That brought to mind the question of what was her interest in the case.

It had been a man driving the car. What was he hoping to find out? Was he the same man that had called me and warned me off the case? It certainly was a possibility. Was he someone who was just keeping tabs on me to make sure that I wasn't getting too close? But, too close to whom, I didn't know. Again, it was a possibility. They were all good questions, but I didn't have any good answers.

I decided that I didn't really want the guy following me. Since I didn't know anything about him or what he wanted, I certainly didn't want him to know who I was talking to. I thought about trapping him in an alley and confronting him, but that might not be a good idea. If I confronted him and it turned out to be someone of any importance, I could be in a lot of trouble with the police.

To my way of thinking I had the right to move around without being followed. The one thing I was sure of was that he was not a policeman. He didn't know how to tail someone without being spotted almost immediately. I knew that the police didn't use fancy cars like that one because they were too easy to spot.

I didn't figure that he would fall for the same trick that I pulled earlier, so I simply found a parking place. The parking place turned out to be near an office supply store. There were very few cars parked on the street which made it easy for him to find a parking space just a couple of cars behind me. I wondered what he was thinking when I didn't get out of my car right away.

I picked up my cell phone and placed a call to Jennifer again. It didn't take me very long to get through to her.

"Licensing, Jennifer speaking."

"Hi, Honey."

"Hi, Peter. I didn't expect to hear from you so soon. Is something wrong?"

"No. Can you look up and find out all the cars that are owned by the people at the address you gave me on the black Lexus?"

"Sure. Give me a minute."

I didn't have to wait very long before she spoke.

"There's the black Lexus, of course, a black Cadillac, and a red Porsche 911."

"A red Porsche?"

"Yes. Is there something special about the Porsche?"

"There might be. One of my suspects drives a red Porsche 911. Who is the red Porsche registered to?"

"Mildred A. Dunberger. The same person who owns the black Lexus and the black Cadillac."

"I find that interesting. Do you happen to know who Mildred Dunberger is?"

"Yes. She is a very wealthy widow with a lot of high powerful friends in the Denver area. Peter, what have you gotten yourself into?"

"Right now, I don't know."

"You better be careful."

"I will. I'll call you later."

"What would you think if I were to come over to your place after work and fix dinner for the two of us?"

"I think that would be great. I have a couple of steaks in the fridge. There are the makings for a salad, too."

"That sounds good. I'll see you at your place."

"Okay."

"I love you."

"Love you, too," I said, then hung up.

After I hung up, my thoughts turned back to the car parked behind me. Now I wasn't sure what to do. It didn't seem likely that Mrs. Dunberger would be involved in anything illegal, especially murder. But after giving it some thought, she wouldn't be the first influential person to be involved in something illegal and have someone killed to avoid being exposed. If she had the kind of reputation that Jennifer hinted at, she would not want any kind of scandal that would involve her. The only question I had at the moment was how far would she go to protect her reputation?

My thoughts turned to the red Porsche. Maybe the Porsche registered to Mrs. Dunberger was not the same red Porsche that I had seen Steuben get into in front of the school. It might be a good idea to find out. I needed to get the license plate number of the Porsche Steuben was driving and check it with Jennifer to see who was the registered owner.

I looked in my rearview mirror and could see that the driver of the Lexus was still sitting there. I thought about it for a moment before I came to a decision. It was time to confront the driver of the Lexus.

I got out of my car and walked down the street along side the parked cars. When I got close to the Lexus, I could see that the driver was looking at me. I reached under my coat and put my hand on my gun. I then opened my coat with my free hand far enough so he could see I was carrying.

As I let my coat fall back over my gun, I motioned for the driver to roll down the window. He did as I requested. The fact that I still had my hand on my gun might have had something to do with his cooperation.

"Put both hands on the steering wheel so I can see them," I said as I moved closer to the driver's door.

He again cooperated. I walked up next to the car and looked inside. There was no one else in the car.

"Why are you following me?"

"I wasn't following you," the man said with a hint of nervousness in his voice.

"This is the second time this car has followed me today. Now let's save ourselves a whole lot of time and trouble, and cut the crap. Who are you?

He appeared rather nervous. He looked at where my hand was before he decided to answer.

"I'm Walter Forsythe."

"Who do you work for, Walter?"

"Mrs. Dunberger," he said somewhat reluctantly.

"Why are you following me?"

"I'm supposed to tell her where you go and who you talk to."

"Why is she interested in what I'm doing?" I asked, not really expecting to get an answer.

"I don't know, sir. She didn't tell me."

For some reason I found it easy to believe him. He didn't act like he had any idea what he was doing. He certainly didn't know how to tail someone.

"What is it you normally do for Mrs. Dunberger?"

"I'm the butler, sir," he said as if being a butler was something special.

I almost laughed out loud at his response. I'm sure being a butler is something special, but it certainly didn't qualify him to tail anyone. This guy had no business trying to play detective. He neither had the muscle nor the training. And he certainly wasn't cut out for it.

"You go back to Mrs. Dunberger, and tell her that I knew you were following me before you did. I suggest that you keep your duties limited to being a butler and leave the detective work to those of us who know what we are doing."

"Yes, sir."

I walked around the front of the car and stepped up on the curb. As he pulled away from the curb, I glanced at the wheels on the car. They looked to be the standard wheels and tires for that model car. I was a little disappointed. I had hoped to connect the car to the one I had seen at Washington Park.

I watched him as he drove away. I was beginning to think that it might not be a bad idea to make a call on Mrs. Dunberger to find out why she thought it was necessary to follow me, but that would have to wait for another time. I needed to talk to D. Preston Nielsen.

I RETURNED TO MY CAR and headed for Nielsen's address. While I drove, I kept a good watch for anyone else who might have decided to follow me. I didn't see anyone.

Nielson's home was located in an area where there were a lot of very nice town houses. It took me a little while to find his town house. When I looked at it, I got the feeling that Nielsen was not a poor man. The town houses were high-end buildings with all the amenities.

I parked in the visitor's parking area and walked up to the front door. I knocked and then waited. I knocked a second time and was beginning to think that there was no one home when the door opened. Standing in front of me was a tall slender woman. The woman was wearing a robe that did little to hide the smooth flowing lines of her figure. In fact, she looked very sexy. It was also open almost to her waist. It was clear that she had nothing on under it.

"Can I help you," she said as she looked me over.

"I'm looking for D. Preston Nielsen.

"I'm D. Preston Nielsen. What can I do to help you?" she asked with a smile that would melt the coldest of hearts.

"Ah – yes. I'm Peter Blackstone. I would like to ask you a few questions about Emily Sutherland."

"Oh. Please come in."

She stepped back and opened the door further. Once I was inside, she closed the door, led me to her living room and invited me to sit down, but she didn't sit down.

"Would you please excuse me for a minute? I would like to get into something more appropriate for a visitor."

I didn't answer her. I simply nodded and watched her as she left the room.

Once she was gone, I took the opportunity to look around. The living room was decorated very nicely. The furniture was very expensive. There were several paintings on the walls that looked as if they might be originals, and also very expensive. I couldn't help but think of June's apartment. It had also been decorated very nicely and expensively, but not as expensively as this town house.

When D. Preston Nielsen returned, she caught me looking at a small framed picture that was sitting on the end table next to the sofa. I didn't recognize the person in the picture, but it was the solid gold frame that had caught my interest. A frame like that would cost several thousand dollars.

"That's a picture of my brother," she said with a smile.

"A very handsome young man."

"Yes, he was," she said as the smile faded from her face.

She walked over to a chair across the coffee table from me and sat down. I got the impression from what she said, and the look on her face, that her brother was dead.

"I'm sure you are not here to talk about my brother. What is it you would like to talk to me about?"

"It is my understanding that you were a friend of Emily Sutherland. Is that correct?"

"Yes. We were friends," she replied.

"Excuse me if I sound a little forward, but it is my understanding that you met at the art school. You don't strike me as a student."

"I'm not a student at the school," she said with a smile. "And I did not meet Emily at the school. I met her at Mr. Slocomb's nightclub downtown.

"Then how is it that you were on the school register as a student?"

"I did attend two figure drawing classes on a whim, but didn't like it; so I quit. That's probably how I got on the school register."

"From the expression on your face when I mentioned Emily's name, I take it that you know she is dead. Is that correct?"

"Yes. Jeff Slocomb told me."

Her answer made me wonder why Jeff hadn't called to cancel my search for her. It may have been that he knew I was now looking for her killer.

"I believe she was murdered. Is that right?" she asked.

"Yes. Do you have any suggestions as to who might have killed her?"

"No, not really."

"I take it that you can think of at least one person who might have killed her."

"I don't know about that, but I know that she was having trouble with one of her instructors at the school."

"Do you know who that instructor might be?"

"Yes. His name is Steuben, Franklin Steuben," she said with a sharp note of dislike for him.

"What makes you think he might have killed her?"

"She had been getting very good grades from him until he made a pass at her and she rejected him. After that her grades fell off quickly in his class. She told me about it and asked me what she should do."

"What did you tell her?"

"I told her to go to the Administration Office and report him."

"Did she do that?"

"I don't know, but I don't think she did. I don't think she had a chance."

"How is that? When did you tell her to go to the Administration Office to report him?" I asked.

"We met for lunch on Wednesday before her figure drawing class. She told me that he would not leave her alone. That's when I told her."

That bit of information moved Steuben to the top of my suspect list, so to speak. If Emily had told Steuben that she was going to report his inappropriate behavior toward her to the administration, he could lose his job. That would certainly give him a motive to kill her. I already knew that he had opportunity.

"Is there anyone else that you can think of that might have wanted to do Emily harm? Maybe someone who was obsessed with her, a classmate that wanted her, but she had rejected. Something like that," I asked.

"No. No. Not that I can think of. She never mentioned anyone like that. I take it you know that she was going out with Jeff Slocomb."

"Do you have any idea how that was going over with Jeff's father?"

"I don't think his father knew about it. I do know that his father didn't like us to date any of the other employees, and that he didn't want his son dating any of the girls that worked for him."

"What would he do if he found out that Emily was dating his son," I asked.

"I'm not sure."

"Why is that?"

"Emily didn't work at any of his private clubs. She only worked at the nightclub downtown."

"At the private clubs, what was the penalty for dating his son?"

"Oh, I'm sure you would be fired immediately."

"That's all? Wasn't he afraid that you might tell the police about his private clubs?"

"No, I don't think so. The police already know he has them, but he moves them around all the time. I never knew if I was going to be working at one of them until that afternoon."

"How do you know where to go and when you are to work?"

"I'd get a call in the afternoon and be told when I would be picked up. I would be picked up at the appointed time and taken to the house. I'd get a ride in a different car each time, and the car would have the windows covered so we couldn't see where we were going. There was always someone in the back seat with us to make sure we didn't peek out."

"Were all the employees treated that way?"

"Yes. The only ones who knew where the gambling was to take place were a few of Mr. Slocomb's closest and most trusted people. Even the dealers and the bartenders didn't know. They were brought to the house the same way I was, in closed cars."

It was no wonder that the police never knew where to raid. Even the employees didn't know where they would be working at any given time.

"I guess that's all for now. Thank you for your cooperation," I said as I stood up and walked to the door.

"Oh, one more question. What does the D stand for, and why do you go by Preston?"

"That's two questions, Peter," she said with a sexy smile. "The D stands for DeeDee. I've never liked DeeDee, and I don't think I look like a DeeDee. I only use Preston in legal matters. I usually go by just DJ. Emily was the only one who started calling me Preston. I think it was to make her parents think that she had a boyfriend, which she did. But it wasn't me. I don't think she wanted them to know who her boyfriend was."

"Why DJ?"

"Oh, I was part of a band in high school. I would announce the songs. Since I didn't like being called DeeDee, they started calling me DJ. It just sort of stuck.

"I see. Again thank you for your cooperation."

"Peter, do you think you can find her killer?"

"I don't know, but I'm going to try."

She simply nodded, then opened the door.

I left DeeDee's town house and got in my car. I left the area and returned to my office.

CHAPTER SEVEN

BY NOW, RALPH SLOCOMB would have been stewing enough that he would be madder than hell. I didn't care if he was mad or not. The only way I would consider taking him on as a client was if he agreed to my conditions, all of them.

It didn't take very long before I was driving into the parking garage of the building where my office was located. I was planning to call him as soon as I got to my office, but there was another problem facing me at the moment.

I noticed a black Lexus was parked off to the side in the parking garage. It was partially hidden by a large concrete column, but there was no doubt in my mind that it was the same Lexus that had been following me.

My eyes were drawn to the wheels on the car. They were the stock wheels and wheel covers that came on that model Lexus. It didn't have the fancy custom chrome wheels I had seen on the black Lexus at Washington Park.

I smiled a bit thinking that the poor butler was just doing what he was told. Giving it some thought, I wondered if there might be someone else in the car this time. Since the butler was bad enough at tailing me that I sent him home, Mrs. Dunberger may have decided that she needed someone else to follow me. She might have hired someone with not only more skill at tailing someone, but with a little more muscle to back him up. Then again, there was the possibility that she was waiting to talk to me. Either way, I would have to be careful.

As I pulled into my parking space, I reached under my coat and pulled out my gun. With my gun in my hand, I got out of my car and started walking toward the Lexus. I kept my hand down at my side and slightly behind me so that my gun could not be seen. I also kept a concrete post close by just in case I needed a little cover.

I approached the driver's side of the car with a great deal of caution as I had no idea what to expect. When I was only a few feet from the car, the driver's side window started to roll down. I quickly stepped behind one of the concrete posts.

"Mr. Blackstone, Mrs. Dunberger would like to talk to you," the driver said.

I wondered if this was a trap. I couldn't believe that Mrs. Dunberger would stick her neck out like this just to talk to me.

"Mr. Blackstone, this is Mrs. Dunberger. I can understand your being cautious, so I will get out of the car and come to you."

It was a woman's voice I had heard, but I couldn't see her. I also heard the door open on the far side of the car. I looked around the corner of the post and saw a woman in her late fifties or early sixties get out of the car. As she walked around in front of the car, I could see that she was dressed like a woman who had money. I decided that it would be okay if I moved out from behind the post.

"It is nice to see you, Mr. Blackstone," the woman said with a pleasant smile.

"You can't blame me for being cautious. I have been lied to, followed, and threatened. As you may guess, I don't like it very much," I said as I continued to hold my gun in my hand while keeping an eye on the car behind her.

"I'm sorry about that, but I think we need to talk."

"Maybe we do, but this is not the place. If you would like to come up to my office, alone, I would be more than happy to talk with you."

"Can't we talk here or in my car?" she asked in a rather pleasant voice.

"I don't do business in a parking garage. I have found it not to be the safest place to talk."

She turned and looked at the man in the driver's seat as if she wasn't sure if she should go with me or not. She looked back at me for a moment then smiled.

"I guess it would be more appropriate to talk in your office," she said, then turned and looked back at the car.

"Norman, wait for me here."

"Yes, Ma'am," he replied.

Mrs. Dunberger started to walk toward me. When she got next to me, I turned and led her to the elevator. I glanced over my shoulder every so often to make sure that Norman stayed in the car.

Once in the elevator, I put my gun away. We rode the elevator to the floor where my office was located without saying a word. When the elevator stopped, I took a quick look out into the hall to make sure that Norman hadn't run up the stairs to get there before we did. The hall was empty.

"This way," I said as I pointed down the hall toward my office.

We walked to my office and went inside. I directed her to a chair in front of my desk where she sat down. As soon as I sat down behind my desk, she looked at me and smiled.

"Mr. Blackstone, I know nothing of any threats that you may have received. However, I did have my butler follow you, but it seems that he is not very good at it."

"That's an understatement. But you didn't come here to talk about your butler's inability to follow someone. What is it you want?"

"I see you are a man who likes to get right to the point. That being the case, it seems that you visited my son at his place of employment. Your questions made him rather uncomfortable. He was very embarrassed having you question him in front of several of his fellow workers. I would like to know what reason you have for harassing him where he works."

I had to think a little about what she had said. I had no idea who her son was, or that she even had a son. It was at that moment I remembered that there was a red Porsche registered to her. I wondered if Steuben was her son. He was the only one that I could think of that I had talked to where any of his fellow workers might have been able to hear us. I looked at her for a moment before I responded.

"Your son wouldn't happen to be Franklin Steuben, would he?"

"Yes. He has a different last name because he is my son from my first marriage."

"I didn't know that," I said. "But I have to tell you, I don't care who his parents are. I simply questioned him about one of his students who was murdered."

Mrs. Dunberger just looked at me without any change in her expression. I wasn't sure if what I said had come as a surprise to her, or if she already knew about the murder of one of his students. My guess would be she knew about the murder. Why else would she have me followed?

"I can assure you that the police will also be questioning your son about it very soon, if they haven't already talked to him," I added.

"What is your interest in the murder of this student? It seems to me that it is a police matter, not a matter for some little-known private investigator," she said with a hint of superiority in her voice.

I can't say that I liked the reference to "little-known private investigator", but then I didn't really care what she thought. If she had a need to feel important by her comment about me, then I hoped it helped.

"Yes, it is a police matter. But it matters to me since the victim's parents had hired me to find her."

"I see, then you have no legal standing in this case at all," she said while looking me right in the eyes.

"You could look at it that way if it makes you feel better. But I can assure you that I am still looking into it," I said as I looked right back at her.

"I would strongly suggest that you do not harass my son again," she said flatly.

"Is that a threat?"

"Call it what you will. But if you try to question him again I will see to it that you no longer harass my son or anyone else."

"Now that was clearly a threat. I don't like to be threatened by anyone. I don't give a damn who it is, and I certainly don't give a damn who you are. I tend to take threats very personally. It also tells me that you are hiding something."

"I can assure you that should you question him again, I will have you arrested for harassing my son," she said as she stood up.

"I will continue to search for the person who murdered Emily Sutherland, and will question anyone I feel the need to question, including your son. I will also be calling the detective in charge of the investigation to tell him that you took time out of your busy day of Bridge playing and your other social activities to come by my office and threatened me. I will also let him know that you had me followed. I'm sure that he will find it interesting that you should take such an interest in my investigation. I wouldn't be surprised if it makes him think that you and your son have something to hide."

"I see you like to make threats as well."

"Oh, no. You misunderstood me. I do not threaten people. That was a promise. And a promise from me is one that will be carried out," I assured her.

She looked at me as if she wondered if I would actually call the police.

"Good day, Mr. Blackstone," she said then turned sharply and started to leave.

"One more thing," I said which caused her to stop, turn around and look at me. "I strongly suggest that you not have anyone following me again. I will not be so nice to the next one as I was to your butler. And by the way, that is also a promise."

She took a minute to look at me as if she was wondering what I might do about it, then turned to leave. I watched as Mrs. Dunberger stormed out of my office. It was easy to tell that she was mad as hell, but frankly, I didn't give a damn. There was little doubt in my mind that she would call the police department and try to get the upper brass to put pressure on Mac to make me back off. It might prove to be in my best interest to call Mac and give him a heads up.

I REACHED OVER, PICKED UP THE PHONE and placed a call to the precinct Mac worked out of, namely Precinct One. The duty officer immediately transferred my call to Mac's office.

"Captain MacDonald."

"Peter. Got a minute?"

"Yeah. What's up?"

"I just had a little talk with Mrs. Dunberger."

"Oh, really? What does she have to do with your investigation?" he asked.

"Her son is one of my suspects, and someone I think you will probably be talking to in the very near future."

"What son. She doesn't have a son."

"Wrong. She has a son from her first marriage. His name is Franklin Steuben."

"Franklin Steuben was one of Emily's instructors at the art school, right?"

"That's right. She made it clear that she was going to sic the police on me and have me arrested if I talked to her son again. She didn't use the word 'talked'. She made it a point of using the word 'harass'," I said. "By the way, I told her that you would probably be by to talk to him."

"That's true enough. I was getting ready to go over to the school to talk to Steuben now."

"I don't think you will find him at the school. If I had to guess, he is probably hiding out at his mother's house and won't talk to you without a lawyer."

"You're probably right, but he will talk to me with or without a lawyer if I have to drag him in here in handcuffs."

"I called to give you a heads up. I think you will be getting a call from the upper brass to step lightly around her and her son."

"Thanks for the heads up, and you're probably right. I think I'll get out of here before I get that call. Talk to you later," he said, then the phone went dead.

I smiled to myself. I knew I had earned a few points with Mac for that phone call, and that was a good thing.

THE LIST OF STUDENTS I had obtained from the Administration Office was right in front of me. It was waiting for me to pick out another student to question. Since I had already talked to the two that I had heard of before I got the list, there was nothing else to do but pick one. I decided to start at the top of the list.

The first name on the list was Sean Albertson. The list showed that he was in his last year at the school and was in the same class as Emily. He was from out of state, but lived in an apartment house near the art school.

I took a quick look at my watch and decided that it was getting on toward dinner time. I had told Jennifer that I'd see her at my place for dinner. I knew she would be getting off work very shortly and would go to my place directly from work. I decided that I would try to contact Albertson tomorrow morning. After all, I had put in a full day. In fact, the last two days had been full. It wouldn't hurt to spend a little time to figure out just what I had found out and what it meant.

I folded up the list of students and put it in the top drawer of my desk, then leaned back to think.

I HADN'T GOTTEN SETTLED IN to think about what I had been told by those I had already questioned when my phone began to ring. I reached over and answered it.

"Peter Blackstone Investigations."

"I left you a message to call me back. I expect you to call me back when I tell you to."

"Good Afternoon, Mr. Slocomb," I said using my best polite and cheery voice.

"Why didn't you return my call?" he asked rather sharply.

"I was busy. Besides, I don't work for you. If you will recall, you turned down my conditions of employment by not sending one of your goons to my office by two o'clock with a retainer check. Therefore, I'm under no obligation to return your call," I said then hung up the phone.

It wasn't but a minute or so and my phone began to ring again. I smiled as I let it ring a few times before I picked up the receiver.

"Peter Blackstone Investigations," I said very politely knowing full well who was probably on the other end.

"You hung up on me. I ought - -."

That was as much as he got to say before I interrupted him.

"Listen! I'll talk to you when and only when you can show me the respect I deserve. You will not tell me what to do, how to do it or when to do it. IF, and I say IF, I work for you it will be under the conditions I gave to your goon. Do I make myself clear?" I asked, then I waited for a reply.

There was complete silence on the other end of the line. I was sure that he was either thinking, or trying to get his temper under control. I didn't care which. I was fairly sure that no one had talked to him like I just did. I halfway expected him to hang up on me this time, but he didn't.

"Mr. Blackstone, I would like you to take me on as a client. I agree with the conditions of employment as were explained to me by my representative. I will send my representative to your office first thing in the morning with a retainer check in the amount you suggested. Would that be satisfactory?"

"Yes, Mr. Slocomb, that would be fine. I will get started as soon as I receive your check."

"Thank you," he said then hung up the phone.

I smiled to myself, but wondered what I would find out if I questioned Slocomb's goons. The answer to that question was probably nothing, but I would give it a try tomorrow when one brought me a retainer check.

I began to think about Slocomb. He said that he wanted me to find out who had murdered Emily to prove he was innocent of her murder. It hardly seemed like a good idea to hire me if he was involved in her death. The only thing I knew for sure was that I didn't trust Slocomb as far as I could throw him.

My thoughts turned to why he wanted to hire me. There had to be some motive, but I couldn't think of what it might be. Then it came to me. He probably thought that since he was paying me, I would be required to turn over everything that I discovered to him. It also meant that I would not be able to tell the police what I found out without breaking the Code of Confidentiality.

However, there was one thing that I had told his goon, aka his representative, in my conditions that would let me off the hook. I had told his goon that I would tell the police everything I knew if he, or any of his employees, lied to me or gave me any kind of a runaround. That was my way out, and I would venture to guess that he was not told that by his goon, or he simply chose to ignore that piece of information.

For now, thinking about Slocomb and his operations would have to wait. It was time for me to go home. I was looking forward to having dinner with Jennifer. A quick look at my watch told me that she might already be at my apartment.

I stood up and left my office, locking the door on my way out. The elevator was busy, so I decided to walk down the stairs to the parking garage. When I entered the parking garage I didn't see any suspicious cars around. I kept my eyes moving as I walked to my car and got in. The drive home was uneventful. I had no one following me and traffic was fairly light, considering the time of day.

I ARRIVED HOME JUST AS JENNIFER ARRIVED in the parking lot. I waited for her to park her car, then walked up to it and opened the door for her.

"Looks like you have great timing," I said as she got out of the car.

"I was hoping to get here before you. I had an idea for a great dinner," she said with a smile as she hooked her arm in mine.

"You always have a great idea for a great dinner," I said as we started across the parking lot toward my apartment. "What did you have in mind?"

Just as she was about to answer, my attention was suddenly drawn to a big black Lincoln Town Car. It had turned into the parking lot of my apartment building, and was accelerating rapidly as it came right at us. I quickly pushed Jennifer between two parked cars so she was out of harms way, then immediately jumped to the other side of the parking lot. The car swerved toward me, turning away from Jennifer. I managed to get far enough away from the car to avoid being hit, but I had fallen on the ground in the effort to keep from getting run over. I sprang to my feet and drew my gun; but by the time I got up, the car had turned out of the parking lot onto the street at the other end. I had not been quick enough to get a good look at the license plate other than to see that it was a Colorado plate.

I looked toward Jennifer. She was sitting up on the pavement where I had pushed her. Her eyes were big, and the fear she felt showed on her face. I could see her trembling.

"Are you hurt," I asked as I ran toward her.

I was afraid that I might have pushed her too hard.

"He was trying to kill us," she said with a note of panic and surprise in her voice.

"Are you hurt?"

She looked at me for a moment and took a deep breath before she answered.

"No. I don't think so. I think I might have skinned my knee, but that's about it."

"Come on. Let's get inside."

I helped her up and took her arm as I led her into my apartment. Once inside and she was settled on the sofa, I went to the phone and placed a call to Mac. The Desk Sergeant told me that Mac wasn't in. I asked him to have Mac call me as soon as possible, then hung up.

I turned and looked at Jennifer sitting on the sofa. She had rolled up the leg of her slacks and was looking at her knee. I could see that she had torn her slacks and scrapped her knee when she fell on the pavement. It was nothing serious, but it was bleeding a little. I went to the bathroom and got a washcloth, soap, a towel, a bowl of warm water, and a first aid kit. When I returned to the living room, Jennifer looked at me. I knelt down in front of her.

"Let me clean this up," I said as I wet the washcloth with soap and water.

"What just happened out there?"

"Someone tried to run me over. You just happened to be with me."

I lightly washed the wound on her knee then dried it. I then put on a little antiseptic ointment and covered the wound with a bandage.

"Okay, Peter. What's going on? What have you gotten yourself into?"

"I'm not sure," I said as I moved over and sat on the sofa next to her. "I was hired to find a young woman that was missing. Actually three people hired me, her folks and her boyfriend. I found her all right, but she was dead. Now I've been hired by a man who is less than honest to find out who killed her."

"Who is this man?"

"Ralph Slocomb."

"There's apparently someone who doesn't want you to find out who killed the woman," Jennifer said.

"I would have to agree with you on that."

"What are you going to do?" she asked as she looked me in the eyes.

"What do you think I should do? I only asked that question because whoever doesn't want me to find the killer, doesn't care who gets hurt in their effort to stop me."

"You mean me."

"Yes. I don't want anything to happen to you."

"What would happen if you gave up the search for the killer?"

"I don't know for sure, but they would probably leave me alone. It would not be in their best interest to continue to go after me."

"Why?"

"First of all, it would just draw more attention to them. I'm sure they would not want that. Secondly, they would have to know that I would be going after them."

"But they might not leave you alone even if you drop the investigation?" she asked.

"Yes. They might not, especially if they think that I have already found something damaging to them."

"So what I'm hearing you say is that even if you drop the case, they might not drop their efforts to kill you."

"Possibly, but not likely."

"What happens if you continue working on the case?"

"I think they would try to stop me. Now that could lead to more attempts on my life. It could also mean that they would use you to get to me."

"I see," she said thoughtfully.

I let her think on that for a minute. She was looking off into space. I couldn't tell what she was thinking, but I was sure what had just happened was playing a big part in it. Finally, she turned and looked at me again. Her eyes told me that she had come to a decision on what she thought should be done.

"I think that you should keep looking for the killer of the young woman," Jennifer said with a determined look on her face.

"Are you sure? I would give it up if you want me to. You mean more to me than anything."

"I know you would give it up for me, but you shouldn't. This is what you do. I knew that from the very beginning. I was with you when you became a private investigator. I love you too much to ask you to give up what you like to do. And I might add, what you do, you do very well."

"What about you. If I keep working on this, it could put you in danger. I wouldn't want to do that to you," I said hoping that she would understand what I was telling her.

"I guess you will just have to protect me," she said then leaned toward me and smiled.

I leaned toward her until our lips met. Even though I was kissing her, my mind was worried about her last statement. The question that ran through my mind was could I protect her.

After a moment or two of her warm lips against mine, I knew that I would do everything I could to protect her. I also knew that she wanted me to find out who had killed Emily.

I leaned back and looked into Jennifer's eyes. I could see the love and trust she had for me.

"I think it is time to fix dinner," she said with a smile.

"Jennifer, I want you to stay here with me tonight."

A big smile came over her face as she looked into my eyes.

"That's what I had in mind all along," she said as she leaned toward me again.

As soon as she kissed me on the cheek, she pulled back and stood up. Jennifer smiled down at me for a moment then started toward the kitchen. When she got to the kitchen door, she stopped and turned toward me.

"This might be a good time to plan your next move. It will take me a little while to fix dinner," she said, then winked at me, turned and went into the kitchen.

I watched her as she disappeared into the kitchen. Almost as soon as she was out of sight, I turned my attention to my case. I began to think about Ralph Slocomb. Almost immediately two people came to mind that I should talk to as soon as possible. The first was Slocomb, the old man, and the second was the last person to leave the classroom on the last day Emily attended class. I had no idea who the last person to see her was, but I was pretty sure that it was someone on the list of students I got from the Administration Office.

I WAS DEEP IN THOUGHT when Jennifer called me to dinner. I got up and went into the kitchen for dinner. I sat down and waited for her to put dinner on the table.

Jennifer set two good sized bowls on the table. I looked at the bowl in front of me. It was a steak salad. There was lettuce, eggs, two kinds of cheese and grilled steak. She had set three different kinds of salad dressing on the table along with a plate that had garlic toast on it. It all looked very good.

"This looks good."

"It tastes even better. Dig in," she said with a smile.

I stuck a fork into the salad after putting some dressing on it. She was right, it tasted very good.

"Have you decided what your next move is going to be?"

"Yes. I'm going to go over the list of students that were in the last class Emily attended. I want to talk to the last one out of the classroom."

"You think one of her fellow students might have killed her?" she asked with a surprised look on her face.

"No, I don't think so. However, it is not something that I plan to ignore. I think someone in her class might have heard or seen something that will help me."

While we ate, I told her about Franklin Steuben and what he had told me about the last class Emily attended. I also told her about how nervous he had become while I questioned him.

"It sounds like you think he might be the killer."

"Let me put it this way, he's on the top of my suspect list," I said. "But I don't know if he killed her."

We ate the rest of our meal in silence. It wasn't until we were cleaning up the kitchen that Jennifer had something more to say.

"Peter, you said that this Steuben was an instructor at the school."

"That's right," I replied wondering what was on her mind.

"Instructors don't make a lot of money. Do you think that he has the resources to hire someone to run you down?"

"Franklin Steuben is the son of Mrs. Mildred A. Dunberger. Do you know who she is?"

"Yes. She is one of the most prominent and influential people in the Denver area. She has friends in high places."

"How is it that you know about her?"

"I looked her up on the internet after you called me about her cars."

"She made it a point of coming by my office. She had the nerve to threaten me if I so much as talked to Steuben again."

"She threatened you?"

"Yes. She threatened to have me arrested if I harassed her son again. She used the word 'harassed' when all I did was ask him a few questions.

"I didn't know she had a son."

"Apparently not many people do."

"She could be a lot of trouble for you."

"I know, but Mac knows that she threatened me."

"That's good," she said thoughtfully.

Nothing more was said about it. When we had the kitchen cleaned up we went into the living room and sat down together. We decided to put the case aside for a while and just enjoy each other's company. We watched Wheel of Fortune and Jeopardy, but Jennifer didn't seem to be very interested in the programs. I was sure that she was still thinking about what I had told her, and what had happened in the parking lot.

After Jeopardy, we watched a movie. It was a pretty good movie, but I don't think either of us enjoyed it all that much. When the news came on, it seemed that Jennifer took more of an interest in it than usual. I certainly wanted to hear what the news media had on the subject of Emily's murder. The topic was announced by the news anchor, a good looking man sitting behind the news desk.

It was clear that the news media didn't really know very much. About all that was reported was that a young woman had been found in a large plastic lawn bag near Washington Park. He said that foul play was suspected, but that the victim's name had not been released pending notification of the next of kin. That was about all they had to say.

Based on what the reporter had to say, they had apparently interviewed several residents in the area, but none of them knew anything about it, except what had been reported. I wondered if the person I had seen looking out the window hadn't seen anything, or just didn't want to get involved.

"I find it interesting that the name of the victim was not released," Jennifer said.

"I got the impression from Mac that he was staying away from the reporters. The rest of the Police Department probably doesn't know much about it, and those that do have probably been told to keep their mouths shut."

"Well, I think it would be a good idea if we did the same, at least as far as this case goes and for the rest of tonight," Jennifer said with a sexy smile. "I would like to spend a little time with you, Peter Blackstone the man, not Peter Blackstone the PI."

"Oh, you would, would you?" I asked playfully.

"Yes."

"Okay," I said as I leaned toward her.

She smiled and leaned toward me. As our lips met, I reached out and pulled her to me. It didn't take long before our kiss became very passionate. It also didn't take long before we found ourselves in my bedroom. We were out of our clothes and in my bed in record time.

We laid side by side wrapped in each other's arms. We were kissing as if we hadn't seen each other for years. The feel of her body against mine, and the feel of her body in my hands drove both of us to want more of each other. In no time at all, we were the only people in the world.

"I want you," Jennifer whispered in my ear.

I couldn't refuse a request like that. I rolled her over and made passionate love to the one woman who had held me in her heart since we had first made love to each other in our senior year of high school. That had been the first for both of us.

After some passionate love making, we curled up in each other's arms and drifted off to sleep.

CHAPTER EIGHT

I WOKE JUST AS THE SUNLIGHT began to creep into the bedroom between the narrow openings in the curtains. I could hear the wind outside my bedroom window. There seemed to be a bit of a chill in the air. I looked over at Jennifer. She was still sleeping. I pulled the covers over her. She moved slightly, but didn't wake up.

As I lay in bed beside a beautiful woman who just happened to be naked under the covers, I began to think about what had happened in the parking lot last evening. It caused me to think about how I was going to protect Jennifer. There was little doubt in my mind that if I continued to search for Emily's killer, there would be more attempts on my life. I couldn't help but think that their failure to get me last night would prompt them to at least think about getting to me through Jennifer.

My first thought was could it be Mrs. Dunberger who was out to get me? The car that had been used to try to run me over had been a high priced car, a Lincoln Town Car. She could certainly afford a Lincoln. The thing that came to mind was that she had three expensive cars registered in her name, but not one of them was a Lincoln. That didn't mean that she couldn't borrow or rent one. She certainly could afford to rent one, which seemed the logical thing to do.

My second thought was Ralph Slocomb. He could afford a Lincoln and may even have one. It was at that moment that I remembered that Preston had told me that she was picked up in different cars all the time when she had to work at Slocomb's gambling houses. He could also use rented cars, and one or more of them could be a Lincoln. I was pretty sure that he wasn't stupid enough to use one of his own cars, but I could check that out. It occurred to me that if he used different cars all the time, he probably had different people rent them which would make it more difficult to prove that he was behind it.

It also occurred to me that just about anyone could rent a Lincoln. That thought certainly didn't help me figure out who had tried to run over me.

I started turning over in my mind everything I knew about the murder of Emily. It seemed that the more I knew, the less any of it made sense. I had a couple of good suspects, but I couldn't help but think that I was missing something or someone. If it was not one of my known suspects, then there was someone out there that had been able to stay under the radar, so to speak. He, or she, was the one I wanted to find.

"Are you all right?" Jennifer asked.

I turned my head and looked at Jennifer. She was so beautiful and sexy lying in my bed. But the look on her face told me that she was worried.

"Yeah. I'm fine. I was just thinking about who I'm overlooking."

"What do you mean?"

"I think there is someone out there I have overlooked. Someone knows something about Emily's death. It could even be someone who was involved in her death in some way. I just can't figure out who it is."

"Maybe it would help if you could figure out why the suspects you already can think of didn't do it, rather than look at why they might have done it."

I looked at Jennifer as if she didn't know what she was talking about. It seemed to me that she was asking me to overlook their motives and look at why they wouldn't want Emily dead. Even the police looked for a motive. It was an essential element in almost every crime. I could come up with a logical motive for each of my suspects for wanting Emily out of the way. I could not think of anyone else who had a motive to kill her. Of course, that didn't mean that there wasn't someone out there that I didn't know about.

The more I thought about what Jennifer said, the more it seemed to make at least a little sense. I got the idea that she was trying to have me look at it from a different angle, rather than ignore the motive.

"Honey, you just might be right," I said as I smiled at her.

"Thank you," she said with a grin.

I began by looking back at when I first found Emily's body. While I was waiting for the police at Washington Park, I had thought about why she had been dumped at the park. The only answer I could come up with was that whoever had killed her wanted her found quickly, but why? It was possible that her killer or killers were getting a little nervous about keeping her hidden for so long. Maybe they were afraid that someone would discover her body. Was it possible that her death could have been an accident? There was evidence that it was possible.

The one thing that I needed to do was to widen my search for Emily's murderer. The best place to start widening my search was with the list of students who had been in her last class, but not just to find out who was the last one to see her at her last class. I would also be looking for someone else that might have a motive or some reason for wanting her dead.

"I need to go to my office and start making some phone calls. I need to see if I can find out not only who was the last person to see her on the day she died; but who didn't like her, or who had a crush on her that she might have rejected. It might lead me to someone else that I hadn't thought of, someone else who may have wanted her dead."

"I know you think better on a full stomach," Jennifer said. "How about breakfast before you go?"

"That sounds good. After breakfast, I'll take you to work. You should be safe there while I'm working," I said.

"I want to take a shower."

"You mind if I join you?" I asked.

"I would like that," she said with a smile.

We rolled out of bed. I took her hand and walked with her into the bathroom. Once the shower was warm enough, we stepped into it. The feel of her body against me made me want to forget about the case. She was so warm and loving.

I have to admit that we spent more time in the shower than was necessary to get clean, but neither of us minded at all. We touched and kissed and even washed each other during our time in the shower.

Once out of the shower, she got dressed while I shaved. By the time I finished shaving and getting dressed, she was in the kitchen putting breakfast on the table. She looked at me as I came into the kitchen and smiled. Her smile quickly faded away when she saw me putting my gun in my holster. I was sure that it was a reminder of how dangerous my job could be.

"Sit down. Breakfast is on."

I sat down across the table from where she was going to sit as she put a cup of coffee in front of my bowl. As she sat down, I poured Cheerios into my bowl then added a sliced banana, a little sugar and milk. I noticed that she had already put a glass of orange juice on the table for me.

"You eat the same thing every morning for breakfast," she said with a grin.

"I guess I do, but I like it,"

"Peter, do you really think that I'm in danger as long as you're on this case," she said suddenly looking very serious.

"I don't really know. What I do know is that it is better not to ignore the possibility that you are. It is better to be safe than sorry."

"Okay. You know more about what you are doing than I do."

"I want you to stay at work until I come and get you. I don't want you to leave the building without me. Do you understand?"

"Yes. I will wait for you to come and get me. I'll even eat in the cafeteria so I don't have to leave the building for lunch."

"Good. I will come to have lunch with you if I can get away, but don't wait for me."

Jennifer and I finished our breakfast then left for work. It had turned cold overnight and there was a light dusting of snow on the grass and bushes in the shady areas. The parking lot was wet, but drying fast in the morning sun. The streets, where there was traffic, were already dry.

When I got to her office building, I pulled up in front. I had her wait in the car while I got out and went around to open the door for her. As I walked her to the front door of her office building, I could see by the look on her face that she thought I was going a little overboard in protecting her, but she didn't say anything. Once we were inside the building, I gave her a quick kiss on the lips.

"I'll try to get here by four-thirty. Stay inside the building until I get here. Don't wait outside."

"Yes, sir," she said with a grin.

I smiled back at her then turned and left the building. I got into my car and headed for my office. I had a lot of phone calls to make this morning.

I ARRIVED AT THE BUILDING where my office was located without a problem. There was no one following me as far as I could tell. I took the elevator to the floor where my office was located. When the elevator stopped, I stepped out into the hall and turned toward my office. I stopped suddenly. I immediately noticed the same big goon that had visited me yesterday was leaning against the wall next to the office door.

"I see that you didn't break in this time," I said as I walked up to him.

"No need. I knew you would want to see me," he said with a grin. "I have a check for you from the boss. He said to get a receipt for it."

I looked at the check then reached out and took it from him. It was in the amount that I had told Ralph Slocomb I wanted before I would even start.

"What's he going to do, use it as a tax write-off?" I asked as I unlocked and opened the door.

"Probably."

He followed me into the office. I walked around to the other side of my desk and sat down. Opening the top desk drawer, I pulled out my receipt book. He didn't say anything while I wrote out a receipt for him. He just stood there watching me. When I finished the receipt, I handed it to him. On the bottom of my receipts was printed the conditions of my employment. I didn't bother to read them as I had already recited them to him.

"Now that I have been retained by your boss, I want you to sit down and answer a few questions," I said

He looked at me as if he didn't know what he should do. He seemed to be thinking about my request.

"And just so we are clear on this, my agreement with your boss included a clause that said I could talk to any of his employees. If they gave me the runaround or lied to me, anything and everything I knew would no longer be confidential. Therefore, I could tell the police anything I learned. Do you understand that?"

"Yeah. I remember that was one of the conditions."

"Good. What is your job with Mr. Slocomb?"

"I mostly run errands for him."

"Do you do anything else for him?"

"Yeah. I drive for him sometimes. You know, I take him places."

"Do you pick up people and take them to his gambling houses?"

From the look on his face, I wasn't sure if he was going to answer that one. I could see he was thinking pretty hard about it.

"If you don't answer me, I get to keep the retainer. Your boss and I have an agreement."

"Yeah, I know," he said, then took a deep breath. "Sometimes I pick up people and take them to his gambling houses, but not very often."

"What kind of a car do you drive?"

"Depends. Most of the time I drive a Lincoln."

"What color is the Lincoln you drive?"

"Silver, why?"

"Just interested, that's all."

I could see that he was getting a little nervous. I didn't want to press him too much and have him completely clam up on me, so I decided that I had asked him enough for now. I could always talk to him later.

"That's all you want to know? What color Lincoln I drive?"

"Yeah. By the way does your boss have a black Lincoln Town Car?"

"No. He has a silver one and his wife has a white one."

"Thanks. I'll see you around. I'm sure your boss would like me to get started."

"Yeah, I guess," he said as he stood up.

I sort of nodded then watched him as he left my office. I was pretty sure that he did a lot more than he told me. The one thing I was sure he did was follow people for his boss. There was little doubt that he would try to tail me to see who I talked to and where I went. I was also sure that he would go directly back to his boss and tell him what I asked him, but I didn't care. After all, his boss had a pretty good idea that I would be talking to his employees.

As I took a minute to think about his answers, I remembered seeing a white Lincoln Town Car in front of Mrs. Dunberger's home. I had no way of knowing if it was Mrs. Slocomb's car. Even if it was, I had no idea what it meant, if anything.

Since he was gone for now, I decided that it was time for me to take a serious look at the list of Emily's classmates on the afternoon of the last day she attended class.

I TOOK THE LIST OF STUDENTS out of my desk and began looking at them. I would contact as many as I could by phone. If I got a hint that there might be something that I needed to follow up on, I would make a personal visit to them.

The first one on the list was Sean Albertson. The information on the list told me nothing about him, or any of the others, except for their address and phone number. I reached over and picked up the phone and placed a call to the number I had for Sean. The phone rang several times. I was about to hang up and try the next one when the phone was answered.

"Hello," a male voice said.

"Hello. I'm trying to contact a Sean Albertson. Is he in?"

"I'm Sean."

"Sean, my name is Peter Blackstone. I'm investigating the death of Emily Sutherland."

"I don't know how I can help you. Am I a suspect or something?"

"No," I said with a slight chuckle in my voice. "I'm just trying to find out all I can about where Emily was and what she did on the days before her death."

"Oh. Okay."

"When was the last time you saw Emily?"

"It would have been the last class she attended. That would have been a little over a week ago. It was the Wednesday afternoon figure drawing class."

"What can you tell me about that class?"

"What do you mean?"

"Did anything happen in that class that was unusual or different?"

"Well, Mr. Steuben seemed to be upset with Emily for some reason. He was pretty hard on her that day. Harder than usual."

"How was he hard on her?"

"It seemed that he was mad at her for some reason. I know she had been complaining about him to her friend, June."

"How is it that you know that?"

"I overheard her talking to June on the phone. She was sitting in a booth right behind me in the café across the street from the school. It was just before the Wednesday afternoon class. I didn't get a lot of what was being said, but I heard enough to know that Emily was worried about her grade in Steuben's class. From what Emily said, it sounded like June was telling Emily to report him to the Administrator, but I'm not real sure what was said before that, or why Emily would want to report him."

"Do you know if Emily reported him to the office?"

"Not for sure, but she might have. She would have had a chance to report him before class."

"What happened during class?"

"Well, during the first half of class it seemed as if Steuben was being far more critical of Emily's drawings than he had in the past. It didn't make sense to me."

"Why?"

"She was really very good, but he was on her case during the entire first half of the class," he said. "When I was leaving the classroom to take our mid-afternoon break, I heard Steuben tell her that he wanted to talk to her. I don't know what happened during our break, but when we came back all of Emily's art supplies were gone from where they had been when we left."

"Does everyone leave their art supplies in the classroom during breaks?"

"Yeah, sure. No reason to take them out. We were going back to the same room when break was over."

"Did everyone leave the classroom during the break?"

"All but Emily and Steuben."

"What happened when you returned from the break?"

"Steuben said that we were going to have a different model to draw. I could hardly believe my eyes when Emily came out of the changing room stark naked. She walked over to the model stand and got up on it. She then struck a pose.

"Steuben told us that she was our model for the rest of the afternoon. Emily had a very nice body, and she did a good job of modeling. She never moved during the ninety minute session."

I heard a hint of something in his voice. He had thought of something, or felt that there was something wrong. It could have been something entirely different.

"But?" I asked.

"She looked like she didn't want to pose for us. I don't know if she was embarrassed, or if there was something else going on, but I know she was not happy about modeling."

"Didn't she model for the figure drawing class before?'

"Yeah, but never completely naked."

"Was there anything else that grabbed your attention about that afternoon?"

"Well, I had seen other girls, and guys, model for us in that class, but this was the first time I had seen Steuben spend so much time so close to the model, close to Emily."

"What do you mean?"

"Usually, he would walk around behind us, the students that were drawing, and look at what we were drawing. Since we worked in kind of a semi-circle, we were all drawing the same model, just at a little different angel; so each of us had a different drawing of the same model," Sean explained.

"I understand that, but what about Steuben?"

"He seemed more interested in Emily than in the rest of the class. He spent a lot of time looking at her and being where she could see him looking at her. He had never done that before in any of the classes I have had with him."

I wondered what had happened during the break. Had Steuben threatened Emily with a bad grade, or even failing her to get her to model naked in front of him? I had been told that he tried to get her to go to his apartment. Then a thought came to me. I remembered something that Mac or the M.E. had told me.

"Sean, have you ever been in the room where Emily undressed before she modeled?"

"Yeah, sure. I think probably every student that ever took figure drawing has been in that room at one time or another."

"What's it like?"

"It's really just a storage room. There's nothing special about it," Sean said.

"What is in the room?"

"It has a lot of shelves with art supplies, paints, and stuff like that on them."

"Is there any furniture in the room?"

"Yeah. There's a bench for the models to sit on or lay on. It is sometimes used by the models to pose on when they want a reclining pose. There's a wooden chair that is used by the models, too."

"What about windows?"

"There aren't any windows in the room. Like I said, it's just a storage room."

"Sean, thank you for your help. Oh, there is one more question. Do you know who the last person to leave the classroom was that day?"

"No," he replied after giving it a moment of thought. "There were at least three others still in the classroom when I left that I know of, not counting Steuben. There could have been others. I'm just not sure."

"Can you tell me who the three were?"

"Let's see. There was Marsha Wallace, Lynn Miller and James Butler. Like I said, there could have been others."

"What can you tell me about them?"

"Marsha and Lynn are good friends. They hang around together all the time. You never see one without the other. I think they have a thing going, if you know what I mean. You never see either of them with a guy."

"I think I get the picture," I said.

"James Butler, I don't know him very well. He pretty much keeps to himself. That might be because he is a little older than most of us. He's a really good artist, though."

"Thanks again for your help. I would appreciate it if you would keep our conversation between us. But feel free to talk to the police should they want to talk to you."

"I liked Emily. She was nice. I never dated her, but I talked to her a few times at school. I was going to ask her out once. When I was told that she had a rich boyfriend, I backed off. I didn't figure I had a chance with her if she had a boyfriend with money."

"Did you know who her boyfriend was?"

"Yeah. Jeffery Slocomb. His family has money," he said as if money was important to Emily.

"Thanks again, Sean."

"You're welcome," he said then hung up.

My conversation with Sean had proven interesting. The information about the storage room gave me the idea that it might be the primary crime scene. A call to Mac might be in order. I placed the call, but he wasn't in. I told the Desk Sergeant to have him call me as soon as possible, then hung up. It was the second time I had called Mac and he wasn't in, but I was sure he was very busy working on the case.

I RETURNED TO THE LIST OF STUDENTS and found the phone number of Marsha Wallace. I placed a call to her. It rang several times, but I didn't get an answer or an answering machine. Since I didn't get an answer at Marsha's number, I tried a call to Lynn Miller. The phone rang several times, and I was just about to hang up when it was answered.

"Hello."

"Hello. My name's Peter Blackstone. I would like to talk to Lynn Miller, please."

"Lynn is busy right now. I'm Marsha Wallace. Could I be of help?"

"Oh. I had tried to call you just a few minutes ago. Would you mind answering a couple of questions for me?"

"No. Lynn might be available by then. What is it you would like to know?"

"It is my understanding that you and Lynn were in the last class that was attended by Emily Sutherland. Is that correct?"

"Yes, it is. What is your interest in Emily?"

"I'm sorry. I'm a private investigator, and I'm looking into her death."

"Oh," she said. "I don't know how I can help. I didn't really know her very well."

"It is my understanding that you and Lynn were the last ones to leave the figure drawing class the last day she attended that class. Is that correct?"

"Not entirely. Actually, I think that Emily, James Butler, and Mr. Steuben were still in the classroom when Lynn and I left. There may have been someone else in the storage room, but those were the ones I remember seeing when we left."

"Did you see Emily leave?"

"No. Actually, the last time I saw her was when she went into the storage room which is also used as the changing room for the models. Emily modeled during the last half of the class that day."

"So Mr. Steuben was still in the classroom?"

"I can't say for sure. I didn't see him leave, but then I wasn't paying a lot of attention to him."

"Why is that?"

"I don't like him."

"Could you explain that?" I asked.

"Sure. None of the girls in that class like him. He's a male chauvinist pig," she said with a strong tone of anger in her voice. "If a good looking girl brushes him off, her grades drop."

"So he makes passes at the girls in the classroom?"

"Sometimes, but it's usually more subtle than that."

"Why haven't you girls gotten together and told the Administration?"

"Administration doesn't listen to students."

"If you got together, they would have to listen to you."

"What good would it do? Steuben's mother practically owns the school."

Now there was a piece of news that I didn't know. That may very well explain why Steuben had a job there.

"I take it she is a big donor to the school?"

"'Big' hardly covers it," Marsha said with a sharp tone to her voice.

"How do you know this?"

"I overheard the president of the school talking to one of the board members just outside the president's office. They didn't know I could hear them."

"What did you hear?"

"I heard the board member tell the president that they couldn't afford to fire Steuben. What do you think that means? It certainly wasn't because they couldn't hire a better instructor."

"I get your point. What about James, James Butler? Did you see him leave?"

"No. When I left the classroom, he was still putting his art stuff away. He was the last student I remember seeing in the classroom when Lynn and I left."

"Do you know him very well?"

"No. He's older than most of the students, and he's kind of weird."

"What do you mean by that?"

"I saw him punch a guy out off the school grounds because the guy laughed at him during one of the computer design classes they were both taking."

I found that bit of information to be interesting.

"Okay. Thanks for the information."

"Do you still want to talk to Lynn?"

"I don't think so. Maybe later. Thanks again," I said, then hung up.

As I hung up the phone, I sat back and began to think about what it all meant. The one thing that came out of it was another suspect, and that would be James Butler. It was possible that he might have heard something that might help me find Emily's murderer, or he could have been the one who murdered her. From Marsha's comment about Butler, it seemed that he might have a rather nasty temper.

My next thought was to call Butler, but it might prove to be more interesting, and more fruitful, if I were to visit him face to face. I decided that I would talk to him face to face, but right now I needed to find out a little more about him.

I left my office and drove to where Jennifer worked. I thought I would stop in and take her out to lunch since it was about time for her to go to lunch.

CHAPTER NINE

I ARRIVED AT JENNIFER'S WORK PLACE just as she was about to leave her office. She smiled when she saw me. I waited for her to come to me, then took her by the arm.

"What brings you here?"

"I thought you might like to go out to lunch with me."

"I'd like that. Where are we going?"

"There's a small café just across the street and around the corner. We could get a booth in the back and enjoy lunch together," I said as I smiled at her.

"Sounds great."

I took hold of her hand and we started out of the building. We walked to the corner, then waited for the light to change. As soon as it changed, I took a step forward. Stepping off the curb, I immediately stopped then quickly jumped back on the curb, pulling Jennifer back with me as a black Lincoln Town Car came speeding around the corner. The car almost hit the curb as it sped past us. I couldn't see who was driving as the windows were tinted very dark. It all happened so quickly that I was unable to get a license plate number before it was out of sight. The only thing I was sure of was that it had a Colorado license plate and it started with two letters.

"That was close," Jennifer said as she turned and looked down the street in the direction the Lincoln had gone.

"Yeah," I replied as I looked down the street.

"Are you all right," Jennifer asked.

"Yes, I'm fine," I said as I looked at Jennifer and smiled.

I looked both ways then stepped off the curb again. We walked hand in hand across the street. I had no idea if the car had cut the corner by accident, or if it was intentional. I tended to think it was intentional. Either way, I planned to pay closer attention to what was going on around me. I kept my eyes moving just in case there was someone else around that wanted to do us harm.

The car that almost hit us had worried Jennifer. I know it bothered me. The thing that seemed to bother me was not so much that I had almost been hit by the car, but the car itself. I couldn't be a hundred percent sure, but my first thought was that the Lincoln was the same one that tried to run us over in my apartment building's parking lot.

We walked on down the street to the café. Once we were in the café and had been seated in a booth near the back, Jennifer looked at me. I was sure that she had something on her mind.

"Peter, I'm not sure, but I think that was the same car that tried to run over us at your apartment yesterday evening."

"I think you are probably right. I didn't get a license plate number."

"I didn't either."

I was about to say something to Jennifer when a waitress came to our booth. We ordered the noon special and coffee, then waited until she had gone before I picked up on our conversation.

"When you get back to your office, could you check to see what kind of cars are registered to Ralph Slocomb?"

"Sure. Do you think it might be him?"

"No, but I would like to be sure. What reason would he have to try to stop me from investigating Emily's death? He hired me to prove that he had nothing to do with it."

"He hired you to prove he didn't kill Emily?" she asked with surprise. "I didn't think you would take on someone like him as a client."

"You knew that he was a client. I told you that last night."

"I guess I didn't connect the name last night," she said looking a little embarrassed.

"Normally I wouldn't have taken him on," I said, then stopped.

The waitress was coming toward our table. I didn't want her to hear any part of our conversation. I leaned back and watched her as she put our lunch on the table. After thanking her, I waited for her to leave.

"Normally I wouldn't take him on as a client, but I did with some very tight restrictions. If he doesn't abide by the restrictions I placed on him, especially the confidentiality clause, my contract with him is void."

"And he agreed to that?"

"Yes, he did. But that doesn't mean that I trust him. He is still on my list of suspects."

"Does he know that?"

"I don't think he knows it, but I wouldn't be surprised if he assumes it. He probably thinks that if he hired me to find Emily's killer, I would think that he had nothing to do with it. Well, as far as I'm concerned, he will be a suspect until I either prove he did it, or prove he didn't do it."

Jennifer looked at me as if she wasn't too sure how that was going to work out. As a matter of fact, neither did I.

We spent the rest of our time in the café eating our lunch. When we were finished, I paid the bill and left a tip on the table. I then escorted Jennifer back to her office building, being very careful to keep an eye out for any danger that might befall either of us.

Once Jennifer was safely in the building, I left and drove back to my office. As far as I could tell, I had not been followed.

After parking my car in the parking garage, I took the stairs up to my office. I decided that the elevator might not be safe. It would be too easy for someone to waylay me on any of the floors.

ONCE I WAS IN MY OFFICE, I sat down at my desk. It was at that moment that I remembered something that I had been told. It was what Sean Albertson had said about James Butler. He had said that he was older than the others in the figure drawing class. I wondered if he was a full-time or part-time student. I wasn't sure what that information would prove, or if it would make any difference. But I knew that a talk with him certainly wouldn't hurt.

I took a minute to look up his address on the student list. It was not very far from the school. A stop at the school to find out a little about him might not hurt. The woman at the counter in the Administration Office had been very helpful the last time I was there. I could only hope that she would be helpful again.

I DROVE TO THE SCHOOL and found a parking space just a little way from the main entrance. I parked then started to get out of my car when I noticed the woman I had talked to in the Administration building coming out the front door. She had a box and several books in her arms. The look on her face was that of a woman that was not feeling well. I couldn't be sure, but she looked like she might have been crying.

I quickly got out of my car and ran over to her. When she looked at me, I could see that she had been crying.

"What's the matter?"

"You ask me "What's the matter"? You're the matter," she said almost hysterically. "I've been fired."

I looked at her then at the box she was carrying. The box confirmed what she had said. The box contained what looked like personal things such as pictures, a flower vase, and some other things that women liked to keep on or in their desks at work.

"It's all your fault."

"I'm sorry that I got you fired. Let me help you with your things."

She didn't say anything for almost a minute. She just looked at me for a moment. She then handed me the box.

"I'm sorry," she said. "I have no business blaming you for getting me fired. I didn't have to give you the information that I did. They fired me for talking to you."

"Are you going to be looking for a new job?" I asked as we walked toward her car.

"I have to," she replied as she stopped at a car in the staff parking lot.

She opened the door and I set the box in on the seat.

"I'm sorry, but I don't even know your name."

"I'm Margery Mellencamp, but my friends call me Marge."

"It's nice to meet you, Marge. I'm Peter Blackstone. My friends call me, Peter," I said with a smile. "Since I was part of the reason you were fired, would you mind if I call a friend of mine and have him call you. He has been looking for someone to head up his office."

"That would be nice of you. What kind of a business does he have?"

"He's an accountant."

"I worked in an accountant's office before the owner retired. I really liked working there. I've never liked working at the school. Too much internal politics."

"Okay. If you give me your phone number, I'll call him and have him give you a call."

Marge gave me her phone number, then left. I returned to my car to think about what my next move should be.

Since Marge no longer worked at the school, I had lost my inside contact. I could see no reason to go inside at the moment. There was little chance that I would get any additional information about students, or staff. I would probably get myself arrested if I ever stepped on the school grounds again. There was one other option I had. That was to call Mac and see what he could come up with on Butler. Again, I had no idea what it might prove, but it was a lead that needed to be followed up.

I DROVE BACK TO MY OFFICE and placed a call to Mac. It didn't take but a few minutes before he answered the phone.

"Captain MacDonald."

"Mac, it's me, Peter."

"I just got in and got your messages. What's up?"

"Could you see what you can find on a James Butler for me?"

"Is he someone of interest to you?"

"Yeah. He might be the last person to have seen Emily alive."

"How so?"

"If my information is correct, he was the last student in the classroom to leave on the last day Emily attended class. I'm still not eliminating Steuben," I said.

"I'll do what I can. I take it you're planning on talking to this guy?"

"Yeah."

"What do you say we go have a talk with him together? He's probably of interest to me, too."

"Sure."

"Where should I pick you up?"

"Pick me up at my office," I suggested. "I have something else to talk to you about, but it can wait until you get here."

"Okay. I'll be there as soon as I get a chance to see what we have on Butler. It may take a little while."

"That's okay. I have a couple of things to do. Just come by when you're ready."

"Okay," Mac said.

As soon as Mac hung up, I placed a call to my friend and told him about Marge. He agreed to give her a call and make an appointment for an interview with her.

While I waited for Mac, I jotted down the address I had for Butler. I had no idea what we would be running into, but I wanted to be ready. I took a minute to check my gun to make sure it was ready to use.

Suddenly, my phone began to ring. I reached over and picked it up thinking that it might be Mac calling to tell me that he was either downstairs waiting for me or on his way.

"Peter Blackstone Investigation,"

"This is Jeff Slocomb. Are you looking for Em's murderer?"

"Yes, I am. I'm sorry about not calling you about finding her, but I immediately started looking for her killer. I found out from one of her classmates that you already knew."

"Yes. I know."

"Since I didn't get right back to you, I'll return the money you paid me."

"That won't be necessary. You did what I hired you to do, that was to find Em."

There was something about the way he talked that didn't set well with me. I wasn't sure what was going on in his head, but he didn't sound very upset that Emily was dead. I knew that he was aware of the fact that she had been murdered. From what he had told me when he hired me to find her, I would have thought that he would have been very upset.

"If you don't mind my asking, how did you find out?" I asked to see if his story matched what I had already heard.

"That's not important. I just wanted you to know that I knew she was dead, and our business is finished. There is no need for you to look for the person who killed her as far as I'm concerned."

His voice was flat and sort of matter of fact. He sounded even a little bit cold about the whole thing. It was the opposite of how he acted when he asked me to find her only a few days ago. The change in him was not what I would have expected if he loved her as much as he had indicated when we talked in my office.

"Jeff, does your father know that you were dating her?"

"I don't think so, but that's not important now."

"Did your father tell you that she had been murdered?"

"Ah – how – ah. No."

I wasn't convinced that he was telling me the truth. That last question kind of caught him off guard. It was something I would have to think about, but at the moment I was pretty sure that he had found out from his father. After all, it was clear that his father had found out quickly enough. Ralph had called me in very short order to hire me to prove he didn't kill her.

"I'm sorry, Jeff. I don't know what else I can say. I know that you cared a great deal for her."

"I'm fine. We weren't all that close. Goodbye," he said then the phone went dead before I could say anything more.

I hung up the phone, then looked up. I was a little surprised to see Mac standing in the doorway looking at me.

"GOT A PROBLEM?" Mac asked.

"I don't know," I said, then stood up. "We best be going. I want to talk to this Butler character."

We left my office and took the elevator down to the ground floor. Mac had parked out in front of the building. We got in his car and headed toward the school and to the address where Butler was supposed to live.

"Were you able to find out anything about Butler?" I asked, hoping that he had at least something for us to go on.

While he drove, Mac filled me in on what information he had on James Butler. It seemed that Butler had been in the Navy, but had been discharged after being court-martialed for fighting with sailors aboard the ship he had been assigned to serve on. It seems he got into fights on a fairly regular basis.

He got into one fight with a sailor over an incident that occurred in Japan. Butler beat the sailor very badly. He put him in the hospital. There were no witnesses to the attack, but during the fight Butler had said something to the effect that he had beat up a Japanese girl in Japan.

Butler's court-martial was held on the ship. It was after the fourth time he had gotten into a fight on board the ship. He was held in the ship's brig until they returned to the states where he was discharged as an undesirable.

"What about the incident in Japan? Was he ever charged with that?"

"I can't find anything that indicates he was charged with it," Mac said, then went on to tell me about it.

"It seems that Butler attacked and almost killed a Japanese girl while on shore leave in Japan. The report stated that the girl was a showgirl at a very respectable nightclub. She had taken a break outside the backdoor of the club when Butler attacked the girl and tried to rape her. When she screamed for help, he slammed her head on the pavement almost killing her. He ran, but was captured sometime later. The girl had suffered so much brain damage that she couldn't identify him or even remember anything about the attack. Since there were no other witnesses, he was released back to the ship with instructions that he was never to come back to Japan."

"This guy sounds like a real winner. It sounds to me like it doesn't take much to set him off," I said.

"It doesn't," Mac confirmed. "He has been arrested several times in Denver and Fort Collins for assault, but let go when the victims failed to sign a complaint. We'll want to be very careful around him. He could be a lot of trouble," Mac said.

"I'll be ready."

"Remember, you are not a cop. If anything goes down, I'm the one with the badge."

"I'll remember," I assured Mac.

I was sure that Mac had too much on his mind at the moment for me to talk to him about the black Lincoln that had twice tried to run Jennifer and me down. I would take it up with him after we were done talking to Butler.

IT DIDN'T TAKE LONG for us to arrive at the address of James Butler's apartment. We got out of the car and walked up to the door of the apartment building. I wasn't sure what kind of reception we were going to get from Butler, but I was ready for almost anything. We walked up to the bank of call buttons and quickly found the one to Butler's apartment.

Mac pushed the call button to Butler's apartment, then waited. We didn't get an answer so Mac rang it again.

"Yeah," a harsh male voice came over the small speaker.

"I'm Captain MacDonald with the Denver Police Department. I would like to talk to you for a moment."

"What the hell for?"

"Either come down here or let us come up there. I'm not going to talk to you over this thing."

There was a long minute of silence before he spoke again.

"All right. Come on up. I'm on the second floor."

The door buzzed and I pushed it open. I followed Mac into the lobby of the apartment building. When Mac stopped, I stopped and looked at him.

"There are two stairs to the second floor. You take the back ones. I got a feeling that he may try to run," Mac said in a whisper.

I nodded that I understood and headed toward the backstairs. From next to the backstairs I could see down the hall to where Mac was standing.

Mac nodded at me, then disappeared. I drew my gun from under my sport coat as Mac went up the front stairs. I moved over to the stairs and looked up. I had no more than started up the stairs when a young man in jeans and a jacket appeared at the top of the stairs. He was looking back over his shoulder and didn't see me.

"Hold it right there," I said as I pointed my gun at him.

He hesitated for a second, then slowly turned and looked at me. I wasn't sure what he was going to do, but whatever it was, it would have to be done quickly. He looked like he was going to reach into the pocket of his jacket.

"Don't even reach in your pocket," I said. "You do and you will die right there."

"Put your hands on your head," I heard Mac say. "You make one wrong move, and it will be your last."

I held my gun on Butler. It was only a matter of a couple of seconds or so before I could see Mac moving up behind Butler.

"Put your hands behind your head," Mac said.

Butler did as he was told as Mac moved up close to him. I kept my gun pointed at Butler as Mac put his gun in his belt holster and reached behind his back for his handcuffs.

Butler was standing one step down the stairs from the top while Mac was standing on the top step. As Mac reached out and took hold of Butler's wrist to put the cuffs on him, Butler quickly twisted around and pulled Mac off balance. Mac lost his balance and fell in front of Butler making it impossible for me to shoot without a strong possibility of hitting Mac. Butler pushed Mac on down the steps toward me.

Butler then quickly ran back up the steps and disappeared from my sight as Mac tried to regain his balance while stumbling down the stairs toward me. I grabbed Mac in the hope of breaking his fall, but he went down hard against the iron staircase railing before I could catch him. He hit his head on the railing and collapsed in my arms. I held onto him and was able to keep him from falling the rest of the way down the stairs.

Mac was out cold and had a deep gash in his head. I wanted more than anything to get Butler, but Mac needed my help now.

While holding Mac, I grabbed my cell phone and called 9-1-1. I remained ready in case Butler decided to come around the other way and finish Mac off, but all I heard was the front door slam shut.

"9-1-1 emergency. What is your emergency?"

"Officer down," I said then gave the 9-1-1 operator the address.

I could hear the operator putting out the call. When she came back on the line, I gave her all the necessary information on what had happened and the name and a description of James Butler.

It wasn't very long before two police officers showed up. They broke in the door and came to me. I was sitting on the steps with Mac's head in my lap.

"An ambulance is on the way," one of the officers said. "Who are you?"

"I'm Peter Blackstone. I was here with Captain MacDonald. We were here to talk to a guy by the name of James Butler. I gave a full description of Butler to the 9-1-1 operator."

I went on to explain what had happened, then why we wanted to talk to Butler. One of the officers took notes while the other waited at the door for the ambulance.

"Get an APB out on him and make sure you tell them he is dangerous."

"Is he armed?"

"I don't know, but he is still dangerous and violent."

It seemed to take forever for the ambulance to get there. I was growing impatient.

"Where the hell is that damn ambulance?" I yelled.

It wasn't as long as it seemed before two EMTs came into the apartment building and very carefully took Mac from me and put him on a gurney. Within a few minutes, they were rushing him out to the ambulance. I followed them outside and watched the ambulance speed away.

Shortly after the ambulance had gone, a detective I didn't know arrived at the apartment. I was just about to get in Mac's car and go to the hospital to see how Mac was doing when the detective stopped me.

"You," the detective called out. "Hold it right there. I want to have a talk with you."

I stopped and waited for him to come to me. I had a feeling it was not going to be a very friendly talk.

"What is it I can do for you?" I asked.

"You can start with who are you?"

"I'm Peter Blackstone."

"Do you live here?"

"No."

"Where do you live?"

I figured that I might as well just tell him the whole story rather than wait for him to ask me all the questions he could think of. It was my first comment that drew a response from him.

"I'm Peter Blackstone. I'm a Private Investigator," I said as I reached for my ID.

As I reached for my inside coat pocket for my ID and Concealed Weapons Permit, he saw the gun on my belt. He stepped back and drew out his gun.

"Hands in the air," he shouted.

I took a deep breath as I put my hands in the air. The two officers who were first on the scene looked at the detective and then at me. They were both wondering what had gotten the detective so uptight so quickly.

"I told you, I'm a PI. I was just reaching for my ID and permit to carry."

"What's going on here?" the senior of the two officers asked, confused by the detective pulling his gun on me.

"Did you know this guy had a gun?" the detective asked sharply.

The officer looked at me than back at the detective.

"Yes. He was here with Captain MacDonald to see a guy by the name of James Butler."

The detective looked at the officer as if he didn't believe him, then looked back at me. I don't know what was going through his mind, but I didn't care as long he let me go. I was about to tell him where he could go when he finally spoke.

"Okay. You can go," the detective said as he put his gun away.

When the detective turned away, I looked at the officer and mouthed the words, "Thank you". I then turned and went to Mac's car.

There was no sense in looking around the area in the hope of finding Butler. Since we knew where he lived, he was not likely to come back there. I got in the car and headed for the hospital to see how Mac was doing.

IT DIDN'T TAKE ME LONG to get to the hospital. I checked at the emergency desk, but they wouldn't give me any information. I decided that I would wait for a little while in the hope of seeing someone who would tell me how Mac was doing.

When I sat down in front of the emergency desk, the woman behind the desk glanced toward me. I noticed the expression on her face suddenly changed. For the first time she saw all the blood on the front of my pants and shirt. She seemed surprised.

"Sir, are you injured?" she asked.

"No."

"You're covered with blood," she said as she looked at me as if I was bleeding to death.

"Oh, that is Captain MacDonald's blood. I was with him when he was injured."

"Oh. In that case you can see him. He's in the third door on the left."

"Thank you."

I walked down the hall to treatment room six and knocked lightly on the door. The door was opened by a nurse. I could see in the room that Mac was lying on a gurney with IV's and several medical personnel around him. It was obvious that he was in good hands and I would just be in the way.

"How is he," I asked the nurse. "I was with him when he was injured."

"He's stable. That's about all I can say for now. Are you all right?" she asked noticing the blood on me.

"Yes. The blood is Captain MacDonald's."

"It will be awhile before we know anything for sure. All I can say for now is that he is stable. You might as well go get cleaned up. It will be quite awhile before you'd be able to talk to him."

"Thanks," I said then watched as she closed the door.

There was nothing else I could do there. I left the hospital and drove to my office. I parked Mac's car in the parking garage and took my car home so I could clean up.

As I drove toward my apartment, I grew more and more angry. I wanted James Butler more than anything I could think of at the moment. But I also knew that getting angry was not going to help me find him. I needed to figure out where he might be.

I began to think more about Butler and where he might have gone than how angry I was. The more I thought about it, the more I wondered if there might be someone on the list of students who might know him well enough to give me a clue as to where I could find him, or possibly where he was hiding.

Then I remembered that I had to pick up Jennifer at work. When I arrived home, I took a shower, then drove to the building where Jennifer worked.

CHAPTER TEN

I ARRIVED AT JENNIFER'S WORK PLACE just as she got off work. I met her in the hall as she was headed for the elevator.

"Hi," she said with her usual smile.

"Hi."

"What's the matter, honey," she asked, the look on her face showing that she could read me.

"Mac is in the hospital. He was injured when he attempted to make an arrest."

"Oh, I'm sorry. Will he be all right?"

"I sure hope so. It's touch-and-go right now."

"When did it happen?"

"Let's talk about it at home. I want you to stay with me again tonight."

"Okay, but can we stop by my place to pick up a change of clothes?"

"Sure."

I drove Jennifer to her apartment and parked as close to the front door as I could. After making sure that there was no one around, I walked her to the front door. When we got to her apartment, I took her key and unlocked the door. I opened the door very carefully, then made a sweep of the apartment. There was no one there, and it looked like no one had been there.

I stood close to the door while Jennifer packed a few things in a small suitcase. When she had what she needed and was ready to go, I led her back out to my car. I kept my eyes moving as she got in the car, then I walked around and got in.

During the drive back to my apartment, I kept a good lookout for anything that didn't seem right. I especially kept an eye out for anyone that might be following us. I saw no one.

When we got to my apartment and pulled into the parking lot, I saw a silver Lincoln Town Car parked out by the curb.

The only one that I knew that owned a car like that was Ralph Slocomb. I wondered if it was one of his thugs, or if it might be Ralph Slocomb, himself. I decided to find out.

"I think that's Slocomb or one of his thugs in the silver car at the curb. I'm going to find out what he wants."

"You be careful. I don't trust him," Jennifer said as she reached out and put her hand on my arm.

"Don't worry, I'll be careful. When I get out, slide over to the driver's seat and keep the engine running. If anything happens, get out of here and go to the nearest police station. Got it?"

"Yes."

I leaned over and kissed her, then stepped out of the car. I waited next to the car while Jennifer slid over into the driver's seat. When she was ready, I drew my gun out from under my sport coat and held it down at my side.

As I started moving toward the Lincoln, the driver's door opened. The "representative" that had visited me in my office and had brought the retainer check to me stepped out. He walked around in front of the car and held his hands out away from his body so I could see them.

"I don't want any trouble Mr. Blackstone."

"That makes two of us. What is it you want?"

"I want to talk to you. I have a message for you from Mr. Slocomb."

"What is it?" I asked as I moved closer to him.

He waited until I was closer and he could talk to me without anyone else being able to hear.

"Mr. Slocomb wants to know if Steuben is one of your suspects."

"Why would he want to know that?"

"I don't know. He didn't tell me."

"You can tell your boss that Mr. Steuben is one of about five suspects, and that includes him."

"He won't like that."

"I don't really care if he likes it or not. This afternoon, one of my friends was injured trying to arrest a guy that is one of my suspects. The guy got away, and my friend ended up in the hospital with a cracked skull. I'm not in a very good mood right now, and I don't really give a damn what Slocomb likes or doesn't like."

"Who was your friend? Maybe I know him," he asked with a tone of real concern.

I was a little surprised by his apparent concern. I was sure that it would change when he found out who it was.

"It was Captain MacDonald of the Denver Police Department."

"I'm sorry to hear that. He's a good honest cop."

"You know him?" I asked, a little surprised by his comment.

"Yeah. He arrested me a few years back. He treated me fairly. He was tough, but fair. I've always had a great deal of respect for him. I hope you will tell him that I wish him the best and that he gets well soon."

"I'd be happy to tell him. By the way, what is your name?"

"My boss calls me Georgie, but it's really George Archer. I'm sure MacDonald will remember me."

"I'll pass your message on to him, George."

"Thanks," George said then he turned to go back to the car.

"George, do me a favor."

George stopped, turned and looked at me.

"What's that?"

"Tell Mr. Slocomb that I have several suspects, but none that I can really pin it on at this time. Will you do that?"

"Sure," George said with a grin.

I watched as George walked around the car to the driver's door. He took a minute to look over the top of the car and smile at me. I nodded and smiled back. He got in the car and drove off.

George seemed like an all-right sort of guy to me. I even thought that we could be friends under different circumstances. I only hoped that he had nothing to do with the death of Emily.

As soon as he was out of sight, I turned and went back to my car. Jennifer shut off the engine and got out. We walked to the front door. After opening the door for her, I took one more look around, but didn't see anything that I felt needed my attention. I followed her inside then locked the door behind me.

Once we were inside my apartment, I called Russell at the First Precinct and told him that Mac's car was in the parking garage where I worked, but that I had the keys at my home. He said that he would send someone over to get the keys. I thanked him, then hung up.

It was only about ten minutes after my call to the First Precinct when there was a knock on the door. I went to the door and looked out the peephole in the door. There was a uniformed officer standing at the door. I opened the door.

"I've come by to get the keys to Captain MacDonald's car," the officer said.

I reached in my pocket and gave him the keys, then told him where he could find Mac's car.

"Have you heard anything on Mac's condition?"

"No, sir."

"Thanks," I said, then watched him walk back to his patrol car. I waited until he drove away before I closed the door and locked it.

JENNIFER MADE one of her "special" dinners. After dinner we watched some television. It had been a long day for both of us. There had been a lot of stress and frustration that made both of us tired. We didn't even wait for the news before we stripped out of our clothes and climbed into bed.

As I laid in the bed with Jennifer curled up against my side, I couldn't help but think of Mac and how he was doing. I had never gotten a chance to tell Mac about the black Lincoln that tried to run us over twice. I sort of smiled to myself as I thought about what George had said about him.

"Are you worried about Mac?" Jennifer asked.

"Yeah. He took a nasty blow to the head."

"Do you think that Butler might have killed Emily?" she asked as she rested her hand on my chest.

"He could have. He has the disposition to kill someone, even a woman. He almost killed a Japanese showgirl he was trying to rape when she screamed for help."

"Why else would he run?" Jennifer asked.

"Scared, maybe. He caused injury to a police officer while resisting arrest."

Jennifer didn't say anything for a long time. It felt good having her lying next to me. I could feel the warmth of her sexy body against me, and feel the softness of her hand as she ran her fingers through the hair on my chest. She was doing what any man would like a woman to do, but my mind was somewhere else.

"Peter, what are you thinking about now?" she asked softly.

I was sure she had a pretty good idea what I was thinking. She had known me most of my life. She often knew what was going on in my head almost before I did.

"Peter?"

"Yeah, Honey?"

"Hold me. Let me take your mind off this case for just a little while. It might help you think better in the morning," she suggested.

I turned and looked at her. A little light from outside was sneaking into the bedroom, allowing me to see the worried look on her face. Maybe she was right. Maybe it was a good idea to make her the center of my attention for tonight. It might help me take a fresh look at things in the morning.

I turned toward her and wrapped her in my arms. I rolled over on my back and drew her up over me. She stretched her shapely body over me as she wrapped her arms around my neck.

As she kissed me, I ran my hands down her smooth back, down over the small of her back and on to her firm shapely behind. She murmured softly as I ran my hands over her sexy body. As she kissed me, I could feel her firm round breasts pressing again my chest. She rose up a little and looked down at me.

"I like the feel of your hands on me," she said softly.

"I like the feel of you," I replied.

"Make love to me," she sighed, then leaned back down and kissed me.

Holding her tightly against me, I rolled her over on her back. I don't know how long we spent making love to each other, but I do know that it shut out the rest of the world for both of us. When our passion for each other had finally subsided, she rolled up against me and we fell asleep in each other's arms.

WHEN MORNING CAME, it came with a bang. At first I didn't know what was going on, but I soon realized that it was raining pretty hard. I could hear the rain as it pelted against the bedroom window.

Jennifer was lying up against my back with her arm over me. I could feel her warm breath against the back of my neck. I slowly turned and looked over my shoulder at her. She was smiling and looking at me.

"That's one hell of an alarm clock you have," she said with a grin.

"Yeah, and I didn't even have to set it," I said just as there was another flash of lightening quickly followed by a loud clap of thunder.

"The only problem with that clock is you can't shut it off." Jennifer laughed as she squeezed me tightly against her.

"Do you know what time it is?" she asked.

I looked over at the clock on the bedside table and said, "Six, forty-five."

"Are you ready to get up?"

"No, but I don't think I will go back to sleep. Are you ready to get up?"

"Can we just lay here for a little while? I like to listen to the rain," she asked.

"Are you sure that we are going to listen to the rain?"

"Maybe, but maybe not," Jennifer said playfully as she rolled over on top of me again.

We ended up having an encore of last night, which neither of us objected to. Afterwards we lay in each other's arms and listened to the rain and the thunder as it moved off toward the east.

It was somewhere around eight-thirty, quarter to nine when we finally rolled out of bed and went to the shower. By the time we got dressed and sat down for breakfast, it was almost nine-thirty. It was almost ten by the time we finished with breakfast, but we were in no hurry. It was Saturday. Neither of us had to go to the office today.

"What do you want to do today?" Jennifer asked.

"It may be a day off for you, but I still have a few things to do."

"Are there any that I can do with you?"

"Well, the first thing I want to do is to go see how Mac is doing."

"I would like to go with you."

I thought about it for a little while. I could think of no reason to keep her from going with me. After all, she had known Mac for a long time, too.

"Okay. Let's go see how Mac is doing."

We got dressed, had breakfast, then grabbed our coats. As soon as we were ready, I went to the door and looked out. There wasn't a soul in sight. I led Jennifer to the car and opened the door for her. She got in and I closed the door.

I had no more than closed the car door for her when I heard several shots being fired and felt a sudden sharp pain in my left shoulder. I knew I had been hit. A second shot hit me almost immediately after the first. It hit me in the upper part of my left leg before I could draw my gun and turn around. The second shot put me down as my leg gave out from under me. It happened so quickly that there was no time to return fire.

The last thing I heard was a car speeding away. My mind quickly turned to Jennifer. I had not heard a sound from her. I had no idea what had happened to her. Using what strength I had, I pulled myself up using the door handle on the car door.

The first thing I noticed was that the side window of my car had been shot out. There were little bits of glass all over. I looked inside and found Jennifer slumped in the seat. There was blood on the side of her head. My heart sank. She had probably gotten hit by one of the first shots.

I managed to get the door open and pulled myself up beside her. I hesitated to touch her, but I had to be sure. I put my fingers on the side of her neck. There was no pulse. She was dead. I let my body slide down onto the ground. As I leaned up against the car, I began to cry.

I don't know how long I was sitting with my back against the car before I heard the sound of sirens. The next thing I knew there were cops all over the place. They were talking to me, but I couldn't hear myself respond to them. I could hear another siren. It was shortly after the siren stopped that I could feel someone touching me on the shoulder and on the leg. I could feel something on my arm, but wasn't sure what it was. I couldn't seem to get my mind to work properly. I had trouble understanding what was going on around me.

Through it all, there was someone standing over me asking a lot of questions. I could not see who it was, but I was sure he was trying to find out who we were and what had happened. I told them what I could, which was not much beyond my name. I heard someone tell someone else we had to go, then a mask was put over my nose and mouth.

The next thing I felt was being lifted up. They put me on a gurney and took me to the ambulance. As I was lifted up into the ambulance, I could see the passenger's side of my car. Jennifer was still in the car and there seemed to be cops all over the car.

I still had no idea how long it had been since the shooting started, but I was able to understand that I had been shot. I had no idea how serious my wounds were, either. I do know that I felt very weak and that I was in a good deal of pain. I closed my eyes as the doors on the ambulance closed and felt it begin to move.

IT DIDN'T TAKE LONG before I was in an emergency room, but I had no idea where it was. I had an oxygen mask over my face. I looked around the room as best I could. I saw an IV bag hanging on a pole along with a bag of blood. Although I wasn't in a lot of pain anymore, I was sore and couldn't seem to move.

There seemed to be several people standing around or leaning over me, but I had no idea who they were or what they were doing. They seemed to be working very hard, and looked very serious about what they were doing. I could feel someone poking at my leg and my shoulder. My eyelids were very heavy and my mind didn't seem to be able to put together what was happening. I closed my eyes again and all the noise sort of faded away. I no longer could feel or hear anything. It was like being in a quiet dark room all alone.

CHAPTER ELEVEN

THE NEXT THING I seemed to be able to understand was that I was in a place that was very dark. There was a noise that I had heard sometime ago, but couldn't quite figure out what it was, or where I had heard it before. It was a slow but continuous beeping sound. Nothing seemed to register in my mind, yet the sound seemed familiar in a strange sort of way. It was like being in a place where nothing made any sense, yet it did.

I decided that I would try to open my eyes. When I did, I found myself in a rather small dimly lit room. It quickly came to me that I was lying in a bed, but it was not my bed.

There was a woman standing next to the bed. She seemed to be leaning over me. I had to admit that she was a nice looking woman. She had a hair net of some kind that covered most of her brown hair. She was wearing pajamas in kind of a faded ugly green. The woman seemed to be leaning over my right arm. I began to realize that she was taking my blood pressure. She looked over at me and smiled.

"Well, welcome back," she said in a very nice voice.

"Where am I?" I asked as I looked into her beautiful brown eyes.

"You are in Denver General Hospital, in the Surgical Recovery Room."

"I am?" I asked with a hint of surprise. "What am I doing here?"

"It seems that you were shot."

"Oh," I said then closed my eyes as I tried to think about what she had told me.

I don't know how long it was before I opened my eyes again, but the woman was gone. I could remember the woman and what she had said. As I thought about what she had told me, it slowly began to come to me what had happened, and why I was in the hospital.

Tears came to my eyes as I remembered seeing Jennifer in the passenger's seat of my car as the doors on the ambulance were closed. My thoughts were suddenly interrupted when the nurse spoke to me again. I looked up and saw her standing near the foot of the bed.

"There is a police officer here that would like to speak to you. Are you up to talking to him?"

"I guess so," I said, but wasn't sure I really wanted to talk to anyone right now.

I watched as the nurse walked away. It took a little while before anyone came back. I could hear the footsteps of street shoes on the hard floor. It wasn't until he came around the end of the curtain that I saw who it was. It was Detective John Edwards from the Second Precinct. I didn't know him very well, but he seemed to be a pretty decent sort of guy. At least I hadn't had any trouble with him in the past.

"Well, Mr. Blackstone, it is good to see you awake. Do you think you could answer a few questions for me?"

"I'm afraid I don't feel much like talking, but I know you have to ask them. Before we start, can you tell me something?"

"I'll try."

"Jennifer," I said then found it hard to say anything more.

"I'm sorry," he said softly, the look on his face telling me all I needed to know.

I turned and looked away. I knew that she was dead, but I guess I needed to know that it was not a nightmare. It took me a couple of minutes before I could gather my emotions enough that I felt like I was ready to answer any questions. Detective Edwards was kind enough not to say anything until I was ready. He simply waited until I turned back and looked at him.

"What is it you want to know?"

"Did you see who attacked you?" he asked.

"No. We were attacked from behind while - - - Jennifer - - - was getting in the car. Actually, she was in the car when the first shot was fired. I had just shut the car door for her."

"We found your gun under your car. It hadn't been fired. How did it get under the car?"

I thought about it for a moment before I answered him.

"I'm not really sure. I remember pulling it out of my holster just as I was hit a second time. I must have dropped it and in the commotion pushed it under the car when I fell."

"Do you know how many shots were fired?"

"At least four or five, but I can't say for sure. There may have been more. Two of them hit me is all I know for sure."

"Do you have any idea who might have had reason to shoot at you?"

I hesitated to answer him. I was sure that he knew that Mac and I had tried to arrest Butler, and that Mac was in the hospital as a result of that attempt.

"I don't know."

"Could it have been this Butler fella that we are looking for?"

"I don't know. I suppose it could have been, but I don't know. I'm sorry, John, but I didn't see anything that would help identify the shooter. For all I know, there could have been two or three shooters."

"Do you think there were three shooters?"

"I don't know. All I know is I was attacked from behind and that I took two rounds. That's about all I know. I'm sorry."

"As far as we can tell, there was only one shooter," he said. "Mac told me that you were looking for the killer of Emily Sutherland. Could the shooting be related to that case?"

"It could, I guess, but I can't think of any connection right now."

"Is there anyone you could think of that might have some interest in that case that would want to do you harm?"

"Yeah, but none that I can say for sure are involved in it."

"Were you getting close to someone, or was there someone that you might have pissed off?" John asked.

I could think of several that I might have pissed off, two for sure. The thing was I had no idea if they were involved in shooting me.

"None that I can think of right off hand."

"Are you working on any other cases at this time?"

"No. Just the one."

I could see that he was getting a little frustrated with me. I needed time to think, time to try and put things together.

"I'm sorry, John. I'm really tired. I just can't think right now. I'll have to talk to you later. Maybe I will be able to make some sense of it when I'm able to think better."

John didn't look like he was ready to call it a day, but what choice did he have. He wasn't going to get anything more out of me now, and he knew it.

"Okay," he said with a note of disappointment. "I'll leave for now and let you get some rest. We can talk again later."

"Sure. Thanks," I said then turned my head away from him and closed my eyes.

I listened and heard him leave the room. I could still hear his footsteps as they faded away down the hall when the nurse returned.

"Are you all right?" she asked.

"Yeah. I'm a little tired."

"I'll leave you for a little while so you can rest. I'll check back on you a little later."

She left the room without waiting for a response. I closed my eyes and let sleep put my mind at rest.

I HAD BEEN IN THE HOSPTIAL for three days before they allowed me to get out of bed. The injury to my shoulder was doing well. The injury to my leg seemed to be doing well, too, but was restricting my mobility. The combination of the two injuries prevented me from using crutches, but they did allow me to use a wheelchair to get around a little. I had to use my good leg to propel it along as my left arm was in a sling. The first place I wheeled to was Mac's room. When I rolled into his room, I found him sitting up in bed.

"How are you doing?" I asked.

"Not bad. I'm still having headaches, but I'll be fine. I think they are going to let me out of here tomorrow. What about you?"

"I'm doing pretty good, but I don't know when I will get out of here. They haven't said. I take it you know what happened?"

"Yeah. Has John Edwards been in to see you?"

"Yeah. We talked a couple of times over the past couple of days, but I'm afraid that I wasn't much help to him. I was attacked from behind. Things happened so fast that I didn't get a chance to see who it was or even return fire. I didn't even get a glimpse of the car, but I know there was one close by. I heard it leave in a hurry."

"I'm really sorry about Jennifer," Mac said as he looked at me. "I liked her."

"Yeah. Thanks," was all I could manage to say.

Mac and I talked for a little while about nothing very important. It seemed that neither of us wanted to talk about the cases we had been working.

After a short time, we found that we were getting a little tired so I returned to my room. I laid down to rest and quickly went to sleep.

THE NEXT MORNING I had a couple of visitors, Jennifer's parents. Mr. and Mrs. Taylor came to see me. I think it was pretty hard for them to talk to me, even though they were pleasant. I got the feeling that Mr. Taylor blamed me for the death of their daughter, although he didn't come right out and say so. It was easy for me to understand since I blamed myself. I mostly blamed myself for not being able to protect her.

Mrs. Taylor told me about the funeral and how nice it was. I was disappointed that I could not be there. They didn't stay very long, but it was okay. As soon as they left, I broke down and cried. I must have cried for an hour before I drifted off to sleep.

When I woke, it was dark in the room. I laid there in the quiet of the night and began to think about what had been taken from me. It wasn't long before I was thinking about what I was going to do about it. I wanted to kill the person that took Jennifer from me, but she would not want me to go after that person for revenge. She would want him to pay for what he did in a court of law.

I couldn't help but think about our last night together and how brave she had been to want me to continue my search for Emily's killer. It was clear what I had to do. I had to find Emily's and Jennifer's killer or killers so that justice could be done. She would want that, but the first thing I had to do was get myself out of the hospital and back in shape.

SHORTLY AFTER BREAKFAST the next morning, I was fitted with a special brace and some kind of pressure dressing on my leg that would allow me to walk a little without reopening the wound, provided that I didn't do something really stupid like try to run. The next day I was discharged with instructions to return in a couple of days to get the sutures removed. I was also instructed on what exercises I could do that would help me regain my mobility and strength in my shoulder and leg.

Since my car had been hauled off for the forensic people to go over looking for evidence, I had to take a cab home. Once I was at home, I laid down to rest. The activities of the morning had made me tired. I found it took a lot of energy just to move around. I spent the next couple of days exercising, resting and working at getting myself back in shape. I also spent sometime with my list of suspects and what I knew about each of them. I had a killer to find, and find him I would.

As soon as I felt that I was ready to get back out there and start looking for whoever had shot me and killed Jennifer, I called a place where I could rent a vehicle. I ordered an SUV, and it was delivered that afternoon.

THE FIRST PIECE OF BUSINESS I had to do was to get the sutures out of my shoulder and leg. I had rented a dark blue Chevy Tahoe. It was parked in front of my garage. Being an SUV, the vehicle had a little more ground clearance than the average car, which made it easier for me to get in and out of with my present injuries.

As I prepared to go to the hospital, I made sure I had my gun neatly tucked in my belt under my sport coat where I could get at it in a hurry. I had taken the sling off my arm so I would have a little more freedom of movement, just is case I needed it. My shoulder was still a little stiff and sore, but not so much so that I could not use it, at least a little. My leg was pretty stiff, but didn't hurt that much if I was careful. Of course, running was still out of the question.

I went to the front door and looked out before I stepped out of my apartment. I wasn't sure if I was still a target or not, but I wasn't about to take any chances. I didn't see anything that I felt would present any danger to me.

I hurried, as best I could with a stiff leg, out to the Tahoe and quickly got in. I started it up and drove out onto the street. I had only gone a couple of blocks when I noticed a silver Lincoln Town Car several cars behind me. It looked as if it was following me. I did a few minor maneuvers to make sure. It didn't take a genius to figure out that whoever was in that car was following me. The only one I knew that drove a car like that was George Archer, one of Ralph Slocomb's enforcers. I wondered why he was following me. I decided that it might be a good idea if I found out.

I quickly checked to make sure that he was still behind me. He was there, following me as if on a leash. I pulled around a corner, then stepped on it. I made a sharp turn into an alley just as he was turning the corner. I wanted him to see the Tahoe turn into the alley. As soon as I pulled down the alley far enough that he would not be able to see the Tahoe until he turned into the alley, I slammed on the brakes and put the Tahoe in park. I opened the door and drew my gun as I stepped out of the vehicle. Stepping out of the vehicle quickly was not easily done without some pain involved, but I managed.

As he turned into the alley, he hit the brakes and came to a stop only a few feet from my vehicle. I could see George sitting behind the wheel looking at me. He knew he had been caught. I had my gun pointed right at him. All I would have had to do was pull the trigger and he would find a 9mm slug come crashing through his windshield and into his face.

"Don't do anything stupid," I said as I looked at him over the barrel of my gun. "Very carefully, step out of the car. Keep your hands where I can see them."

George was not a stupid man. He put both hands out the side window. With one, he reached down and lifted the door handle and opened the door. Keeping both hands on the door where I could see them, he stepped out of the car. He put his hands up in the air and stepped out around the door so he was in front of it.

"Why are you tailing me, George?"

"I was told not to let anything happen to you," he said as he looked at me, but kept his hands up.

"Who told you to do that?"

He looked around and took a deep breath while still holding his hands above his head. He then looked at me again as if he had decided he would answer my question.

"Come on, George. I thought we had an understanding. Who told you to keep watch over me?"

"I did," he said with a hint of surrender.

"You? When did you become my guardian?"

"When you started looking for Emily's killer."

"I don't get it. Would you be so kind as to explain it to me?"

"Can we go somewhere private where we can talk?"

I looked at him wondering what was going on. My thoughts turned to the last time we talked. He seemed like a nice enough guy. He had been civil, and didn't seem to hold any feelings of resentment against me for knocking him over in my office chair and sticking a gun in his face the first time we met. In fact, the last time we had talked, he was downright friendly.

"Okay. By private, I take it you mean some place where anyone who knows us would not be likely to see or hear us talking together?"

"Yeah."

"Okay. Put your hands down," I said as I lowered my gun to my side. "There's a small café on the corner of Fourth

Avenue and Thirteenth Street. Meet me there, but don't follow me."

"Okay."

I watched him as he got in his car. I put my gun in my belt and got into the Tahoe then drove on down the alley. When I got to the end, I turned right and headed off toward the café where we were to meet. I looked out my rearview mirror and noticed that he had turned left. It took me a few minutes to get to the café, but I had done a little driving around to make sure that no one else had been tailing me and was tailing me now.

When I got there the silver Lincoln was parked across the street from the café. I didn't see anyone in the car when I drove by. I parked at the end of the block on the other side of the street from George's car. I walked back to the café and looked in the front window as I walked to the door.

I didn't see George until I entered the café. He had found a booth in a corner. I walked back to join him there. He motioned for me to sit down across the table from him. He had ordered coffee for both of us and it was sitting on the table. I sat down across from him.

"You can see anyone coming in from there, since I'm sure you don't trust me," he said with a grin.

"Okay, George, what's on your mind?"

"First, I would like to say that I'm sorry about Miss Taylor. I'm sure she was a nice lady."

"What are you saying? Did you have something to do with it?"

"No!" he said sharply, then looked around to see if anyone might have heard him.

Keeping his voice down, he continued.

"I wouldn't do anything like that. I've never killed or beat up anyone, except while I was in the Marine Corp. My job with Slocomb has always been just to be a driver, run errands and to be a bodyguard for Mr. Slocomb from time to time. That's all. But sometimes I hear things," he said.

"Like what?"

"I'm not sure, but I overheard Mr. Slocomb talking on the phone. He was talking about you to someone. I'm sure of that.

I didn't get who the other person was, but he kept telling whoever it was on the phone not to worry. He said something about keeping an eye on you, and that you wouldn't be any trouble."

"Any idea who he was talking to?"

"No. I didn't get a chance to hear very much of the conversation. I came in in the middle of their conversation. One of Slocomb's enforcers came in the room before he was finished so I didn't get to hear the rest of it. I saw him coming before he saw me. I was able to move away from the door to the coffee machine. I was pouring a cup of coffee when he came in the room and saw me. He went on into Mr. Slocomb's office without saying anything to me."

"Do you think that he might have guessed that you heard Slocomb?"

"I don't think so."

"What is your interest in Emily's death?"

George looked at me for a moment, then looked down at his hands. He didn't say anything, but I got the feeling that he might have liked her, maybe a lot. He took a deep breath, then let it out slowly as he looked up at me.

"I really liked her. She was nice to me and she would talk to me," he said as he looked up.

"Are you sure it wasn't more than just "like"?" I asked.

He again hesitated to talk. I don't know what it was, but I got the feeling that he and Emily were close. I just didn't know how close.

"Yeah, it was more, a lot more. Emily and I were lovers. We tried very hard to keep it a secret."

"Why did you want to keep it a secret?"

"Because Mr. Slocomb would have had my hide if he found out that I was dating one of the girls that worked for him. He didn't like any of his employees dating the girls, not one bit."

"Did you know that Jeff was dating her?"

"No, he wasn't dating her. She had turned him down several times when he asked her out, but she never dated him."

"She had a picture of him on her dresser. Did you know about that?"

"Yeah, sure. She told me about it."

"It didn't bother you?"

"Of course not. She told me that Jeff gave it to her in case his father had someone search her apartment. He knew that his father did that sort of thing. You see, Mr. Slocomb didn't trust his son to keep away from the girls, with good reason."

"Wasn't she one of his girls?"

"Mr. Slocomb wouldn't mind all that much if Jeff dated one of the girls that only worked in his nightclub. He didn't want his son to date any of the girls that worked at his gambling houses or in his escort service. Most of the girls that worked for his escort service also worked at the gambling houses, but not Emily."

"So Emily was not a call girl."

"No!" he said rather sharply."

"How were you able to date Emily and still keep it secret?"

"We have an apartment in Aurora. Emily lived there. Her apartment near the school was just a cover. My days off, we would spend together in Aurora. We didn't go out where we might be seen by anyone who might tell Mr. Slocomb. We were planning on getting married, but she said not until she was finished with school, and we both quit working for Mr. Slocomb. I gave Mr. Slocomb my notice a month ago. Tomorrow is my last day."

"You gave notice before Emily was killed?"

"Yeah. She was going to graduate in just a few months."

"What are you going to do now?"

"I'm hoping that you will let me help you find who killed her. I'll do whatever you want."

I got to thinking about what he was going through all by himself. I could sympathize with him having just lost Jennifer.

"Are you sure you can do what I tell you? I can't afford to have you running off half-cocked. It could get us both into a lot of trouble."

"I promise to do what you say. I'll give you no reason not to trust me," he said, the look in his eyes seemed to be pleading with me to let him help.

"George, what will you do after we find her killer?"

"I'll finish my computer classes, get my degree and get a job. Then I'll get on with my life."

"You're taking computer classes?" I asked with a hint of surprise.

"Yes. Why, don't you think I'm smart enough?"

"No, it's not that. I didn't know you were going to school."

"Well, I am. I don't want to work for someone like Slocomb all my life. I need something that I can make a living at for a long time without fear of being arrested for something my boss did."

"I can understand that. Okay. When will you be free of Slocomb?"

"I'm to collect my final pay tomorrow morning and turn in the Lincoln. Then I'm free."

"What will you do for a car?"

"I have a car at my apartment in Aurora. I can get a cab to take me there after I turn in the Lincoln."

"When you get done and have your car, come by my office. You can park in space 19 in the parking garage. I'll be in my office all morning going over what information I have on all my suspects. We'll work together on this case."

"Thanks."

"Does Slocomb know what kind of a car you have?"

"No. I just got it last week. I keep his car at my place all the time, so he hasn't ever seen my car."

"That's good."

"What do you want me to do today?"

"I think it's a good idea if we are not seen together. I'll be going to the hospital to get my sutures out. When I'm done with that, I'll be going back to my office."

"Okay. Why don't you go ahead and leave first. I'll pick you up outside and follow you around for the rest of the day," George said.

"Okay. Keep an eye out for anyone that might be following either of us. I want you to especially keep an eye out for a black Lincoln Town Car that might be following me," I replied as I reached for the money to pay for the coffee.

"I'll get it," George said with a smile.

I smiled back, then turned and left the café. I walked down the block to my car. As I was getting in the Tahoe, I saw George leave the café and walk across the street to the silver Lincoln. I left the area and found him on my tail within five blocks. I couldn't help but smile. I looked to see if there might be someone else on my tail, but didn't see anyone.

When I got to the hospital, I pulled into the parking lot near the emergency entrance. I saw George pull into the parking lot, but he parked off to the side where he could see my vehicle.

I ENTERED THE EMERGENCY ENTRANCE and went to the check-in desk. After telling the receptionist why I was there, she had me take a seat and called for someone. It took about five minutes before a young woman in scrubs came out of a room and called my name. I stood up and followed her into an examining room.

Once in the examining room, I took off my pants and shirt. The nurse removed the sutures from both my leg and shoulder. After the doctor examined my wounds, he told me that I could go, but not to put too much stress on the wounds. He said that they were healing well, but needed a little more healing time. He also told me that I didn't need to return unless I had a problem.

I left the hospital for my SUV. As I got in, I looked around. George was still parked some distance away, but I could see him sitting behind the wheel.

CHAPTER TWELVE

I LEFT THE PARKING LOT and headed back toward my office. George followed me out of the parking lot and hung back a ways as he tailed me. I had never liked being followed, but under the circumstances it was nice to have him back there, especially since he was on my side.

It didn't take me very long to get back to my office. I hadn't been there very long when there was a knock on the door. I took my gun from under my coat and held it in my hand under the desk.

"Come in," I said from behind my desk.

George came in and walked up to my desk. I put my gun back in my holster under my coat.

"Expecting trouble?"

"No, but no sense being unprepared."

"How'd it go at the hospital?" George asked as he sat down in front of my desk.

"Pretty good. All I have to do is avoid any stress on my wounds, and I should be okay in about a week to ten days."

"Good."

"I hope no one saw you come up here."

"Are you kidding. I'm good at tailing people, and I'm good at making sure that I'm not being tailed," he said with a grin.

"Hey, I knew you were following me within a couple of blocks from my home this morning," I reminded him.

"Yes, you did. But that was because I wanted you to know that I was following you."

We had a laugh over that, but it was time to get serious.

"What do we do now?" George asked. "I know that you want to find out who shot you and killed Jennifer."

"You're right about that. I want whoever it was, and I want him before the cops get him. That is how I feel."

"I know how you feel, I really do. I feel the same way about finding Emily's killer. But we have to put our feelings aside and figure out what our next move is."

"You're right, and I know that," I said as I took a deep breath. "I also know that we really need to look at it with an open mind. We need to stick to the facts and do our best to keep our emotions under control and out of it."

"Okay, but it won't be easy."

"I agree. We just might have to help each other in that regard," I said. "We need to go over what we know, then go from there."

"Okay. You're the investigator. I'll follow your lead."

George and I sat down at the table in my office. I started out by telling him what I had learned so far about Emily's death. I followed that up with what I had learned from the interviews I had had so far.

Once that was done, we went over the list of students that had been in the last class Emily had attended. George was able to recognize a couple of names. They were girls that worked for Mr. Slocomb. He told me a little about them. One of them was DeeDee Preston Nielsen.

I told him that I had already talked to DeeDee, but he gave me a little more information about her. That information included the fact that Jeff Slocomb was sleeping with her, and had been for almost a year. That came as a bit of a surprise to me, but not as much of a surprise as I thought it would be. The last time I talked to Jeff, he didn't seem all that concerned with Emily's death, at least not as concerned as I had expected him to be. I got a hint of why from my talk with George in the café. Now I knew why.

When I took a minute to think back to my interview with DeeDee, I remembered how she looked when I first arrived at her apartment. She not only looked very sexy, she looked as if she had just gotten out of bed. I wouldn't be surprised if Jeff had been in her bedroom listening to everything she told me."

"June Parker Cullen was also a friend of Emily's," George said. "Have you talked to her yet?"

"Yes. She was very cooperative. She told me a little about Steuben and what he was like. She was one of them that told me that Steuben was making passes at the girls."

"Did you talk to Lynn Miller?" George asked.

"No. When I tried to call Lynn, Marsha Wallace answered the phone. She gave me a lot of information."

"I'm not surprised that you got hold of Marsha at Lynn's place. They practically live together. You almost never see one without the other."

"What can you tell me about them?"

"Not a great deal. What I know about them is pretty much second hand."

"Tell me what you do know even if it is second hand," I said.

"Emily mentioned one time that they often sleep together. She also told me that Lynn is a real man hater and the dominate one in their relationship. Lynn gets extremely jealous of any woman that even shows the slightest interest in Marsha, even just to be friendly. From what Emily had told me about Lynn, Lynn tends to get violent if Marsha even talks to another woman, or a man for that matter."

George's last comment gave me something to think about. Was it possible that Marsha had made a comment to Lynn about how sexy Emily looked while they were drawing her in the figure drawing class? I had heard from several of the students that Emily had a very nice, even a very sexy body. I had seen pictures of Emily, and there was little doubt that she had a very nice figure and a pretty face.

"Do you think that Marsha might have commented to Lynn on how nice a body Emily had, and that Lynn got so jealous that she killed Emily? Maybe Lynn was afraid that Marsha would dump her and try to get together with Emily."

"Emily was not like that," George said sharply.

"No. No. I wasn't implying that Emily was. Not at all. But if Lynn was the type to get violently jealous over just a hint that she might lose Marsha to someone else, do you think she might kill to keep Marsha's affections?"

"I hadn't thought about it that way, but I suppose it's possible. Do you think that might be the case?" George asked.

"I don't know. It seems a little far out to me at the moment with the other suspects we have, but we can't rule out anyone. People have been killed for a lot less. Some emotions are hard for some people to control, especially jealousy. Some are even harder to understand."

George looked down at the table in front of him. He didn't say anything for several minutes. He let out a sigh, then looked up at me.

"It's hard to think that Emily was killed because someone was jealous of her when there was no reason to be," George said with a note of sadness in his voice.

"Then there's the fact that I was shot at. Why would Lynn shoot at me and Jennifer?"

"Good question. Do you have an answer?" George asked.

"No, but I doubt that Lynn would have tried to kill me once the threat of losing Marsha was gone. So I don't think that was the case."

"I agree. I guess that puts Lynn close to the bottom of your suspect list," George said.

"Yeah. I would think so."

"Who are you leaning the hardest toward?" George asked as he looked at me.

"It's hard to say. Butler is right up there on the top of the list as far as I'm concerned, with Steuben a close second."

"Is the reason for Butler being on the top of the list because he caused injury to MacDonald, and because he ran?"

It was not hard for me to see what George was doing. He was trying to make me think in terms of who might have actually killed Emily and Jennifer, rather than in people I might be upset with. I wasn't very happy with his question, but it did help me focus on the killings.

"I'm convinced that the murders of Emily and Jennifer are connected in someway. I don't know how, yet. Do you agree?" I asked.

"I don't think there is any doubt they are connected. Yes. I agree."

"Then we need to focus on the one that we have the most information on and the most suspects. That would be Emily."

"Okay. Who do we have as suspects in Emily's murder?" George asked.

"Right now, I'm still leaning toward Butler. He is the type that would attack a woman and even kill her. The fact that he almost killed a woman he attacked in Japan lends credence to it," I said.

"We have a witness that Butler beat up a guy for something he said in one of the classes he had with Butler," I said. "We also have a witness that indicated that Butler was one of the last ones to leave the classroom where Emily was last seen. In fact, we have a couple of witnesses. Now, how reliable those witnesses are seems to have come into question."

"Okay. I agree. Who's next?" George asked.

"The next one would be Franklin Steuben. He got really shook when I talked to him. The last thing he would want would be to get caught up in a scandal. We have strong indications that Emily was probably going to report him to the president of the school."

"Do you think that would get him fired with his mother being the largest supporter of the school?" George asked.

"It might, although I'm not sure. I doubt that she would like the morning headlines if her son was arrested for murder, or was arrested for sexual advances toward female students. I wouldn't be surprised at anything that woman would do to avoid a scandal. She might even help cover up a murder to protect her son. Some people would do just about anything to keep their family secrets private."

"So she's a suspect, too," George said.

"Yes, I would think so. She even threatened me with arrest if I so much as talked to her son," I said. "She seems to be very protective of him. I could see where she might hire a hit man to lessen the chances of her son being arrested. Do you know that she has friends in high places in the police department, in the city and in state government?"

"I didn't know that. We keep her as a suspect," George said. "I take it Mr. Slocomb is also a suspect?"

"It's possible, but I'm not leaning too hard that way at this time. If he had anything to do with it, it would be mostly to protect his businesses or his son. Either of those would be his motivation. But on the other hand, he does have the people to carry out a hit."

"You think maybe his son had something to do with Emily's death?" George asked.

"I don't have anything to make me lean that way at this time, but I wouldn't eliminate him."

"Okay. Where do we start?" George asked.

"We start by looking for Butler. I want to find him and ask him a few questions."

Finding Butler was easier said than done. I had no idea where to start looking for him. I needed something that might give me a direction, and his apartment might just do that for us.

"I think we need to take a look at Butler's apartment. We might be able to find something there that would give us an idea of where he would go to hide."

"Will his apartment be crawling with cops?"

"I doubt it. I would think that the forensic investigators would be done with it by now.

"Do you think that they might be watching the place in case Butler returns?"

"They might, but we can get by them," I said with a smile. "I doubt that they would have the place under a full-time stakeout. But I'm sure they will have a rolling stakeout around the area in case Butler tries to come back to his apartment. I don't think they have the manpower to keep a continuous watch on the place for very long. Probably not more than a couple of days."

"It's been longer than that already," George said.

"The cops know both of us. We need to get into the building undetected."

"I've got a friend that lives there. I'll have her meet me somewhere so I can go into the building with her. That should avoid drawing any suspicion for my being in the building," George said.

"Good idea. I'll meet you there. When you get inside, make sure that the backdoor is unlocked."

"I can do that."

"Okay. Lock up when you're done here," I said as I stood up and walked to the door.

Just as I left, I looked back over my shoulder and saw George picking up the phone. I took the elevator to the parking garage.

As I stepped off the elevator, I saw a black Lincoln Town Car pull into the parking garage. My heart began to beat faster. I immediately reached for my gun and sidestepped behind one of the large concrete pillars. I readied myself for a confrontation with whoever was in the car.

I took a breath when I saw a man that I knew worked in one of the offices on the third floor get out of the car. His name was Martin Wingate, an insurance agent for a local insurance company. I slipped my gun back in my belt and stepped out from behind the pillar.

As I walked toward my car, he smiled and gave a slight wave of his free hand. He had a briefcase in his other hand.

"Nice car," I said as I walked by him.

"Yeah. I just got it," he said with a big smile as if he was proud of it.

I nodded back and continued toward my Tahoe. I got in the Tahoe and left the parking garage for Butler's apartment.

WHEN I ARRIVED at the building where Butler lived, I drove on around the block. I didn't see any cars that had anyone in them that looked like they might be watching the building. I didn't see anyone standing around as if watching the building, but that didn't mean they weren't there. They could be watching from the building across the street. I drove around the corner and parked the Tahoe near the entrance to the alley that ran behind the apartment building. I was pretty sure that no one would think twice about the Tahoe as I had only had it a short time.

I sat in my SUV waiting to hear from George. I had been there only about twenty minutes when my phone rang.

"Blackstone," I said.

"George. I'm just parking outside the building. Give me about five minutes."

"Okay," I said then hung up.

After waiting the five minutes, I got out and looked around before I started down the alley. There were lots of bushes, high fences and garages along both sides of the alley. Most of them would prevent anyone in any of the other nearby buildings from seeing someone walking down the alley. I started down the alley staying close to one side near the bushes.

I was about halfway down the alley, between the corner and the back of the apartment building where Butler had an apartment, when I saw a black-and-white start to turn into the alley at the far end. I quickly ducked into some bushes. I could see the police car from where I was hiding, but doubted that they could see me. I only hoped that they didn't drive down the alley.

The police car had turned into the alley then stopped. It just sat there at the end of the alley. With the glare on the windshield, I could not see what the officers inside were doing. All I could tell was that there were two officers in the car, and they were just sitting there. There was nothing else I could do but wait and watch, and hope they left soon. I would be out in the open if I tried to move either way.

It seemed like an hour before they backed out of the alley and drove away, but it was only a few minutes. I quickly stepped out of the bushes and moved to the backdoor of the building where Butler's apartment was located. I tried the door, but it was locked. I couldn't wait very long. If another police car came into the alley from either end, I would be spotted.

Just as I saw the front fender of a black-and-white start to turn into the alley from where I had come in, the door came open. I quickly ducked inside to find George standing there. I shut the door and looked at him.

"Your timing was perfect. In fact, you cut it a little close."

"Better close than not at all," he said with a grin.

"You got that right. Let's get a move on. I don't want to get caught nosing around Butler's apartment."

"Let's take the service elevator," George suggested. "When it opens, it will put us just a few feet from Butler's apartment door."

"Good idea," I said, then followed him to the service elevator.

When we got to the second floor, we stepped off the elevator unseen and went directly to the front door of Butler's apartment. The door was locked, but it only took me a few seconds to get it open. We quickly ducked inside, closed and locked the door.

"Don't touch anything," I said as I took rubber gloves out of my coat pocket and put them on. "We don't want any fingerprints left for the cops to find if they should decide to come back."

"I wouldn't know what to look for. I'll leave that to you. I'll just keep an eye out."

"Good idea," I said."

I stood in the living room and looked around. Where in this place would he hide something that would tell us where he might be hiding? I decided that it would be best if I checked out the other rooms in the hope of finding something.

The first room I went into was set up like an office. I decided to start there. I went over to his desk and looked it over. There was a computer on the desk, but little else. I tried to open the desk, but it was locked. I quickly picked the lock and began rummaging through the desk.

The drawers of the desk held nothing of interest to me until I found some mail in the second drawer on the left. I rummaged through the mail, looking at each piece. There were two utility bills. I noticed that one of them was for a different address in another part of town. I found that a little strange. I rechecked the addresses. What was a utility bill for a different address doing there? Both bills were made out to James Butler.

I tucked the bill into my coat pocket then continued to search the desk. People often hide things, especially small things, under drawers and behind drawers. I started pulling out the drawers. As I did, I looked at the underside for anything that might be taped there, or on the back of the drawer. Once they were all out, I checked out the inside of the desk.

"Bingo," I said as I reached in and pulled a small white envelope from the inside back of the desk.

"Did you find something?" George asked as he stood in the doorway to the room.

"I found something, but I'm not sure what."

"We've got company. A couple of cops just pulled up out in front. They're looking up at the front of the apartment building. We best get the hell out of here."

"Got yah."

I quickly put the drawers back in the desk, then took a quick look around. Everything looked like it did when we walked in. I stuffed the envelope in my coat pocket as I ran toward the front door of the apartment. George was standing outside by the time I got there. I stepped outside the apartment, closed the door and made sure it was locked.

I was about to head for the backstairs when George grabbed my arm and quickly led me to an open apartment door. We hustled in, and he closed the door just as the downstairs front door opened. I looked around and saw a very nice looking woman sitting on a sofa. She was smiling at me.

"How do you do?" I asked with a smile.

"Very well, thank you. And you?" she said with a smile.

"Very well," I replied.

I turned to see George looking out the peephole in the door. He turned and smiled.

"Looks like we made it. It was the cops, by the way. The apartment manager is just letting them in Butler's apartment."

"That was close," I said. "Now, would you mind introducing me to this lovely woman who has just saved our necks?"

"Not at all. This is my sister, Julie."

"Nice to meet you. I didn't know George had a sister."

"This is Peter Blackstone. He's a private investigator."

"How did the two of - - - ." she said, but was interrupted by a knock on the door.

I looked at the door then at George.

"You can hide in the other room," she said as she stood up. George pointed toward a door. I quickly went into the room while George sat down on the sofa. I left the door ajar so I could hear what was going on. The next thing I heard was the front door to Julie's apartment open, then I heard Julie.

"May I help you?" she asked very politely.

"I'm Detective Edwards with the Denver Police Department. I would like to ask you a few questions about your neighbor."

"Come in, Detective."

I could hear the door shut. I was sure that he was going to want to know who the man sitting on her sofa might be, but Julie was one step ahead of him.

"This is my brother, George Archer," Julie said. "Which neighbor are you interested in?"

"James Butler."

"Is that the one that lives in the apartment at the end of the hall?"

"Yes. What can you tell me about him?"

"I'm afraid that I don't even know him. Of course, I've seen him in the hall on occasion, but I've hardly talked to him except to say 'hello'."

"You've never talked to him?" the detective asked as if he didn't believe her.

"Other than to say "hi", no. He doesn't seem very friendly. In fact, Mrs. Turner, who lives on the other side of the hall, was saying just the other day that she didn't think he was very friendly, either. I don't think he talks to anyone in the building."

"Do you know anything about him?" Detective Edwards asked.

"Not really. I don't see him very often. We seem to move in different circles. I have seen him a couple of times with one of those big portfolios cases. You know, the kind that artists put their paintings in. He might be an artist of some kind."

"He does attend an art school here in Denver."

"Well, it seems you know more about him than I do. I do know that he injured a policeman here in the building a couple of weeks ago. I wasn't home when it happened, so all I know about it is what I have been told. By the way, how is the officer doing?"

"He's doing well."

"That's good to hear," she said. "I'm sorry that I'm not much help."

"That's fine." Edwards said as he turned and looked at George. "Sir, do you live in this building?"

"No. I don't live here. I'm just visiting my sister."

"Oh. Well, thank you for your time. If you should happen to see Mr. Butler, would you be so kind as to give me a call?"

"Certainly," Julie said as she took the business card Edwards held out to her.

I didn't hear anything until I heard the door close again. I stepped out of the room and joined George and Julie in the living room.

"That was interesting. Why do you think he stopped by here?" George asked.

"That was Detective John Edwards. He has been investigating the incident that got Mac injured. There's that and someone watching the place might have recognized you. He probably wanted to know what you were doing here."

"What's in the envelope you found?" George asked.

"Don't know," I said.

I took the envelope out of my pocket. It was not sealed. I opened it and found a piece of paper in it with three names. Beside each name was a phone number, except for one of the names that had two phone numbers. The name with two phone numbers was Franklin Steuben.

"This is interesting. What do you make of it," I said as I handed it to George.

He looked at it for a minute or so, then he looked at me.

"I have no idea what it means, but it must be something important if he went to all the trouble of hiding it."

"I agree. I think we need to go back to the office and check out these phone numbers," I said as I looked at George.

"I guess we need to go," George said to his sister.

"How are you going to get out of here with the police still hanging around?"

"She's got a good point there," I said to George. "Have you got a good answer?"

"No," he said.

"I have," Julie said, with a slight grin. "Why don't you check out the phone numbers from here while I fix dinner for all of us?"

I looked at George and he looked at me. He didn't look like he had any objections. I then turned and looked at Julie. She was looking at me with a very pleasant smile on her face.

"I think that is a wonderful idea. It would be an honor to have dinner with you," I said.

"The phone's over there," she said with a grin as she pointed toward a desk in the corner of the room. "The telephone book is in the top drawer on the right."

"Thank you," I said and walked over to the desk.

I sat down and took the phone book out of the drawer as George pulled a chair up beside me.

"Let's start at the top," I said as I gave him the piece of paper.

"Albertson, Sean," he said then gave me the phone number.

"I talked to Sean on the phone a while back," I said as I thumbed through the phone book looking for his phone number.

When I found Albertson's number in the phone book, it was not the same as the one on the piece of paper. The one in the phone book was the number I had used when I called him, and was the one listed on the student list. The only thing I could think of was that the number on the paper was a cell phone number.

"Looks like that's a cell phone number," I said. "Wonder if the others are cell phone numbers that wouldn't be listed in the phone book."

"Only one way to find out," George said. "The next one is Jeff Slocomb."

The phone number we had was not the same as the one in the phone book, but it looked familiar. I had to think about it for a minute before it came to me.

"Jeff's number is his cell phone. He gave that number to me when he asked me to find Emily," I said.

The two for Steuben were also cell phone numbers. I wondered why he had two.

"Well, what do we do now?" George asked.

"That is a good question. I have to think about it for a while."

I pushed back in the chair and looked at the wall in front of me. There was only one of the numbers that I believed I could call without raising too much suspicion, and that was Jeff's. He was the only one on the list that had actually given me his cell phone number.

I started to reach for the phone, but stopped. If his phone had caller ID on it, he would know where I was calling from. I didn't want him to have that information. I certainly didn't want to put Julie in any kind of danger. Instead, I reached into my pocket and took out my cell phone. I punched in the numbers from the paper and listened as it rang.

"What do you want, now, James?" Jeff said with a harsh tone to his voice.

"This is not James. This is Peter Blackstone."

"Ah – I – I thought it was James."

"James who?"

"Oh, ah – just a friend of mine," he said.

I got a hint that he might have said more than he wanted to say, especially to me. I was also sure that he was lying to me.

"It wouldn't happen to be James Butler?"

"Ah- No!" he said rather sharply. "It's another James I know. Ah – I don't really know James Butler. He goes to the art school is about all I know about him. I think Emily must have mentioned him to me."

Jeff rattled on saying much more than I would have expected him to say if he didn't know Butler. I had made him very nervous.

"Oh. Well, the reason I'm calling you is that I would like to get together with you and return the money that I figure you have coming since I didn't do any real investigation into finding Emily."

"That's okay. I told you that you didn't need to return any of it since you did find her."

"Well, I would also like to talk to you about James Butler."

I thought I heard a sudden intake of a breath.

"What about him? Like I told you, I don't really know him. All I know is that he had a couple of art classes at the school with Emily." he said, his voice sounding nervous.

"I'd like to talk to you in person, if you don't mind."

"Ah – yeah, sure. What about tomorrow morning at your office?"

"That would be fine. What time?" I asked.

"Ah – nine?'

"That would be good. I'll see you then. Have a good evening."

"Ah – yeah – you, too," he said then hung up.

I smiled to myself as I closed my cell phone and looked at George. He was smiling, too. He had heard the entire conversation because I had the speaker on.

"What do you think?" I said.

"I'd say he was a bit nervous. But he did tell us one thing. He is involved with Butler in some way. As far as I'm concerned that puts him up higher on our suspect list."

"I have to agree. It also told us something else. James is not with him, at least at the moment. The only problem I have is where was Jeff when we called. If he was at DeeDee's, James could be hiding out in Jeff's place."

"I thought Jeff was living at home," George said. "At least that was what I heard his father tell one of his customers at the nightclub the other night."

"Do you think that Jeff might live at home, but in a private section of the house? Maybe some part of the house that would allow him to come and go without being seen or detected? The house is certainly big enough."

"That could be. I've been in that house several times. There are a lot of parts of the house that could be shut off from other parts easy enough," George said. "It wouldn't be very hard for someone to come and go without anyone knowing."

"Do you think that he might be hiding Butler there?"

"It certainly would be possible," George said.

"We might have to stake out Slocomb's house."

"That won't be easy, but it can be done," George said with a grin.

"We'll look into it tomorrow after I talk to Jeff."

George and I talked about the others on the list, but decided that we wouldn't do anything about them until after I talked to Jeff in the morning. It wasn't long before Julie joined us in the living room.

We spent the rest of the afternoon and a good part of the evening just talking. Julie was an excellent cook and an interesting woman to talk with. It became clear that George and his sister were very close.

When it came time to leave, I thanked Julie for hiding me, for an excellent dinner and pleasant conversation. George provided me with a hat and coat to make it difficult for any policeman to identify me when I left.

I walked around the corner, got into my Tahoe and went home. It wasn't long and I was home and sound asleep.

CHAPTER THIRTEEN

I WOKE TO THE SOUND of my alarm clock buzzing as if it were in pain. I reached over and shut it off, then rolled over on my back and looked up at the ceiling. The first vision that came to mind was that of Jennifer lying next to me in my bed. I turned my head and looked over at the pillow next to me. Of course, she wasn't there. But in my mind I could see her as she looked on the morning of the last night we had spent together.

Tears came to my eyes as I began to think about the fact that I would never have her lying next to me again. I could remember many of the moments that we had shared over the years. The nights we had made love and the nights that we just spent talking about our lives. Now she was gone forever, and there was nothing I could do about it. But there was something I could do about the person who had taken her from me.

My thoughts turned to yesterday. George and I had set out to find whoever it was that had taken our lovers from us. I had to consciously force myself to focus on what had to be done. I couldn't let my emotions get in the way. I had to use my skills and ability to find the killer and see to it that justice prevailed. Legal justice, not the kind of justice I felt the killer deserved.

With that thought firmly planted in my mind, it was time to get up and get to work. The first thing I needed to do was to take a shower. A shower always helped me think better, and put things in perspective.

I rolled out of bed and went into the bathroom. As I stood under the warm shower, my mind began to think in terms of my known suspects. I was going to have a talk with Jeff Slocomb this morning. The difference between today and yesterday's talk with him on the phone was that he would be prepared to answer questions. I would not have the advantage of catching him off guard.

While still in the shower, I thought about how I was going to approach the subject of Butler with Jeff. By the time I got out of the shower I had some idea of what I would ask him. I sat down at the table to eat my usual breakfast and continued to think about what I thought Jeff might know and how I might get it out of him.

My breakfast was suddenly disturbed by the ringing of the phone. I got up and walked across the room to answer it.

"Hello."

"Peter, this is George."

"What's up? Have you already finished your business with Mr. Slocomb?" I asked as it was not even eight in the morning.

"No. I was thinking. The other day you said that you wanted me to come to the office as soon as I was done with Slocomb. If I do that, I could get there about the time you are talking to Jeff. I'm not sure you want Mr. Slocomb to know that we are working together. I'm sure the kid would tell his old man."

"You're right about that. What I would like you to do as soon as you are finished with Slocomb, is spend a little time watching the Dunberger house in Cherry Creek.

"Why there?"

"That's were Steuben lives. He is Mrs. Dunberger's son."

"I didn't know that."

"Apparently not many people do. Steuben might not even be there. But if he is, I want you to follow him if he leaves. Call me if anything happens."

"Okay, but I might not be able to get there before nine."

"If you're lucky enough, he might still be there. He drives a bright red Porsche 911. Chances are the car will be in the garage if he is there. If he doesn't leave, you may never see it. We have to start somewhere. It might as well be there."

"Okay, I'm with you," George said.

"If nothing happens, meet me at the office at noon. I should be done with Jeff by then. Call before you come up just in case he's still there."

"Okay. Talk to you later," he said, then the phone went dead.

I knew that sending George out to watch for Steuben could prove to be a waste of time. There was the possibility that Steuben would be gone by the time George got there. If he was there, it would be clear that he wasn't going to leave the protection of his mother's house. But on the other hand, it might pay off. I just didn't want Jeff to see George at my office.

I sat back down and finished my breakfast. I got to thinking about Steuben again. I had touched a nerve the last time I talked to him. It had been enough to get his mother to come to his defense. I wasn't sure, but that alone made me wonder what it was he was hiding.

It was time for me to go to my office and get ready to talk to Jeff. It would be awhile before he was scheduled to meet with me.

I ARRIVED AT MY OFFICE just a little before eight. I was pretty sure that Jeff would not be there early this time. Talking to me would not be what he would want to do, but I had really left him with little choice.

As I unlocked the door to my office, I heard the elevator door open. After having been shot, there was little doubt that I was being alert to any kind of trouble that might come my way. I quickly opened the door and stepped into my office. I closed the door leaving just enough of a crack that I could see anyone who was getting off the elevator.

A man in his mid-thirties stepped off the elevator then stopped. I watched him as he looked up and down the hall. It was obvious that he was looking for something. I took note of him. He was tall, maybe six-two, and probably weighed around two-twenty-five. He carried himself with a hint of confidence. Actually, he reminded me of someone I had seen before, but I just couldn't place him.

He suddenly looked at a door down the hall and smiled. He walked up to the door and knocked. It was the door of an attorney that handled divorce cases. It was a great relief that he was not there to see me. I was still not physically ready to take on some big bone breaker.

I closed the door to my office, then went to my desk in the inner office and sat down. I took a look at the list of students I had gotten from the school. I looked at each name and studied them carefully. Actually, I was hoping that something would pop out at me, but nothing did. None of the ones on the list that I hadn't talked to had been mentioned by anyone I had already contacted. Those I had talked to were the ones that had hung around after class and were likely to be the last to have seen Emily alive.

I decided that I would work the ones I already knew about. If nothing came of it, I would start talking to the rest of them on the list. However, there was one that I had not talked to that I probably should. I had not talked to Lynn Miller, the man hater. I wondered what an interview with her would be like, or if she would even talk to me. Only time would tell. I would go to see her in the afternoon. She was one that I thought might be best to talk to in person.

I turned around and spent a little time looking out the window of my office. I mentally took my time to think about each one of my suspects. I guess you could say that I sort of rated each one of them. I was trying to figure out which ones to believe and which ones were lying to me. It was hard, but the more I thought about it, the more I was convinced that there were two, other than Jeff, that I needed to talk to in person. They were Albertson and Miller. Of course, Butler was also someone I wanted to talk to, but so did the cops.

My thoughts were suddenly interrupted when I heard a knock on my door. I turned around to find Jeff Slocomb standing in the doorway looking at me. He didn't look like he was very happy to be there.

"Come in, Jeff," I said as I pointed at the chair in front of my desk.

"I still don't understand why you want to talk to me again. You found Emily, case closed," he said with a certain confidence in his voice he didn't have last night on the phone.

"The case is not closed. I want to talk to you about James Butler," I said.

When I spoke to him, I looked him right in the eyes. I noticed that he looked down at his lap before he looked back at me.

"Like I said last night, I don't know him. The only thing I know about him is what Emily told me. I think she might have been a little afraid of him."

"Why would she be afraid of him?"

"I don't know. She never said."

His body language told me that he was lying to me. I had some serious doubts that Emily even talked to him about Butler.

"I want to clear up something I discovered."

"What's that?"

"It has to do with you and Emily," I said as I leaned back in my chair.

I could see that he was getting very nervous. I was sure that he was wondering what I might have found out about them.

"Emily was never your girlfriend, was she?"

He hesitated to answer, so I continued.

"She had a boyfriend, someone else that you knew nothing about. I hear that she actually rejected your advances."

"She never did. She didn't have to. It's true. I have a girlfriend."

"Who might that be?"

"That's none of your business."

"It's DeeDee Nielsen, isn't it?"

"How do you know that?" he asked.

"How I know it is not important. What is important to you is that your father doesn't know it. Am I right?"

I waited to see what kind of an answer I was going to get from him. I had a pretty good idea that if his father knew he was sleeping with DeeDee, he would be in big trouble with his old man. That was to say nothing about what might happen to DeeDee if the old man found out his son was sleeping with her.

"I think you know that your old man hired me to prove he had nothing to do with Emily's death. My question is did you have something to do with it?"

"NO!" he said sharply. "I liked Emily. I wouldn't hurt her."

Now that was the first thing he said that I tended to believe. "Last night when I called you, you thought it was James calling. Was that James Butler? And don't waste my time lying to me," I said sharply as I sat up and leaned toward him.

Jeff sat there looking at me, but didn't answer my question.

"Jeff, what's going to happen if your old man finds out that you have been sleeping with DeeDee? I know you were in her bedroom when I stopped by and talked to her," I said, knowing that I was guessing.

"How do you know that?"

"You just told me," I said with a grin. "Where's Butler now? I know you're hiding him."

"I don't know where he is."

"But you knew where he was when I called last night, didn't you?"

"Yes," he admitted reluctantly.

"Where was he last night?"

"He was in my apartment."

"You don't have an apartment."

"Yes I do. It's attached to the back of the garage of my parents' house. It has a private entrance off the alley that runs behind the house."

"Is he there now?" I asked.

"No. After you called, I told him to get out of there before the police came by. I told him that you suspected he was there, and that you were looking for him."

"I have just one other question for you. Did your father have anything to do with Emily's death or the death of Jennifer Taylor?"

"I don't think so," he replied.

"I take it, by that, you don't know?"

"I don't, honest. I don't know why he would. Neither of them could be of any harm to him or his illegal businesses."

"So you know about his other businesses?"

"Sure. DeeDee told me about them. She works for him. How else do you think she can afford that fancy town house?"

"Do you have any idea where Butler might be hiding now?"

"No. I wouldn't tell you if I did. Butler is crazy, and he's dangerous."

"Are you afraid of him?"

"Yes," he replied. "You would be too if you knew him."

"Okay. I guess that will be all for now. You can go."

"Are you going to tell my father about DeeDee and me?"

"No, not at this point. But if I find out you lied to me, I might hint at it and let him find out for himself."

"I didn't lie to you. I don't know where Butler is."

"Okay. You can go," I said.

I remained seated behind my desk while I watched Jeff stand up. He looked at me for a moment then turned and left my office. I was sure that I had him worried. He was probably wondering if I would tell his dad, but I had told him I wouldn't. Besides, what good would it do? On the other hand, if I didn't tell his old man, I would have something to hold over his head in case I needed more information from him.

I leaned back to think about what I had learned from Jeff. Jeff had some connection to Butler, but I still wasn't sure what it was. I knew he had hidden Butler for a while, but I doubted that Butler was still in Jeff's home apartment. If he was, he wouldn't be within a few minutes. Jeff would probably call Butler and tell him that I knew where he was hiding, if he hadn't already left. I wondered what kind of a hold Butler had over Jeff to make him take such a risk by hiding Butler. He had to know that Butler was wanted by the police for assaulting a police officer.

JUST THEN MY PHONE BEGAN TO RING. I reached over and picked it up.

"Peter Blackstone Investigation."

"Peter. George here. Has Jeff left?"

"Yeah. Where are you?"

"I'm in the parking garage."

"Come on up," I said, then hung up.

It didn't take George long to get to my office. He walked in and sat down in front of my desk.

"Did you get everything settled with Ralph Slocomb?" I asked.

"Yeah. He asked me to stay on, but I told him I had other plans," George said.

"Did you tell him what your plans were?"

"Yeah. Well, some of them. I told him that I needed to devote more time to my computer classes," he said with a grin.

"Well, that's not entirely a lie."

"No, I guess it isn't. How did your talk with Jeff go?"

"It went pretty well. He had been hiding Butler in his apartment at his old man's house."

"I figured that. I went by there, but didn't see anyone leave the rear apartment that Jeff uses."

"I thought you were going to watch Steuben?"

"I did. I got there just as Steuben was leaving in his red Porsche 911. I followed him to the art school. I figured he would be there most of the day, so I took a run over to see if Butler might be hanging out at Slocomb's."

"Good thinking. Have you got any idea what kind of a hold Butler has on Jeff to get him to hide Butler out at his place?"

"No, but I've got an idea," George said.

"You want to tell me about it?"

"I happen to know that Ralph Slocomb is into selling drugs. He's not big into it, but it sort of goes with the territory, so to speak. When you're into all the other things he's into, it seems that it's the next step. I think Jeff is using drugs. He may not be heavy into them, but he's a user. I can't prove it, but I think that Butler might be one of Ralph's dealers. If not, then he is a supplier for Jeff, maybe both."

"That sort of makes Butler or Jeff, maybe both of them, prime suspects in Emily's death," I said as I thought about what George had just told me.

"How so?"

"The ME says that Emily was given cocaine by force before she was killed. From what he said, she was held down and forced to inhale cocaine. He said she showed no signs of ever having used it before."

I could see by the look on George's face that he was very angry. It was apparent that he didn't know that she had been forced to use cocaine. I could only imagine what was going through his mind at that moment.

"If that little son of a bitch forced Emily to use cocaine, I will personally kill him."

"Listen to me. I know how you feel, George, but we can't let our personal feelings get in the way of proving who the killer or killers are. We have to be able to prove it."

"Yeah. I know, but if the law doesn't get him, I will."

I had no problem understanding what George was feeling. I wanted the same thing for whoever had killed Jennifer. Right now, we needed proof.

"We need to do two things right now. We need to find Butler, and we need to have a talk with Lynn Miller," I said.

"What does Lynn Miller have to do with this?"

"She might know who the last person left in that classroom was on the day Emily was murdered."

"Okay. Do we go talk to her together?"

"I just thought of something I almost forgot," I said. "I want to get into that storage room off the classroom, the one that the models change in."

"Why? Is there something special about it?"

"I don't know, but it might be important. Remember, the classroom was the last place that anyone I have talked to saw Emily alive."

"It shouldn't be too hard to get in there."

"No. It shouldn't, because I'm going to walk right in," I said.

"I'll go with you."

"Not this time. If we go waltzing in there together, we might find ourselves tossed out or escorted out by the police. Besides, I've got a job for you. I want you to find Jeff and follow him wherever he goes. I want to know who he talks to and what he does. If I know him, he's rather nervous after our talk this morning. He will probably go to DeeDee's, but he might try to find Butler as well. I want to know where Butler is hiding. I want to talk to him. You said you were good at tailing someone without them knowing it. I'm counting on that skill."

"Okay."

"I'm sure you know what kind of car Jeff drives. Find that car and you will probably find Jeff."

"I'll get started. I'll grab a bite to eat on my way."

"Good. Don't expect me to answer if you call me on my cell phone. I will have it off while I'm at the school, but leave a message and I'll get back to you as soon as possible," I said.

"Okay. Call me if you need any help. See you later," George said as he stood up.

I watched as George left my office. I sure hoped that he didn't take things into his own hands. As I thought of that, I really began to feel that he knew how important it was to get proof rather than revenge. I was hoping that our revenge would come in a court of law.

A quick look at my watch told me it was just shortly before twelve. By the time I would get to the school, it would be in the middle of lunch break. It would be the perfect time to get into the storage room.

I got up and left my office for the parking garage. I left the parking garage and drove to the Denver School for Artists. On my way to the school, I kept an eye out for anyone following me. I didn't see anyone.

I ARRIVED AT THE SCHOOL within fifteen minutes. That would give me time to get into the storage room, and hopefully out, before the afternoon class got started. I parked and walked into the school as if I belonged there. As I passed by the Administration Office, I noticed that they were rather busy, which was a good thing for me. The place was full of students wanting this or that. I was sure that no one even noticed me as I walked past the office.

It didn't take but a couple of minutes to find the classroom where Steuben held his figure drawing classes. I wasn't sure if he would be in the classroom or not, but I wanted to see that storage room. I only hoped that Steuben was in the instructors' lounge having his lunch.

I took a quick look around and didn't see anyone in the hall. I opened the classroom door and stepped inside. Luckily, there was no one in the classroom. I closed the door and went directly to the storage room. The last thing I wanted was to get caught and tossed out before I had a chance to look around.

Once inside the storage room, I closed the door behind me and just stood there as I looked around the room. It was a fairly large room that was well lit by several florescent ceiling lights. The room was cluttered with all kinds of art supplies and fixtures, like easels, stands for paints and even a few stools.

There were a number of shelves on one wall that had all kinds of art supplies on them, such as brushes, paper and framed canvases in an assortment of sizes. There were cabinets along another wall. When I opened them, I found all kinds of paints and thinners of the kind that would be used by artists who used a variety of different kinds of paint.

Off to one side I saw a bench and a wooden chair. I found the bench to be of immediate interest. The bench was about six foot long and about two and a half feet wide. It had a soft cotton sheet over it. I took the cotton sheet off the bench and discovered the bench was padded and covered with a smooth vinyl material. It met all the criteria for what the ME had said Emily was on when she was murdered.

My first thought was that I had found where Emily had been murdered. The next step was to prove it. For that, I would have to have something that would get Mac to send out a forensic team to go over the bench, chairs and the complete storage room with a fine tooth comb.

As I continued to look around the room, I wondered how anyone would get a body out of there without someone seeing them. I didn't see a door except the one I used to get into the storage room. I knew that the school had evening classes. That would mean that there would be people in the building until it closed, probably around midnight. Getting a body out when the building was closed might be a little tricky, too, since I knew there was a night watchman and a custodian in the building all or most of the night. There had to be another way out.

I continued to look around while trying to think of how to get a body out of there without being seen. There were no windows in the room. It seemed like it would be almost impossible, but it had obviously been done because I had almost run over Emily several miles away from the school.

Suddenly, I heard voices coming from the classroom. If it was the model, he or she would be coming into the storage room to change to get ready to pose for a classroom full of students. I hadn't counted on anyone coming in before the lunch hour was over.

There was a tall, narrow piece of plywood board in the corner of the room. It was just barely big enough that I could hide behind it. I quickly moved behind the board and discovered a door in the corner. I hesitated to open it because I had no idea where it went, but I had little choice if I didn't want to get caught.

I looked the door over then tried the door knob. It opened easily. I slowly opened the door and looked inside. There was a staircase that went down a level. Since I was on the ground floor of the building, I assumed that it must go to the basement.

I stepped onto the landing and closed the door as quietly as possible. I got it closed only seconds before the door to the storage room opened. I stood next to the door and listened.

"I don't like the way that Steuben looks at me when I model," a female voice said.

"Just model and don't think about him. If he makes a pass at you, tell him that you are going to report him to the police," a male voice said.

"What good will that do? It will be his word against mine, and who do you think they'll believe?"

"I'll stick around after you model to make sure he leaves you alone."

"Thanks, Dave."

I stood on the landing wondering how long it would be before I could get out of there without being seen. I looked down the stairs and began to wonder what was in the basement. Was there a way out of the building from the basement? If there was, I might have not only found my way out without being seen, but I might have found the way they got the body out of the building. The only other question was where had they kept the body cold for almost a week.

I moved down the steps very carefully in order to keep from making any noise. I soon found myself in a small room that had only one small window in it. The window let in just enough light so that I could see around the room.

On one side of the room was a stack of old school desks. There were several large tables with a bunch of chairs piled near them. But the thing that caught my eye was back in a corner. Until my eyes adjusted to the dim light in the room, I had not seen it. It was a fairly large refrigerator, like the ones that might be found in a restaurant or a school kitchen. I wondered what it was doing there. It looked like it had been there for years.

I walked over to it and noticed that there was a heavy coating of dust on it. I also noticed that there was no dust on the handle on one side. That told me that someone or something had removed the dust. On a closer look, it was clear that someone had opened the refrigerator. I wondered if it was big enough to hold someone the size of Emily.

I took my rubber gloves from the inside pocket of my jacket and put them on. The last thing I wanted to do was leave my prints all over the place. I then carefully opened the refrigerator and looked inside. On the side that had no dust on the handle, there were no shelves. From the size of it, there would have been ample room to put someone as small as Emily.

I would have liked to examine the refrigerator closer, but I didn't have a flashlight. I checked to see if it was plugged in. It was not, but there was an electric outlet close by, but nothing was plugged into it. The plug for the refrigerator was on the floor under the outlet. From the looks of the plug, it had been used recently. I was pretty sure that I had found where Emily's body had been kept until it was taken to Washington Park.

Now, the only thing left for me to do was to find out how they got her body out of the school without being seen. I first checked for doors leading off the room. There was only one, the one that I used to get into the basement. I then studied the window for several minutes. I noticed that there were indications on the glass and on the frame that the window might have been opened recently. Dust and dirt on the window and window frame had been disturbed. It became clear to me that Emily's body could have been taken out the window. Even I could get out that way if I crawled out.

What was outside the window was the next question that came to mind. The window was fairly high on the wall, but close to the ground on the outside. It could be easily reached if one of the tables across the room was moved under the window. It would also make it easier for someone to push Emily's body out the window if he was standing on a table. A quick look at the tables revealed that two of them had been stood on. There were scuff marks and shoe prints in the dust from tennis shoes. It was obvious that the prints in the dust had been made fairly recently.

I felt that it would take at least two people to get her body out the window. I remembered that there had to be at least two people in the car that took off from the park after dumping her body there. The question was, who were the two people?

I needed to get out of the storage room without messing up any evidence. That meant that I could not go out the window. The way I figured it, I had two choices. The first was to remain in the basement until class was over and the room had cleared out. The other was to simply walk out through the classroom as if it was the most normal thing in the world.

The last idea was very tempting, but not all that good an idea. If I simply walked out, Steuben might get the idea that I had found the basement and the refrigerator. That would not be good. By the time I could get the cops there, he could either ruin the evidence, or he could be gone making finding him very difficult. He certainly had the resources to disappear.

I decided to sit tight for a couple of hours, or until the classroom cleared. If nothing else, it would give me time to think.

CHAPTER FOURTEEN

TIME PASSED SLOWLY while I was in the basement of the art school. I didn't dare sit down on any of the chairs or tables for fear of leaving evidence that I had been there, or disturbing evidence that was already there. I decided that I would try to contact George and see how things were going with him. I turned on my cell phone, but left the ring to vibrate so it would not make any noise if someone should call me.

"Hello."

"George?"

"Yeah. What's up, Peter?"

"I was wondering what is happening with you."

"I found Jeff's car. He doesn't have a clue that he is being followed. His car is parked in front of DeeDee's apartment."

"Are you sure he's in there?" I asked.

"Yeah. I saw him go up there just a little while ago. He hasn't left."

"Any idea where he was between the time he left my office and arrived at DeeDee's?"

"No. I picked him up here."

"Have you seen anything of Butler?"

"No, not yet. Did you expect me to see him around here?"

"Not really, but I can hope," I said.

"If I see Butler, do you want me to follow him or stay on Jeff?"

"Follow Butler. He's the one I want right now. I'm not sure, but I think Jeff may be involved; but I don't think he is a principal player. At least I don't have anything to point me in that direction at this time."

"Okay. By the way, where are you?"

"You wouldn't believe me."

"Give me a try," he said with a chuckle in his voice.

"I'm in a small basement room in the school. I think I've found where Emily was killed and where she was kept until I found her in the park."

"You mean she was kept at the school until she was left in the park?" George said not really believing what I was telling him.

"Yes. Based on the information I have, there is every indication that she was killed here and her body was kept here for a week. Why she was kept here for so long I can only guess."

"I'm coming over there," he said.

I detected the sound of anger in his voice. I couldn't have him running around and making a mess of what little evidence I had been able to find. If he came barging into the school, whoever was involved could destroy all the evidence that might be in the basement room before the police could get there.

"You stay on Jeff," I insisted. "He is the one who might very well lead us to Butler. It's important that we find Butler."

I could hear George take a deep breath. I knew how he felt, but I needed him to stay away from the school.

"Okay," he said reluctantly. "Are you coming over here?"

"I'm afraid not. I have not been able to find a way out of here without being seen. I'm going to have to wait until class is over and everyone leaves."

"How long do you want me to follow Jeff?"

"As long as you can. Remember, he is the key to getting Butler. By the way, I never asked anyone, but does Jeff have a job of any kind?"

"Sort of. He works for his old man."

"What does he do?"

"From what I've seen and heard, he mostly tries to boss people around at the nightclub. I've never had much to do with him."

"So I take it he works a lot of evenings?"

"I guess. Like I said, I didn't have much to do with him. I worked mostly days driving Mr. Slocomb around and running errands for him or his wife. I went to school in the evenings."

"But you know about the gambling houses?"

"Sure, I know about them. Like I said, I hear things. Most of Slocomb's muscles didn't have much to do with me. They do almost all the work when it comes to the escort service and the gambling houses. I've only driven to one or two of the gambling houses."

"Well, I'm going to be here for awhile. Just do what you can as far as Jeff is concerned, then go home for the night. I'll talk to you in the morning, but call me if anything comes of it."

"Okay. See you in the morning," he said, then the phone went dead.

I began to think about George. I hoped that he wouldn't do anything that would screw things up to the point where we couldn't get the guilty parties put away.

There was very little I could do until I could get out of the basement. As I looked around, I could hear a woman talking in the storage room, but I couldn't understand what she was saying. I looked up toward the door to the storage room and thought about it. From the look of things, there was very little chance that anyone would come down here. I decided that I would go back up the stairs to the landing. If I was closer to the door, I might be able to hear what was going on in the storage room.

I started up the stairs being very careful not to make any noise. The steps were pretty solid and had been built well so they didn't make any noise when they were walked on. I was able to get to the landing at the top of the stairs without making a sound. I leaned over close to the door and listened.

"Class should be having their break as soon as Steuben finishes checking their work," a female voice said. "Can we get out of here for a little while?"

"Yeah. Steuben said that he had to go to the office to get some grades. We should be able to get out of here in the next few minutes," a male voice said. "Get dressed and we'll go get a coke across the street."

"I'd like that," the female voice said.

I didn't hear anything else except for the moving around of someone in the storage room. I was relieved to think that I might be able to get out of the basement in a few minutes. I would have to make sure everyone was out of the room. I continued to wait.

When I didn't hear any sounds at all, I slowly and carefully turned the doorknob. It turned quietly. I slowly opened the door, then stepped out behind the plywood board. I looked around it and didn't see anyone in the storage room.

The door to the storage room from the classroom was partway open. I quickly moved up to it and looked out into the classroom. It, too, was void of anyone. I hurried across the classroom to the door. The hall was full of students, but no one seemed to be paying any attention to anything. I simply stepped out of the classroom and acted like I knew where I was going and what I was doing. The fact was I did know where I was going. I was getting out of there before I was seen by someone who might not like the fact I was there.

ONCE I WAS OUTSIDE the building, I went to my car. I got in it, but didn't start it. Instead, I sat there looking at the building. I was thinking about how Emily's body had been taken out of the building without anyone seeing it.

While I was in the basement, I had only seen two ways out of the room. One was through the classroom, but that left too big a risk that they would be seen removing the body. The second was through the basement window, which seemed to be the most likely way out. From what I had seen while in the basement, the window appeared to be the way that was used. I began to think about the window.

With the size of the window, it would not have been possible to get her through the window without some bumping or dragging of the body against the window and window frame. That might explain at least some of the post mortem bruising on the body. The large plastic lawn bag that I saw at the park was too big to get out the window with a body in it without tearing it open. That would mean that she had to have been taken out of the basement before she was put in the lawn bag.

I had to think in terms of two or more people moving her out the window, since I had already concluded that it would take more than one person to get her out of such a small window. There was also the fact that the window showed signs of having been opened recently from the inside.

The next question that came to mind was the wet leaves. Where did they get them and the large plastic lawn bag? Did they already have them? I doubted that they did.

As I looked down the side of the building, I noticed a man in coveralls was cleaning up a small grassy area along side the building. That got me to thinking. We had had a pretty bad wind and rain storm a day or so before I found the lawn bag with Emily's body in it at the park. I remembered seeing a lot of people out raking branches, twigs, and leaves off their lawns over the next couple of days after that storm. It had also rained on the day I found the lawn bag at the park.

I couldn't see any branches, twigs or leaves on the grassy area next to the building. It had obviously been cleaned up, and I had a good idea where some of those leaves had gone. They had gone into the lawn bag that also contained Emily's body.

Now I was sure I had found the primary crime scene. It was the storage room. I had also figured out where they had kept Emily's body until they could move it, and that was in the refrigerator in the basement. I also knew how they got her out of the building. All I had to do now was prove it. The other problem I had was to figure out who "they" were, the ones that had killed her.

As I looked at the school, I noticed the groundskeeper was working along side the building. I decided that it might be a good idea to have a little talk with him. I got out of my car and walked over to him.

"Excuse me, sir. Could I talk to you for a minute?"

"Sure. What's on your mind?" he asked as he leaned against his rake.

"Have you been working here very long?"

"You mean at the school?"

"Yes."

"Oh, about eight years or so."

"Do you remember the windstorm we had a few weeks ago?"

"Sure do. That was a doozy. I had six bags of leaves and branches to clean up just along side the building. You wouldn't think there could be that much with so little lawn, but there was."

"Can you tell me when they were picked up?"

"Well, let me think. That storm was on a Tuesday, I raked it up on Wednesday, - ah – yeah. I took the bags out to the dump on the Friday morning after the storm."

"You took the bags out yourself?"

"Yap, I got them out of here myself. I took a pickup load out to the dump on that Friday morning."

"Thanks," I said.

I started to turn and head back to my car when he spoke again. What he said caught my attention immediately.

"I remember it well. It was kind of strange."

I turned back and looked at him. He was just standing looking off into space as if he was thinking about something.

"Why was it strange?" I asked hoping he had something that would help me.

"When I raked them up on that Wednesday after the storm, I filled six of those large plastic lawn bags full with leaves and stuff. You know the kind of stuff I mean."

"Yeah, I know the kind," I said.

"I counted the bags so I would be sure to get a truck big enough so I would only have to make one trip to the dump. But on Friday when I went to pick them up, there were only five full bags. One of the bags had been dumped out and the bag taken. Now who would want a used lawn bag? I had to rake up the mess and put it in another bag," he said with a confused look on his face.

"Was the sixth bag as full after you raked it up the second time as it was when you filled it that Wednesday?" I asked not sure if he had even noticed.

"You know, it's funny you should ask that. The new bag was the same size as the ones I had used when I first filled them. But when I raked up the leaves that had been dumped out, it didn't seem that the new bag was near as full. Maybe the leaves dried out a little making them smaller, you think?"

"Maybe," I said. "Where were the bags between the time you filled them and you took them to the dump?"

"Up close to the building. Right over there, just this side of that window," he said as he pointed toward a basement window.

He had pointed to an area where the lawn bags would have blocked off a view of the window from the street. A quick look around gave me the impression that it would be rather dark along side the building at night.

"Thanks for your help," I said then returned to my car.

I had gotten a lot more information than I had expected to get from the groundskeeper. Now I knew what had happened. I was pretty sure that I could put together a timeline between the time when Emily was last seen in the classroom and when I found her body. I was sure that Mac would like to know. My next step was to have a little talk with Mac.

I started my car and headed for the police station where Mac had his office. I had no more than turned the corner when I noticed a black Lincoln Town Car. It was just two cars behind me. I decided that it would be okay with me if it followed me to the police station. I was pretty sure that it wouldn't stick around there very long.

It didn't take me long to get to the police station even with my tail. I guess he wasn't all that interested in me, because when I pulled into the police station parking lot, whoever it was drove on by. I sort of smiled to myself, but the smile went away rather quickly. Whoever it was, I was sure I would find them waiting to follow me when I left the parking lot.

I WENT INSIDE THE POLICE STATION and asked for Mac. It was only a few minutes before he came out of an office and walked down the hall to where I was waiting. Without saying a word, he motioned for me to follow him to his office. Once inside his office, he shut the door then sat down behind his desk.

"Have you got something for me?" he asked as he pointed toward a chair.

I sat down before I answered.

"Yeah. I think I found were Emily Sutherland was murdered, where her body had been kept, and where the leaves and plastic lawn bag that I found her in came from," I said more than just a little pleased with myself.

"Can you prove it?"

"Not at the moment, but I think your forensic people should be able to prove it."

"Where is this place?"

"It's at the Denver School for Artists."

"Are you sure?" he asked.

"Yes. I'm sure."

"You're sure, but you have no proof."

"Right. Say, what the hell's going on here?"

"The next thing you are going to tell me is that Steuben murdered Emily?"

"He might have, but I don't know for sure. Whoever did it had help."

"I see," Mac said, then turned and looked out the window.

Mac had a strange look on his face. I got the impression that he believed me, but for some reason that I didn't understand, I got the feeling that he wasn't going to do anything about it.

"What's going on, Mac? I thought you were interested in finding the primary crime scene?"

"I am, but I can't go barging into the school and upset everything without some kind of proof. I wish I could," he said, then there was a long pause before he spoke again.

"Peter, I'm sorry. I'm no longer investigating the murders of Emily Sutherland and Jennifer Taylor," he said sort of formal like. "I've been taken off the cases. In fact, I'm not investigating any cases. I've been put on administrative duty for a while. I was told that I was to turn over all investigations to John Edwards until I get a medical release to go back to full duty. In other words, until I can go back to investigating murder cases again, I can't get involved."

"What? I thought you were doing fine. Are you having problems since your head injury?" I asked concerned that he was not doing as well as I had thought.

"None at all. I'm not having one damn problem," he said a little sharper than one would have expected.

"What's going on?"

"I don't know. I'm not even supposed to talk to you or anyone else about any of the cases that I was working on until I'm released to full duty. Somebody is pulling strings around here."

"Any idea who that might be?"

"Yeah, but I can't prove it."

"What about Edwards?"

"What about him?"

"Will he go after whoever he thinks is involved, or will he follow orders from someone else?"

"He's a team player. He'll follow whatever his senior officer says. I can assure you that he will not be let loose on this. I suspect he will be on a short leash."

"So that's it. Emily's and Jennifer's cases will be left to rot in some old file room for years from now until they're reopened as a cold case?"

"That's about it," Mac said.

"And you're not going to do anything about it."

"I wouldn't say that, but I'm being watched. I think my phone is tapped. I'll give you a call first thing in the morning. Now it would be best if you just left before they find a reason to pull your license."

I wouldn't say we were good friends or even just friends, but I got the feeling that he was not going to let it go. It pleased me to know that he would still help as much as he dared.

It didn't take a genius to figure out what was going on. I was beginning to wonder if maybe Mrs. Dunberger had carried out her threat and had gotten someone in the upper brass to get Mac off the cases by putting him on administrative duties. I knew that Mrs. Dunberger was a big contributor to the school, and that she had a lot of influence with some of the upper brass and a few local government officials.

I didn't really think that Mac would let that kind of pressure stop him from investigating a crime, and it looked like I might be right. I would have to wait and see what he had to say in the morning. From the look on his face, I would have to say it bothered him to think that one or more of the upper brass would do such a thing.

I also knew that he didn't have any choice if he wanted to keep his badge. If he got caught investigating either of the two murders, he could be suspended or even fired. If he had decided to help me, off the record, he was risking his career. I would have to be careful to make sure that I didn't do anything to help the upper brass get rid of him.

I got up and walked to the door. I opened the door and saw one of the detectives that I knew, but didn't like. He was standing down the hall a little ways. As he looked at me, I noticed that he had a smug look on his face as if he had heard something that made his day.

I turned back and looked at Mac.

"I get it," I said with a disgusted tone in my voice. "I'll see you around."

I turned and walked down the hall. I made it look like I was storming out of the police station. I only hoped that everyone who saw me would think that I was mad as hell. If the truth be known, I was mad as hell; but not for the reason they might think.

As I left the police station, I wondered what I was going to do now. The one thing that had come out of my meeting with Mac was that I wasn't going to get any help from the police department with Mac off the cases. I was pretty sure that I wouldn't get any help from Edwards, either.

It was time for me to go back to my office and regroup. I knew that George would not be very happy about what happened. I was sure that he would be ready to take things into his own hands, and I could certainly understand that. I was about ready to do it myself. The more I thought about it, the angrier I got. No one was going to stop me from finding out who had killed Jennifer. I would not let her down. I would find her killer with or without help from the police.

The one consolation I had was that Mac had not completely let me down. He would help me as best he could with his limited access to information on the cases.

As I drove toward my office, I saw that damn Lincoln tailing me again. Being mad as hell with the turn things had taken, I was about ready to take it out on someone. As far as I was concerned, the guy in that Lincoln would be as good as anybody. All I needed was a private place to meet him face to face.

I led him around for a little while to make sure he was tailing me. I was sure that it was the same Lincoln that had tried to run over me, twice. It didn't take long before I was satisfied that he was tailing me. I quickly made a turn, then sped up. By the time he was making the turn, I was turning into an alley. I slammed on the brakes, put the Tahoe in park, then quickly stepped out of it. I drew my gun just as he turned into the alley.

The Lincoln squealed to a stop when the driver saw me pointing my gun at the windshield. He found himself looking down the barrel of my gun. I could see the look on the face of the driver. He was shocked to have found me pointing a gun at him.

I seriously thought about putting a couple of 9mm holes in the grill of the Lincoln, when he slammed it in reverse and stomped on the gas. The back wheels of the car suddenly spun and the car went backwards at a high rate of speed. He backed out into the street almost hitting a delivery truck. He turned and sped off down the street.

I got back in my Tahoe and drove out the other end of the alley before anyone saw me. I was sure that the next time he followed someone into an alley, he would be a bit more careful about it.

I drove back to my office and parked my vehicle in its normal parking space. As I got out of my vehicle, I looked around to make sure that there were no unusual vehicles in the parking garage. I saw none.

ONCE I WAS IN MY OFFICE, I sat down behind my desk. I still wasn't sure what my next move was going to be. What I did know was that no one was going to stop me from finding out who had killed Jennifer. Justice was going to be served if I had to serve it myself.

Someone had taken my Jennifer away from me forever. In order to get rid of me, she had become collateral damage. There was no reason to kill her. She had nothing to do with it. She was killed because she was with me.

As I sat behind my desk, I slowly began to think like a real investigator. In short, I got my emotions and my temper, mostly my temper, under control. It was not like me to get so angry, but I felt I had good reason. I was going to have to find out who had killed Jennifer on my own, and the place to start was with Butler. I set my first goal in my effort to find her killer, and that was to find Butler. I would put all my effort toward that goal.

I couldn't help but think that the place to start was with Jeff. I had a feeling that he knew where Butler was hiding, and he was going to tell me, one way or the other. I didn't give a damn who his father was, or how many thugs he had.

Just then my phone began to ring. I was not in the best of moods, but I couldn't just let it ring. I took a deep breath, then let it out slowly in an effort to get myself under control. I then reached over and picked up the phone.

"Peter Blackstone Investigations," I said with the most professional voice I could muster.

"Is this Peter?" a pleasant female voice said.

"It is. Who am I talking to?"

"This is Julie Archer."

"Oh, hi, Julie. George isn't here right now."

"I wasn't calling for George. I was calling for you."

"Oh. Well, what can I do for you?"

"You could come over to my apartment for dinner tonight."

"That's a very nice offer and I'm honored, but I'm afraid I wouldn't be very good company tonight. It's been kind of a bad day."

"George told me about Jennifer, so I understand. But I also think it would be good for you to have someone to talk to."

"I appreciate your offer, but I don't want to burden you with my problems."

"Peter," she said in a way that got my attention. "I would like to get to know you. What better way to get to know you than to listen to you and your problems. I might even be able to help you deal with them. It certainly wouldn't hurt, and you have to eat anyway. You might as well eat with me."

"I admit it might be nice to have someone to talk to," I said after thinking about it for a moment.

"Good," she said with a cheery tone in her voice.

"What time and what would you like me to bring?"

"Just bring yourself. By the way, do you like steak and salad?"

"Very much."

"Good. About six o'clock?"

"Six would be fine.

"I look forward to seeing you at six," she said, then the phone went dead.

I leaned back in my chair. My thoughts turned to Julie and the other night when I had enjoyed her and her brother's company. She had taken my mind off my troubles for at least a little while, and that was a good thing. It gave me something else to think about, which sort of cleared my mind. It actually made me think a little clearer the next day, too.

I wondered if her brother would be there, too. For some reason, I didn't think he was invited.

MY THOUGHTS WERE INTERRUPTED when George came into the office.

"How did things go with you," he asked.

"Not good. They took Mac off the cases. He's on administrative duties, supposedly for health reasons. I think it was because someone didn't want him talking to Steuben. As a result, we've lost our connection to the police department."

"Damn, that's going to make things tough."

"It sure does, but we are not giving up. We'll just have to work harder. We'll need some good solid proof, gotten legally, before we go to the police. And if that doesn't work, we'll take our proof to the DA. And if that doesn't work, we'll take it to a judge."

"Where do we go if that doesn't work?"

"We go to the press. They're always looking for something juicy to print."

George nodded his approval.

"Where do we start?" George asked.

"We start tomorrow morning looking for Jeff. I think Jeff is the key to getting to Butler. I want Butler. I think he knows what happened."

"Okay. What do you want me to do tonight?"

"Take the night off. I'm going to dinner tonight, if you don't mind."

"Why would I mind?"

"I'm going to have dinner with your sister. She called me and asked me to dinner at her apartment. What do you think?"

"I think she could do a lot worse," he said with a smile.

"Gee, thanks."

"You won't have any problem with me. Just treat her right."

"I will. Besides, it's just for dinner and to get to know each other a little."

"Great. Have a good time. I'll see you in the morning," George said with a big grin on his face.

"What are you doing this evening?" I asked.

"I've got class tonight."

"You might want to give me your class schedule so that I don't ask you to do something that would cause you to miss class."

"Thanks. I'll do that."

"See you in the morning," I said as I watched him leave the office.

Shortly after George left the office, I went home. I watched very carefully for anyone following me, but saw no one. When I got home I took a shower, shaved and dressed in something casual but nice to go have dinner with Julie. I found myself looking forward to spending a little time with her, but then why not. She seemed to be smart, pleasant and friendly. She was also very pretty.

CHAPTER FIFTEEN

I ARRIVED AT JULIE'S apartment about five minutes to six and knocked on the door. Julie answered the door within a minute or so.

"Come in," she said with a big smile.

I entered her apartment, then waited for her to close the door. I followed her into the living room.

"It will be a few minutes before dinner is ready. Would you like to come out to the kitchen?"

"Sure," I said then followed her to the kitchen.

"I was just fixing a salad. I didn't start the steaks, since I don't know how you like yours."

"Medium rare to Medium would be fine. Is there anything I can do to help?"

"No. I have everything under control. Would you like a drink?"

"Sure. What do you have?"

"I have a nice zinfandel wine or scotch or a beer if you prefer. It's Heineken."

"I'll take a Heineken, please."

"I'm being rather informal tonight, so would you like it in a glass or bottle?"

"A bottle's fine."

I sat down on a bar stool at the end of the counter with the beer and watched her while she made the salad. We talked a little while she made dinner. When it was ready, we decided to keep it casual and ended up sitting on bar stools and eating at the counter. During dinner we shared a little small talk, mostly about her and what she did for a living. It turned out that she was a surgical nurse at Denver General.

After dinner, I helped by clearing the counter where we ate while she put the dirty dishes in the dishwasher. When we were finished we went into the living room and sat down on the sofa.

"How is your investigation going into the death of your friend?"

"We had a little setback today. Actually, it was a big setback."

"What happened?"

She sounded very interested in what was going on. I wasn't sure why, but it was nice to find someone I could share it with.

I took sometime to tell her what happened that I considered a setback. I also told her about how I thought the death of Jennifer and Emily were connected, but I was having a hard time proving it.

I wasn't sure if her interest in it was because it involved her brother and the death of his girlfriend, or if it was because it involved my girlfriend and me. Maybe it was a little of both.

I found Julie very easy to talk to. She seemed interested in my relationship with Jennifer, what I liked and didn't like, and even in how I became a private investigator.

Julie seemed very open to talking about herself, too. She had grown up on a ranch in eastern Colorado, went to nursing school in Denver, got her degree in nursing and went to work at Denver General Hospital. She seemed to be the kind of person who liked to help others.

As the time went by and we shared a little of our life stories, we seemed to be able to talk freely and openly to each other. I found myself liking her very much. I enjoyed our evening together, and felt comfortable with her. In fact, we talked so much that time got away from us. It was very late when we finally bothered to look at a clock.

"It's getting pretty late," I finally said. "I want to thank you for the great dinner and for a very pleasant evening. As much as I have enjoyed myself, I think I should be going."

"I enjoyed your company, too."

"Can I see you again?"

"I would like that very much," she said with a pleasant smile.

I stood up and walked to the door. She followed me to the door. I turned around and looked at her. I had this feeling that I would like to kiss her goodnight, but I wasn't sure if she was ready for it. There was only one way to find out.

"Would you mind if I kissed you goodnight," I said as I looked into her beautiful blue eyes.

"I might be a little disappointed if you didn't," she said as she stepped up close to me.

I reached out and put my hands on her narrow waist and drew her closer to me. She reached up and put her hands on my shoulders as I leaned down to her. She tipped her head up to meet me. Our lips met in a soft warm kiss. It was not a passionate kiss, but a kiss that sort of told her that I liked her and would like to spend time with her again. I ended the kiss and looked into her eyes. She smiled up at me.

"Would it be all right if I call you tomorrow?" I asked.

"Sure. I get off work at four in the afternoon."

"I'll call. Goodnight, and thank you for a very nice evening."

"You're welcome," she said with a smile.

I turned and walked down the hall to the stairs. I looked back as I started down the stairs. She was standing at her door watching me. I waved at her then left her apartment building.

During the drive home, I had a lot of very pleasant thoughts about Julie. She had filled a void for me even if it was just for an evening.

As I drove to my apartment, I couldn't help thinking of Julie. She was a very nice looking woman in her early thirties. She had long blond hair and deep blue eyes. She had been wearing medium brown slacks that fit her shapely hips and narrow waist very nicely. The blouse she had on fit her well and complimented her figure. She had a wonderful smile. But the thing I liked about her the most was she seemed to care about people, and she had a very pleasant personality.

I HADN'T BEEN PAYING close attention to what was going on around me as I drove toward my apartment. I suddenly realized that I had a car coming up behind me rather fast. Being able to only see the headlights, it was impossible for me to see what kind of car it was.

When it got very close to the back of my vehicle, it swerved into the lane to my left and moved up beside me. I glanced over in time to see the passenger looking toward me. He had a gun in his hand and it was pointed at me.

I immediately slammed on the brakes causing him to shoot on by me. I then stood on the accelerator. I quickly moved up on them and hit the car in the right rear corner. As soon as my bumper made contact with their car, I stepped on the gas and pushed the back of the car around in what the police call a pit maneuver. It caused the car to start sliding around and the driver to lose control. The black Lincoln swerved off across the right lane in front of me and crashed into a streetlight pole.

I slammed on the brakes and backed up to where the Lincoln had crashed. I pulled my gun out from under my sport coat as I got out of my SUV. With the SUV between me and the Lincoln, I worked my way closer to the car. The driver was just starting to come around. I smashed out the side window with my gun, then hit him in the head with it. He slumped over the steering wheel. He was out cold.

His partner, the one who had tried to shoot at me, was trying to shake off the crash when he turned toward me. He started to lift his hand with the gun in it.

"Go ahead. I'd love an excuse to blow your brains out," I said with my gun pointed at his face. "Pitch the gun out the window or die."

He looked at me for a second as if he was thinking about taking a chance at me, but decided better of it. He let out a deep breath, then tossed the gun out the car window.

"I want to know who wants me dead. You've got two seconds to tell me who you work for."

I wasn't sure that he was going to tell me. In fact, I was pretty sure that he wouldn't. If he did, he would not live very long.

"Okay," I said when he didn't answer. "Put your hands on the dash."

After he did as I told him, I carefully walked around the front of the car to the passenger's side while keeping an eye and my gun on him. I moved closer to him until I got around to the passenger's side of the car. I quickly reached down and picked up his gun. I had kept my gun pointed at him the whole time.

"Give me your wallet," I said as I tucked my gun in my holster, but kept his gun on him.

He didn't move.

"That was not a request. Give me your wallet," I said then fired a shot through the seat between his legs.

His eyes were as big as saucers and he was shaken, but he complied with my request immediately. I took his wallet and slipped it into my coat pocket. While keeping an eye on him, I moved to the front of the car and put two rounds from his gun into the grill of the car. I then walked back to my SUV, got in and drove off.

I turned at the next corner and drove on down the street. I hadn't gone more than a couple of blocks when I heard a siren. I saw a police car speeding toward me then went on by. It was headed in the direction of where I had left the Lincoln leaking antifreeze and oil on the street. I smiled to myself as I went home.

When I got home, I parked the SUV in my garage. I took the hit man's gun and stashed it in a lockbox on a high shelf in the garage. I didn't want the police to get it with my fingerprints all over it.

A quick look at the front end of my rented SUV showed that the front had sustained some minor damage as a result of the pit maneuver. I only hoped that I would not have to explain it to the police. I was pretty sure that the two in the Lincoln would not want to tell the police anything, even though it would be hard to explain the holes in the front of their car and the damage to the rear end.

When I went inside, I checked out my apartment to make sure that I didn't have any unwanted guests hiding in it. As soon as I was sure that it was clear, I took the hit man's wallet out of my coat and put it on the table. I sat down at the kitchen table and began going through the wallet.

I quickly found out that the hit man's name was William Baker, but I had some doubts that it was his real name. It was a Michigan driver's license that showed an address in Detroit. It suddenly became clear that someone out there with money had hired a hit man. Someone was feeling very threatened by me. That thought made me sit back in my chair to think.

As I thought about it, I could think of two people on my suspect list who had the kind of money that it would take to hire a hit man. Two hit men, if I counted the driver. Mrs. Dunberger and Ralph Slocomb were the only two that I believed had enough money and might have contacts in Detroit. But what reason would they have?

As I sat there thinking, I wondered if Mrs. Dunberger would go to that extreme to get me to drop the case. It was not unheard of that rich people would do almost anything to protect their reputation and keep their secrets from the public. In her case, she might feel that she has a son to protect, too.

Slocomb might want me out of the picture, but only if he was involved in something that he believed I was getting too close to. But why? Why would he hire me in the first place if he had something to hide? That didn't seem to make sense.

I suddenly found myself yawning. I guess the day was catching up with me. The day had been a real roller coaster ride, and I still wasn't up to par after being shot. I was sure that I would not get anything settled in my mind until I got a little rest.

I went into my bedroom and got ready for bed. With all that had happened, I decided that it might be a good idea if I kept a gun close by. I set my 9mm automatic on the bedside table and my .38 caliber pistol under the extra pillow next to me. With my guns next to me, I felt a little more secure and was able to drift off to sleep.

WHEN MORNING CAME, I found the sun was up and it looked like it was going to be a very nice day. I looked at my clock only to discover that I had slept in. I got out of bed and took a quick shower, then dressed.

I was just sitting at the kitchen table eating my usual breakfast when I heard someone pounding on my front door. I quickly grabbed my gun and started for the door. I stepped up to the edge of the front window and peeked out. George was standing at the front door.

"Peter!" he yelled then hammered on the door with his fist again.

I went to the door and opened it. The look on George's face showed me that he was worried. I had no idea why.

"Come in," I said. "What's the problem?"

"I got worried when you didn't show up at the office this morning."

"I had a little trouble on my way home from your sister's apartment, and got in late. I just slept in."

"What kind of trouble?"

"I'm eating my breakfast. Come out to the kitchen. Can I get you something?" I asked as I walked to the kitchen.

"No. I've had breakfast," he said as he followed me.

We sat down at the table. I began to eat the rest of my breakfast.

"What kind of trouble did you have?"

"I had a couple of hit men try to ambush me while I was driving home."

I went on to tell him about the incident. He didn't seem all that surprised.

"Do you have some idea what's going on? You don't look very surprised that someone tried to put a hit on me."

"No, but I have to wonder if we haven't gotten into something more than just Emily's murder, or maybe we're getting close to why she was murdered," George said.

"I thought about that while I was showering this morning. I've even thought about who we might have touched a sensitive spot on."

"Any ideas?" George asked.

"Yeah, I have a couple. I also have an idea about how to find out."

"What can I do to help?"

"Does Butler know you?"

"Yeah. I've seen him around Slocomb's nightclub. He may not know me by name, but he probably knows I worked for Slocomb."

"We need to find him. I'm going to find Jeff and he is going to tell me where Butler is hanging out."

"How are you going to do that?" George asked.

"Jeff worked last night, right?"

"Yeah. I'm sure he did," George said curious as to what I was thinking.

"He will probably be sleeping in with DeeDee. We are going over there and disturb his rest," I said with a smile.

I HAD JUST FINISHED my breakfast and had put my dishes in the dishwasher when the phone began to ring. I looked at George, then reached over and picked up the phone.

"Hello."

"Peter?"

"Yeah."

"Meet me at the bakery on Colfax at Cook," the voice said then the phone went dead.

I hung up the phone and looked at George. He had a puzzled look on his face.

"I think we might have something."

"Who was that on the phone?"

"Captain MacDonald. He wants to meet me at a bakery. Let's go. We'll take your car."

George and I left my apartment and headed out to Colfax and Cook. George did the driving while I watched for anyone following us. I noticed what looked like an unmarked police car about three cars behind us.

"George, we've got a tail. The green Ford about three cars back."

"Yeah. I see it. Any idea who it is?"

"I got the impression from Mac that he suspected he was being watched since they put him on administrative duty. They don't want him talking to us."

"It looks like we are the ones being watched. What do you want to do?" George asked.

"There's a small café in the next block past the bakery. Pull in there and park where the car can be seen from the street."

George did as I told him. We then got out of the car and went into the café. We picked a high backed booth near the rear of the seating area and sat down. The café was old and not very big. I was sure that they would not follow us into the café because we would see them. When I was sure that they were not coming into the café, we ducked out the back and went down the alley to the bakery. We entered the bakery from the alley. We found Mac sitting in a booth out of sight from anyone walking by the front of the bakery.

"What's up, Mac?" I asked as I slipped into the booth.

Mac was looking at George as he slipped into the booth beside me. From the look on Mac's face, he wasn't sure he should say anything.

"Mac, this is George Archer. He has been working with me on the Emily case. He was Emily's boyfriend."

"Hi, Mac. I'm sure you remember me. I can understand if you would prefer that I was not here, but I don't work for Slocomb any more. I'll leave if you want me to."

"No. If Peter says its okay, it's okay with me."

"Thanks," George said with a smile.

"Why all the secrecy, Mac?" I asked.

"For some reason that I don't understand, I've been cut out of any information on Emily's and Jennifer's murder cases. Someone doesn't want me to find out what's happening," he said, then took a quick look around. "But I still hear things."

"What did you hear?"

"Last night, two thugs were arrested with outstanding warrants on them. They were from Detroit. They were picked up after running into a light pole. The two thugs work for a drug ring that operates out of Detroit. They're hit men, and I think that they are here to kill you."

"They tried last night. That's why the police have them."

"Did you put the holes in the engine and in the front seat of the car?" Mac asked with a smile that told me that he already knew the answer.

"Yeah. I figured it would keep them there until the police arrived."

"You best be careful. I doubt that will be the end of it."

"Right now, I'm more concerned with who brought them here," I said.

"The way I hear it, the two thugs probably didn't come here to kill you. That was ordered after they got here. The narcotics division thinks they came here to deliver drugs to the headman for this area."

"Any idea who that might be?"

"Not for sure. However, before they put me on a desk some of the narcotics investigators that I know pretty well were taking a serious look at Ralph Slocomb," Mac said. "They seem to think he's branching out."

I sat back in the booth and took a minute to think. Emily was found with cocaine in her system that she had been forced to inhale. The ME thought it was the first time for her. If she was killed where I think she was, then I had two real good suspects. I also had a theory as to what might have happened.

"You're thinking pretty hard over there," Mac said. "Have you got an idea?"

"No, but I'm working on it. The problem is that I can't prove what I believe without the help of forensic evidence. I think I know where Emily was killed, and I think I know where she had been kept for a week. I also think I know how she was moved from where she had been kept to the park where she was dropped off."

"Do you know who murdered her?"

"Not for sure."

"What would it take to get the proof you need?" Mac asked.

"Are you offering to help?"

"If I can."

"I could get the proof I need myself, but I question if it would hold up in court coming from me."

"Why's that?" Mac asked.

"I would have to bend the law just a little to get it. That could get it tossed out of court. Mac, I think it would be better for all concerned if you don't know what I have in mind."

"The only thing I can say at this time is keep your head down. I've got a couple of ideas of my own," Mac said. "I'm looking into who had me put on administrative duty. If I can find that out, it might help you with your case."

"It might. But you might take a little of your own advice and keep your head down."

"I will. And you be careful around Edwards. It makes me nervous when a cop acts like he's investigating something, but never comes up with anything at all."

"You think he's part of the problem?" I asked.

"I don't know, but it's beginning to look like it."

"We better get out of here before someone gets to wondering what happened to us," I said.

"I'll give you a few minutes head start," Mac said as George got up from the booth.

"See you around," I said as I slid out of the booth.

George and I left the bakery out the back door, then returned to the café by way of the back door. We walked out the front door of the café and went directly to George's car. George drove out of the parking lot and back onto the street. We almost immediately had that same car on our tail.

"Where to now?" he asked.

"I need to find a place where I can get a set of wheels just like the ones I have. I sort of wrinkled the front bumper last night."

"Where is the one you have?"

"It's in my garage. I don't want the police to see it. If they do, they will know it was the one that ran the Lincoln into the light pole last night."

"I've got a friend that will be more than willing to fix it for you. No one will ever know that you wrinkled it. He'll even come and get it, and replace it with an SUV just like it."

"Can he be trusted?"

"Yes. He'll call when it's done, deliver it to your garage and take the other one back."

"Great."

We returned to the office where George made a couple of phone calls. I made a couple of calls around and found that there was a rental place just a few blocks from where I lived that had a Tahoe just like the one I had already rented. While

George and I were at the office, he had his friend pick up the new Tahoe and take it to my place. He then took the damaged Tahoe out of the garage and replaced it with the new Tahoe. He took the wrinkled Tahoe to his place where he could repair the damage I had done to it. I would use the new one until the old one was repaired, then we would trade them back.

While the shifting around of the Tahoes was being done, George and I drove over to DeeDee's town house in his car.

IT WAS JUST A FEW MINUTES past eleven in the morning when we arrived at DeeDee's town house. George went around to the back of the town house while I went to the front door and knocked on it. It took a couple of minutes before the door was answered by DeeDee.

"Well, I didn't expect to see you again. Come in," she said with a smile.

"Thank you."

I stepped into the entryway and waited for DeeDee to shut the door. I noticed that she was wearing slacks that didn't go very well with the top she had on. It looked as if she had dressed in a hurry. That got me to thinking that she might not have been up very long.

"What is it I can do for you this time?" she said with a sexy smile.

"You can tell me where I can find Jeff Slocomb," I said as I looked her in the eyes.

"Now, how would I know where Jeff is?"

"That shouldn't be too hard a question. In fact, it is probably the easiest question I have, and one that should require very little thought on your part. His car is parked just outside your door, you are sleeping with him, and you dressed so fast that your clothes don't match. A woman of your style would never dress like that if she had time to pick out her clothes."

"I see you are a very observant man, but he is not here."

"In that case, you wouldn't mind my looking in your bedroom."

"I certainly would. I believe you have to have a warrant or something to go searching my home."

"Cops have to have warrants. I'm not a cop, but I am in a hurry. So I will make this simple. Produce Jeff now, or I will take this place apart. By the way, it won't do him any good to try and sneak out the back. I have a friend out there just waiting for him if he tries."

"You're bluffing," she said.

"No, he's not," Jeff said as he came out of the bedroom. "I saw George out back waiting for me."

"What is it you want?" Jeff asked.

"I want to know where Butler is."

"I don't know where he is."

"I have about had it with people giving me the run around or lying to me. I'm about ready to tear someone's head off and it might as well be yours," I said with a strong note of anger in my voice.

"You would never get away with it, but I will tell you this. He is in hiding, that much I can tell you. I don't know where. He didn't tell me where he was going."

"Why should I believe you?"

"You probably shouldn't. I can also tell you that there is nothing he would like more than to kill you."

"It has already been tried. The two thugs that were hired to kill me are currently in jail. It will be a long, long time before they get back to Detroit," I said as I watched him for a reaction.

Jeff should never play poker. I could tell by his body language that he knew something about the thugs, but he didn't know that they had been jailed. If he knew about the thugs, then there was a pretty good chance he knew something about the drugs. Either he was the one who was handling the drug part of his father's businesses, or he knew that his father was in the drug business. I wondered if the narcotic division knew. I wondered if he might be using drugs, but that would have to wait. I didn't think beating the hell out of him would get me any closer to finding Butler, but it might get more people looking to end my career.

"I'll see you around," I said as I turned and left the town house.

As I stepped out on the front porch, I called to George. I knew that George and I would probably hear from Ralph Slocomb with loud threats and a lot of yelling. He might also sic his enforcers on us. I still wanted Butler.

Just as George was coming around the corner of the town house, Jeff stepped out on the porch. He looked like he might want to say something.

"We're leaving," I said.

"If you don't say anything to my father about DeeDee and me, I won't say anything about you and George coming here."

I looked at him for a moment. It sounded like a pretty good deal to me. If he kept his word, it might keep Slocomb's enforcers off my back for awhile.

"Okay. You have a deal. But if your dad sics any of his goons on us, I can assure you that he will know about the two of you in a heartbeat."

Jeff nodded his head in agreement then turned and went back inside. I turned around and joined George at his car.

"You think he will tell his father?" George asked.

"No, I don't think so. He's more afraid of his father than he is of us."

"Did you find out where Butler is?"

"No. I don't think he knows, but he knows something about the thugs that tried to take me out last night."

"Where to now?"

"Back to my place. I want to pick up the new Tahoe."

CHAPTER SIXTEEN

WE ARRIVED BACK AT MY APARTMENT a little after twelve noon. George drove me around to the garage and dropped me off. He then left for his place in Aurora. He said he needed to hit the books for awhile before his evening computer class.

I went to the garage and opened the garage door. There was a dark blue Tahoe parked right where the other one had been. I looked it over and found it to be just like the one I had wrinkled, but without the wrinkles. I opened the door and found the keys on the seat. Now if the police decided to check out my Tahoe for bumps and scraps, it would be clean.

As I turned and headed for the back of my apartment, I remembered the envelope with a utility bill that I had taken from Butler's apartment. The bill had been for utilities for a different house or apartment in another part of town. I wondered if that was where he was hiding.

I went inside, then to my closet. I found the coat I had been wearing that evening. I searched through the pockets and found the bill. The address was about halfway across town from where he had been staying. If my memory was right, it was in an older part of town.

I left my apartment and drove to the part of town where Butler might have a second apartment. When I found the address, it turned out to be a small brick house with a one car garage. It looked like it was in pretty good shape for as old a house as it was. The lawn was well taken care of and the shrubs were nicely trimmed. For some reason, it didn't look like the type of house that Butler would have. That being the case, it seemed to make a good cover for him.

I drove around the block and parked at the corner. The house was in the middle of the block on the opposite side of the street. I noticed that there were no cars parked out in front. The door of the single car detached garage was closed so I had no idea if there was a car in the garage. I sat back to wait and watch.

It was over an hour before I saw any activity at the house. A car drove up and stopped in front of the house. It was a car that I had never seen before. It was a four or five year old red Ford four door sedan. I watched as a young man got out of the car, walked up to the door and knocked. While he waited for someone to come to the door, he looked around. When he looked my way, I got a good look at him but I didn't recognize him. He was fairly average in height, about five-ten or eleven, but a little on the slim side. He probably weighed in the neighborhood of a hundred and forty to a hundred and fifty pounds. He was dressed in jeans and a sweatshirt with a small logo on the left side that I couldn't make out. He had on white tennis shoes.

My attention was drawn to the door as it opened. James Butler was the one answering the door. I noticed that he smiled when he saw the young man at the door. He immediately stepped aside and let the young man in. Butler looked around outside before he stepped back inside and closed the door.

I wondered what was going on inside. There were a number of things that I could think of as I continued to watch the house. They ran from just a friend stopping by for a few minutes to the young man buying drugs from him.

It was only about ten minutes before the front door opened again. I saw the slim young man start out the door. He then turned and said something to someone inside the house. I couldn't see who he was talking to, but it was for just a few seconds. He then turned and left the house.

I saw Butler look out of the house as the young man walked to his car and got in. As the young man drove off, Butler stepped back inside and shut the door. I still had no idea what was going on. Well, I had a couple of ideas, but nothing I could prove.

As I sat there watching the house, I thought about what had happened up to now. I couldn't get over the idea that Butler was a big part of it. One of the questions that ran through my mind was did Butler own the house. It made a pretty good place to run his drug business out of if that was what he was doing.

Suddenly, a thought occurred to me. I was driving around in a brand new big blue Tahoe in a neighborhood that probably didn't see many brand new vehicles. It was time to switch to a car that fit in with the rest of the cars in the neighborhood before I continued my surveillance of the house.

I reached down and started my vehicle. I then drove down the street for a few blocks before heading back to my office. I could pick up my surveillance of Butler's house later. It might take me a couple of days to figure out what was going on there, but I would find out.

I LEFT THE AREA and drove back to my apartment. I parked the Tahoe in the garage in the hope that no one would know that I returned. Keeping an eye out for trouble, I walked up to the backdoor of my apartment. I didn't see anyone as I went inside.

I took off my coat and put my gun in the drawer in the end table next to the sofa. My thoughts turned to Julie. I had asked her if it was all right if I called her. I was thinking that maybe it would be best if I didn't see her anymore, at least until I finished what I had to do. Only then would I be free to get to know Julie. I reached over, picked up the phone and placed a call to her. The phone rang only three times before it was answered.

"Hello," Julie's pleasant voice said.

"Hi. It's me, Peter."

"Hi. How was your day today? Did you get a lot done?"

"I don't know if I got a lot done, but I did find out where one of my suspects is hiding."

"Does it happen to be the guy that lives here, ah – James Butler?"

"Yes, it does. He has another place on the other side of town."

"Can I ask you to be careful around him? From what you said the other night, he's dangerous."

"Yes, he is that. I think he's also a drug dealer."

"George was telling me that someone had forced Emily to take cocaine. Do you think it might be him?"

"It might be. I've got a plan that I hope will tell us who it was that killed her."

"Do you think it will bring you any closer to who killed Jennifer?"

I thought I could hear a little concern in her voice because of mentioning Jennifer's name. I wasn't sure how she felt about talking to me about her.

"I think that whoever killed Emily had something to do with killing Jennifer."

"I hope you don't mind if I asked you about Jennifer."

"No, its okay," I said, but I wasn't totally sure that I meant it. "Well, I thought I would give you a call and see how you're doing. I didn't mean to disturb you."

"You didn't disturb me. I just got home before you called. I like to hear your voice," Julie said.

I took a minute to take a deep breath. I wasn't sure how Julie would take what I had to say.

"Julie, I would like to see you again, but right now I have to get this settled. It's like closing one door before I open another. I really would like to see you again. I hope you understand."

There was silence for a moment before she spoke. Her silence made me wonder what she might say.

"I understand," she said softly. "I like you and I would like to see you again, too."

"Do you really mean that?"

I couldn't believe what I had asked. It sounded sort of stupid.

"Yes. I really would like to see you again."

"I'm sorry that sounded so, I don't know. You know, maybe it would be better if I just shut up," I said.

I could hear a little bit of a chuckle in her voice.

"When you get done with what you have to do, I'll be expecting you to call me and come have dinner with me. Then we can see where it might go from there. Okay?"

"Okay. I would like to call you and have dinner with you. I'll say goodnight for now."

"Goodnight, Peter. Be careful out there. I'll be waiting for you to call."

"I will, and I will. Goodnight, Julie," I said then slowly hung up the phone.

I looked at the phone for a minute or so just thinking. I then got up and went out to the kitchen. As I fixed myself something to eat, I thought about the evening I had spent with her at her apartment. It was a pleasant evening. I wondered if something could come of it once this investigation was over, but right now I had other things to think about.

I forced my mind to return to thinking about Butler. I would have to plan how I was going to find out what part he played in the deaths of Emily and Jennifer. The one thing I knew I had to do was find proof. It had to be strong enough proof that the police couldn't ignore it.

While I sat at the table and ate my dinner, I came up with a plan to get the evidence that would make the police take notice. And I knew just the guy to help me. I would pay a visit to my close friend, John Farrell, but it would have to wait until tomorrow.

Right now, it was time to get a little rest. My leg was beginning to hurt a little. It was still early evening, but I went into the bedroom and got ready for bed, anyway. It wasn't long and I was in bed trying to relax. I had a ton of things going through my mind. It took a while, but I finally dozed off.

IT WAS EARLY in the morning when I woke. I got out of bed and took my usual morning shower. After I showered and dressed, I sat down my breakfast. When I finished my breakfast, I drove to the Crime Lab in Lakewood. I parked in the parking lot and went into the building. The girl at the counter paged John for me. I didn't have to wait long before he came out to meet me.

"Hi, Peter. What do you need now?"

"Information mostly."

"Okay. Come back to my office. We can talk there."

I followed John down that long white hall to his office. I couldn't help but think how sterile the place looked. I was sure it was necessary in order to assure that any evidence brought in would not be contaminated. Once I was in his office, I sat down in front of his desk while he sat down behind the desk.

"Okay, what can I do for you?"

"I need some advice. I need to know how I can get evidence of a crime from private property that would stand up in court, and without a warrant."

"You never come to me with something simple," John said with a chuckle in his voice.

"If it's simple, I wouldn't need to come to you."

"I take it you are serious?"

"Yes. I know as a PI, I have a few more liberties than the police. I guess what I'm really asking, is how do I protect the chain of custody of evidence and prove that it was obtained from where I say it was?"

"That is difficult. The best way is to have a witness. But if the witness is not a credible one, it won't do you much good. You might be able to get a judge to issue you a limited warrant that would allow you to get evidence from a very specific location, but you have to find a judge that believes in what information you have and trusts you. That is usually very difficult, because judges rarely issue warrants to anyone other than the police or the DA."

"What if I get just some evidence from the crime scene? I would think that any other evidence that might be found there after I took some of it would be considered compromised."

"You're probably right."

"I guess I'm going to have to find another way to get the evidence I need. Thanks for your help."

"I'm sorry I couldn't be of any help to you," John said with a disappointed look on his face.

"Wait a minute. I understand you did the toxicology tests on Emily. Is that right?"

"Yes. What's on your mind?"

"If I could get a sample of cocaine, could you tell if it was the same cocaine that was given to Emily?"

"I'm sure I could, but what good would that do?"

"It could lead me to who had given it to her." I said. "If I got a sample of the cocaine and it proved to be from the same batch, then maybe I could trace it back to the dealer and find out who he had sold it to. It might take a little, shall we say, convincing to get the dealer to talk to me. But it might work."

"Just how do you plan to get a sample of the cocaine?"

"That might not be a good thing for you to know."

"I see your point. If you get me the sample, I'll test it. But I don't want to know anything else, at least for now."

"Thanks. I'll be in touch," I said as I stood up.

"Be careful out there," John said as I left his office.

"I will," I said, and started down the hall to the front door.

I returned to my SUV in the parking lot and got in. I sat there for a few minutes as I thought about how I was going to get a sample of cocaine from either Butler or Jeff. I was convinced that one of them was the dealer and one was the dealer's supplier. I just didn't know which was which.

I was about to start my SUV when my phone began to ring. I opened my cell phone and saw that it was George.

"What's up, George?"

"I was wondering if you have something for me to do? I'm available for the next four or five hours."

"Yeah. I found out where Butler is hanging out. I want you to drive over there and just watch the house. Do you have a camera?"

"Yeah."

"I want you to take pictures of everyone that goes in or out of the house. If Butler leaves, follow him," I said then gave him the address of the house.

"Okay. What are you going to be doing?"

"I'm going to have a face to face talk with one of the students I talked with on the phone. He seemed to know a little about Butler. Call me if you need something."

"Okay," George said, then he hung up.

I started my SUV and headed for Sean Albertson's apartment. It was located not very far from the school. I didn't know if he had a class, but I would soon find out.

I PULLED UP IN FRONT of Albertson's apartment. It was a large old house that had been converted into about four or five apartments. After checking the mailboxes, I found his apartment was located on the second floor in the rear. There was a note at the mail boxes that said there was a rear outside stairway up the back of the house. Since I had no idea what to expect, I made sure that my gun was easy to get at.

When I started around to the back of the house, I noticed the same car that I had seen at Butler's house parked in a parking area off the alley. It was a good indication that Albertson was the young man that I had seen at Butler's earlier.

As I came around the corner, I heard the door at the top of the stairs close. I stepped up to the stairs and looked up. Albertson was just leaving his apartment.

Albertson had taken only about three steps down the stairs when he saw me. He suddenly stopped and quickly looked around as if looking for a way to escape.

"There's no place to go, Sean."

He started to come on down the stairs. I had noticed that he had one of those plastic art boxes I had seen at the school. When he got close to the bottom of the stairs, he tossed the box at me then started to run. I ducked the box and took off after him. It was no race. With the injury to my left leg, there was little doubt that he could out run me. I was not about to let him get away.

"One shot and you are dead," I yelled, then fired a round into the ground near me.

I never saw anyone stop so quickly. He put his hands in the air and just stood there. I needed to get out of there before I had cops all over the place. I wanted to talk to him before the cops did.

"Get over here," I ordered.

Sean turned around and walked back toward me. As soon as he was near enough, I had him turn around and put his hands on his head and interlace his fingers. I then moved up behind him and grabbed his hands. With his fingers interlaced and my free hand squeezing his fingers together, he was more than willing to do whatever I said. Squeezing someone's fingers together like I had his could prove to be very painful if he decided to be uncooperative.

I marched him up the stairs and back into his apartment. Once we were inside, I dropped him onto the sofa. He looked up at me. I guess the gun did a lot to make him behave himself. I sat down on a chair right in front of him. My leg was hurting like hell, but I wasn't about to let him know it.

"You paid a short visit to James Butler yesterday. What did you go there for?"

It was a question that I was sure I already knew the answer. I just wanted him to know that I had seen him at Butler's place.

"Nothing," he said, but not very convincingly.

"I'm not a very patient man, Sean. I would just as soon shoot you as look at you, but that would be too messy and too noisy. Since you don't want to talk to me, I will turn you over to a friend of mine who is very good at making people talk, and very good at disposing of their remains after he is done with them."

"You wouldn't dare," he said, but his reaction didn't convey the same message as his voice.

"Are you going to tell me what you were doing at Butler's house, or do I call my friend?"

I gave him a minute to think about it before I reached for my cell phone.

"Okay, okay. I'll tell you," he said, but didn't say anything more.

I opened my cell phone and began pressing a few numbers.

"Okay. I was buying some cocaine from him."

"Do you still have it?"

"Yes," he said with a confused look on his face.

"Where is it?"

"In my bedroom."

"Go get it," I said as I stood up.

Sean stood up slowly. I got the impression that he was afraid that I would shoot him. It was not a bad impression for him to have at the moment. I followed him into the bedroom.

"Where is it?"

"In the dresser."

"Get it out and put it in this," I said as I handed him a small plastic sandwich bag that I used when I gathered evidence. "If anything else comes out of that drawer, it will be the last thing you do."

Sean opened the drawer and reached inside. He looked at me for a second before he pulled out a small bag of cocaine. He put it in the sandwich bag and held it out to me. I took it and put it in my pocket.

"Now, I'm going to leave. If you say anything about this to anyone, including Butler, your life won't be worth a nickel, but I don't think I have to tell you that," I said, then turned and left.

I LEFT ALBERTSON'S apartment and drove out to the Crime Lab in Lakewood. As soon as I got there, I asked for John. He didn't happen to be busy and was able to see me right a way.

"What do you have for me this time," he asked.

"A packet of cocaine. I got it from Sean Albertson. He had purchased it from James Butler yesterday."

"Are you sure?"

"As sure as I can be. I would like you to test it and see if it is from the same batch as the cocaine Emily Sutherland was forced to inhale. You might also want to see if there are any fingerprints on the packet."

"That's a good idea. Have you touched the packet at all?"

"No, just the sandwich bag that it's in."

"I'll see what I can do with it and give you a call as soon as I can."

"Thanks," I said then turned and left John's office.

I got in my SUV and returned to my office. When I arrived at my office, I immediately placed a call to George.

"Yeah," George said as he answered his phone.

"Where are you?"

"I'm just down the block from Butler's place."

"Keep a close watch on his place. He may decide that it's time to disappear."

"Okay."

"Has he had any company?"

"Yeah. He's had a couple of scroungy looking guys stop by. They were there just a minute or two then left. I figure that they were buying drugs."

"You can count on it."

"You want me to grab Butler?" George asked.

"No. I may have some help. If everything works out like I hope it will, we'll have help grabbing him. Right now, I'm thinking it is time for me to talk to Mac again."

"You think he will help?"

"I think he will. He's a good cop. I'll talk to you later."

I HUNG UP THE PHONE and placed a call to Mac at the precinct. It didn't take but a minute for Sergeant Russell to transfer my call to him. His phone rang just a couple of times before it was answered.

"Captain MacDonald, may I help you?"

"Hi Mac. Do you have a minute to talk?"

"No. In fact, I'm not supposed to talk to you," Mac said then hung up on me.

I smiled to myself. There were only two possible reasons for him to have talked to me like that and hang up on me. It was because he had someone in his office who might report him for talking to me, or he knew his phone was bugged to make sure that he didn't talk to me.

It was getting on toward lunch time. I decided to wait and have my lunch later in case Mac was able to get away from the office to call me.

It was about five to twelve when my phone rang. I answered without identifying myself right away in case it was Mac and he only had a second or two to talk.

"Hello?"

"Meet me at Joe's Barber Shop on Broadway," Mac said then hung up.

I immediately left the office for the parking garage. I looked around to make sure that there was no one in the garage that might be a problem for me. I saw no one.

I GOT IN MY CAR and started down Broadway toward the barber shop. I watched for anyone following me. There was a car that seemed to be following me. If I tried to ditch it, it might turn into a problem for Mac. I decided to let it follow me.

Instead of going to the barber shop, I went down Broadway to a restaurant that was over a mile from the barber shop. I parked in the restaurant's parking lot and then headed for the front door. I saw the car that had been tailing me park across the street in a used car lot. I went inside and got the hostess to seat me where I could see out the window. I set the blinds on the window so that I could see outside, but doubted that I could be seen. I then called Mac at Joe's Barber Shop on my cell phone. It rang only a couple of times before it was answered.

"Joe's Barber Shop."

"Yes. Is MacDonald there?"

I could hear him ask if there was a MacDonald in the shop, and heard Mac respond.

"This is MacDonald."

"I'm in a restaurant about a mile south of you on Broadway. I had a tail. I figured that if I ditched him, it might be a problem for you."

"Good thinking. What did you want to talk to me about?" Mac asked.

"I'm going to need your help. I think I will be able to prove that Butler was the one that killed Emily. I got a packet of cocaine from one of the students who goes to the art school."

"You better stay away from that school. If you go there you will be arrested for trespassing. The word is out."

"I didn't get it from him at the school. He bought the cocaine from Butler. I have it at the Crime Lab being tested to see if it is from the same batch as the cocaine found in Emily. I'm also hoping to find Butler's fingerprints on the bag. Butler and Steuben were the last people in the classroom when the figure drawing class ended."

The phone was silent for a little while. I got the feeling that Mac was thinking about what I had said.

"What kind of help do you want from me?"

"I know that you would be risking your career, but I would like you to arrest Butler."

There was silence again before he said anything more.

"You say Butler is selling drugs?"

"Right."

"You know where he is?"

"Yes."

"I've got a friend on the force that works in narcotics. I'll have him make the arrest, that way I can stay out of it for now. I can get him to ask the questions that we need answers to. If we get the right answers, I will get right back in the mix. Who do you think is responsible for Emily's death?"

"I think there are two, Steuben and Butler. The way I see it, Steuben tried to force himself on Emily in the storage room after class. He had Butler hold her down. Butler forced her to breathe in the cocaine to make her more cooperative, but she accidentally inhaled too much. It ended up killing her."

"That could very well explain why I was put on administrative duty. Steuben's mother knows he was involved in it. She is a big, and I mean 'big' contributor to the school," Mac said.

"That's the way I figure it."

"Okay. I'll sic my friend on Butler. I'll call you when it goes down. Give me Butler's address."

I gave Mac the address where Butler could be found and told him that I had a guy watching the house.

"Is Butler there now?"

"Yes."

"I'll get them on it."

"Thanks, Mac. I owe you one."

"You owe me a lot more than that," he said then hung up.

I sat back and thought about what was going on. Mac was about to put his career on the line. There was a chance that even if he got Butler for dealing in illegal drugs, we might not be able to get Steuben. We also might have trouble getting either of them for murder.

My thoughts turned to who had put out the hit on me that had caused the death of Jennifer. I had two ideas on that. The first was Mrs. Dunberger in order to protect her son. There was also the possibility that she felt she was protecting her reputation in the community as well.

The second was Slocomb to protect his son. That was assuming that he knew his son was dealing in drugs. I found it hard to believe that he didn't know what was going on with his son.

It suddenly occurred to me that I should give George a call to give him a heads up. I placed a call to him on my cell phone. He answered it immediately.

"Yeah?"

"There might be a narcotics raid on Butler's house."

"What do you want me to do?"

"Nothing. Just watch it go down then come to the office when you know the results."

"Okay. Any idea when it might happen?"

"Could be anytime soon. Mac is arranging it with a friend of his in narcotics."

"Is that good or bad?"

"At this point, I don't know. It all depends on if they get Butler, and if they can keep him locked up. I'll talk to you later," I said then hung up.

I looked across the street and could still see the car in the used car lot. The sunlight on the windshield had changed enough that I could see that there were two men in the car.

I smiled then motioned for a waitress. She came over and took my order for lunch. I figured that if I had my lunch, it would keep the guys following me busy for another thirty minutes or so. That would give Mac time to get back to the office and the two tailing me would have nothing to report except that I had had lunch alone.

CHAPTER SEVENTEEN

AFTER I HAD MY LUNCH, I returned to my office. The two guys who had followed me to the restaurant followed me to the parking garage, but drove by the entrance after I pulled in. I was sure that they had no idea that I had seen them. They would probably find a place to park somewhere along the street where they could watch and wait for me to leave again.

I took the elevator to the ninth floor where my office was located. When I stepped off the elevator, I noticed that the door to my office was open. I didn't think that George would be there as he was supposed to be watching Butler's house. Since he had not called me, I was sure that the raid on Butler's house had not gone down, yet. I opened my sport coat as I walked toward my office. I wanted my gun where it was handy.

As I got closer to the office door, I could hear voices. I thought I recognized one of them. With my hand on my gun, I stepped into my office and found Ralph Slocomb sitting in one of the chairs in front of my desk. Standing against the wall just a little ways from the door was one of his enforcers.

"I find it interesting that you feel you can barge into my office whenever you want. Just because we have an agreement doesn't give you the right to break into my office."

"What am I supposed to do, stand out in the hall and wait for you?" Ralph said sarcastically.

"You could do that, or you could call for an appointment. Now what is it you want?"

"I want to know how you're coming on proving that I had nothing to do with Emily's death."

"Well, I know where she was murdered. I doubt that you would have been there at the time of her death. So, I would have to say that if you are charged with her murder, I would be able to show that you were not at the scene of the crime."

"What about my son?"

"What about him?"

"Did you prove that he didn't do it, either?"

"You didn't ask me to prove he didn't do it."

"Don't get smart with me," Ralph said sharply.

"You want me to make him tell you, Boss?" the enforcer said.

"You make a single move from where you are, and you will be dead before you can get two steps," I said as I looked the big guy in the eyes. "I'm in no mood to put up with either of you."

"That's enough. No one is going to do anything. I found out what I wanted to know," Ralph said as he stood up.

"Next time you want to talk to me, you either call or leave your apes at home. If you decide to break into my office again, I won't hesitate to either shoot you or call the cops and have you arrested for breaking in. You got that?"

"Yeah, I've got it," Ralph said rather casually as he walked out the door.

As soon as they were gone, I sat down in the chair behind my desk and took a breather. As I thought about Ralph Slocomb's visit, I began to think about his question regarding his son. I wondered if he thought his son might have killed Emily. My answer might have made him think that I wasn't interested in his son. If that were the case, he might assume that I didn't think his son had anything to do with it due to my apparent lack of interest in him. Little did he know that I had not scratched his son off my suspect list.

My thoughts were interrupted by the ringing of my cell phone. I answered the call.

"Hello?"

"Peter, it looks like the narcotics guys just arrested Butler. He's in cuffs and they're putting him in the back of a police car. I can see several policemen carrying out several boxes of stuff. I can't tell what is in the boxes, but my guess would be drugs. What do you want me to do now?"

"Do you have class tonight?"

"Yeah, but I can skip it if you need me. I have class from seven to nine."

"In that case, why don't you pack it in for today. I'll see you tomorrow morning in the office."

"Okay. You can call me after nine if something comes up."

"I'll see you tomorrow."

I hung up then sat back again. I began to wonder how I was going to get a chance to talk to Butler. I was sure that they would charge him with selling a controlled substance and assaulting a police officer, namely Mac. There could be other charges, but I wasn't sure what they would be. I didn't know the arresting officer so I had no "in" with him. All I knew was that I wanted to talk to Butler.

I decided it was time to tail Steuben. A quick look at my watch was all I needed to figure out that his class would be over shortly. I had time to get over to the school, find his car and begin following him. I had no idea what good it would do, but I would give it a try. I wouldn't know what it might produce without trying it.

I got up and closed my office. As I locked the door, I thought that maybe tomorrow I would call a locksmith and have a new and tougher lock put in.

The elevator showed up just as I turned from my door. I quickly slid my hand under my coat and put it over my gun. From the way I was standing, anyone getting off the elevator would not be able to see my hand or my gun.

A young woman got off the elevator and started down the hall away from me. Having been shot at a couple of times made me a little nervous and a lot jumpy. I took a breath, put my gun away, then continued toward the elevator. I got to the elevator just as the door started to close. I put my hand in the door and stopped it from closing. The door opened again and I got in. I took the elevator to the parking garage where I got into my rented SUV and drove out onto the street.

MY TAIL PICKED ME UP almost immediately after leaving the parking garage, but that was no surprise. I had expected them to follow me. However, I didn't want to be followed this time. I would have to find a place to ditch them, and with rush hour the interstate was just the place to do it.

I drove out to Interstate 25 and headed north with the heaviest traffic. I changed lanes a couple of times which put me toward the center of the highway. My tail followed along. I continued for several miles until I found an opening that would allow a sudden lane change just before an exit ramp.

I had just passed a very long semi-truck when my opportunity came. With my tail just starting to pull up along side the semi, I darted across two lanes and got on the exit ramp just in time to get off the interstate. The two following me had no chance at all to get off at the same exit without causing a major accident.

Once off the interstate, I started heading back toward the area where the school was located. I kept a watch for anyone else that might be tailing me, but saw no one.

As I turned the corner about a block from the school, I saw Steuben's red Porsche 911 pull away from the curb about a half a block in front of me. I followed him. I knew if he knew how to drive such a high performance car, I would never be able to catch him if he decided to take off. About the only thing I had going for me at the moment was I didn't think he knew what kind of a vehicle I had.

Steuben hadn't gone more than a few miles when he pulled into a liquor store parking lot on South Broadway and parked at the far end just off the street. I pulled into the lot and parked around at the side of the store where he could not see me. I was able to watch him by looking through the store windows. He didn't get out of his car, he just sat there.

It was becoming clear that he was waiting for someone. I sat back in the seat while I watched and waited. I had no idea how long I would have to wait, but it could be a long time.

Time went by slowly and he continued to just sit there. I did notice that he looked at his watch a couple of times. He appeared to be getting impatient. I was beginning to think that whoever he was waiting for had stood him up. It crossed my mind that he might be waiting for Butler. If it was, he had a very long wait, probably at least ten to twenty years.

We had been there for about an hour when he started his car and pulled out of the parking lot. I started my car; and after giving him a bit of a lead, I followed him. I ended up following him all the way to his mother's home in Cherry Creek where I knew he lived.

As Steuben pulled up in front of the garage, I slowed and then stopped near some shrubs close to the curb. I could see the garage door open, then he pulled into the garage. I noticed something in the garage. It looked like fancy chrome wheel rims and tires lined up against the inside wall of the garage. I wasn't a hundred percent sure, but there was a very good chance that they had been on the Lexus that his mother had arrived in when she paid me a visit at my office.

I reached for the glove box of the SUV, but remembered that my binoculars were in my car. I thought about driving into the drive so I could get a better look at the rims to see if they were the same kind that I had seen the night I found Emily. I hesitated because I was sure that the minute someone realized who I was, they would call the cops. By the time I decided that I would take a chance, the garage door was closing.

Now I had a bit more information that led me to believe that Steuben was involved in Emily's death. The problem was I didn't have enough proof for the police to get a search warrant, and it would take a lot since the wheel rims were in Mrs. Dunberger's garage. The one thing it did help with was it gave me a good idea of who the two involved in Emily's death were, and helped to convince me that my theory that two people were involved was right. All I had to do now was prove it, which was not going to be easy. It was never easy when wealthy people with influence were involved, especially if their influence was with the upper brass of the police department.

I left the area just in case someone saw me and called the cops. As I drove back toward my office, I got to thinking. I had a pretty good theory about how, where, and when Emily was murdered. But I didn't have a reason or motive.

I tried to look at it objectively. My two prime suspects were Steuben and Butler. One of my problems was what did they have in common. The only thing I could think of was the school. One of them was a student, while the other was an instructor at the same school. I knew Butler was in at least one of Steuben's classes, but did their relationship go beyond that? I also knew that Butler was a drug dealer. That brought up another question. Did Steuben use drugs? If he did, was Butler his supplier? It seemed likely.

I had no answers to my questions, just assumptions. I was hoping that John would come up with something that might help me. I had time to get back to my office and call him before he would leave from work for the day. I headed straight for my office.

AS I PULLED INTO the parking garage at the office building, I saw a man standing near the elevator. He looked a little familiar to me, but with his back to me I wasn't sure. I parked my SUV, took my gun from under my coat and then got out of the SUV. As I got out, the man turned around and I could see his face. It was Captain MacDonald. I put my gun away as I walked toward him.

"Aren't you taking a chance being here?" I asked.

"Probably, but I think you can help me and I can help you," he said.

"You want to come up to my office to talk or would you like to sit in my SUV?"

"Let's sit in your car."

Mac and I went to my SUV and got in. I looked at him and wondered what was on his mind. Just talking to me could get him into a lot of trouble with the brass.

"What do you want to talk about?"

"I called Detective Rushmore in narcotics. He's the guy that arrested Butler. He told me that Butler isn't talking. I suggested that he have you come by and try to talk to Butler."

"Why would Butler talk to me?"

"Because you know more about him and his activities than we do, and you're not a cop."

"That's pretty lame if you ask me, but I would like to talk to him. I think he was the one who killed Emily, or at least made her inhale the cocaine. That means he was there and probably participated in killing her," I said.

"It might shake him up a little if you told him what you think happened in the storage room. If you are right, he could spend some serious time in jail. And if he had anything to do with the death of Jennifer, he could get the needle. It might help you find out who killed her."

I had to think about what he said. There was no doubt in my mind that Butler was a major player in the death of Emily, but did he know anything about the death of Jennifer? I had my doubts. I couldn't see him having enough money to be able to put out a hit on me or anyone else for that matter.

"Okay, but with one condition. I get him alone."

"You know I can't let that happen," Mac said. "As much as I would like to let you have at him, I can't risk it. I'm already sticking my neck out for you."

I knew he was sticking his neck out for me. I wasn't sure what good it would do me to talk to Butler; but if Mac thought it was worth a try, I would talk to Butler. If nothing else, they would be able to get him for dealing drugs.

"Okay. I'll do it. When do I get to question him?"

"Right now. Detective Rushmore is waiting for you. Start the car and let's go."

I started the SUV and drove to the police station where Butler was being held. He was being held at the Second Precinct, Mac worked out of the First Precinct.

WE ARRIVED at the police station where the narcotics division had their offices. We went in the backdoor and up a rear elevator to the third floor. When we got off the elevator, Mac led the way down a hall to an interrogation room. We entered the room together.

Sitting in a chair on the far side of a table was Butler. Detective Rushmore was standing close to the table, while another detective I didn't know was leaning against the wall next to the door.

"Hi, Butler," I said with a slight grin on my face. "We meet again."

"Who the hell are you?" he asked sharply.

"Oh, I'm just a private investigator who knows a lot about you."

"You're not a cop?"

The look on his face showed that he wondered why I was there if I wasn't a cop. He looked rather nervous. This was not something that had ever happened to him before. He was confused by it all.

"No. I'm not a cop. What I am is your ticket to a little room at the state pen with a narrow, hard, flat bed and a very sharp needle."

"What the hell's going on here?" he yelled out as he looked for help from Rushmore and Mac.

"I'll tell you. Let's start with a Wednesday afternoon awhile back. Emily Sutherland was modeling for a figure drawing class at the Denver School for Artists. She was modeling in the nude. You were in that class. When the class was over and the rest of the students had gone, you and Franklin Steuben went into the storage room where Emily was starting to get dressed. Steuben and you were going to force yourselves on her and rape her, but she resisted. She turned out to be a lot stronger than you expected. These farm girls get pretty strong working on a farm.

"You gave her a little cocaine to calm her down. It didn't work very well, so Steuben started to strangle her in order to keep her quiet. Steuben was about to panic when he realized that she was dead. He thought he had killed her, but it was the cocaine that had done it. You came up with a plan to hide the body until you could figure out how to dispose of it. The two of you took Emily into the basement and put her in the old refrigerator that was being stored there. I'm not sure how you knew that it worked, but you did. By the way that makes it premeditated."

"You don't know what you're talking about," Butler said, but without much conviction in his voice.

"As I was saying. The two of you were having a hard time figuring out how to dispose of the body that you had in the basement, but you were pretty sure no one would find her there. That gave you time to figure out how to get rid of her.

"About a week later there was the wind and rain storm that dumped a lot of leaves and twigs on the grassy area along side the school building. You noticed the day after the storm that the groundskeeper had raked up the leaves, put them in large plastic lawn bags and stacked the lawn bags near the window to the basement. That's when you got the idea to put Emily in one of the lawn bags and dump her at Washington Park. By the way, whose idea was it to dump her there?"

"I don't know what you're talking about," Butler said, but his voice showed I had him worried.

"It doesn't really matter. I almost ruined your plans when I came around the corner and almost caught Steuben. I saw him run to the car that you were driving. When you took off, you weren't used to handling a car like his mother's Lexus and slammed into the curb damaging those fancy chrome rims."

"I didn't - - ah - - you're full of it."

"Am I? I found the damaged rims in the garage at Mrs. Dunberger's home. They're along the wall in the part of the garage where Steuben parks his fancy red Porsche 911.

"After you damaged the rims, you put the stock tires and wheels back on the Lexus so it would be harder to identify. You probably had to take it some place to have the front end of the car realigned. I'm sure the police will be checking that out. There will be a record of it somewhere."

I knew that a lot of what I had to say was guessing. I also noticed that Butler was looking a little green around the gills, so to speak. He was beginning to accept the fact that he had been caught, but wasn't quite ready to give it up.

"You can't prove any of it," he said, but didn't look like he was as convinced as he sounded.

"With all the charges against you, I would think that you would want to cooperate in the hope of getting a lighter sentence. Right now, it looks pretty good for the needle.

"Oh, and as far as proving it. Once the forensic team starts doing its thing in the storage room and basement of the school, they will have you cold," I said with a bit of emphasis on the word 'cold'."

"I've got nothing to say."

"Well, that's okay. I'm sure that Steuben with have a lot to say."

"He won't talk."

"Oh. Thank you. You just filled in one of the empty blanks."

"What do you mean?" Butler said.

"I wasn't one hundred percent sure just how much Steuben was involved, but now I am. Are you so sure Steuben will not talk that you are willing risk your life on it? Are you so sure he won't talk to save his own ass? I've talked to him. I'd be willing to wager that he will sing like the proverbial canary as soon as he is questioned."

Butler just looked at me with a blank stare. It was clear that he was trying to figure out how to get out of all this. I was sure that he was beginning to realize there was no way out. Probably the only thing he could do was to talk to keep from getting the needle. There was little doubt that he would be going to jail for life.

"If you have something to say, now is the time to say it." I said.

He looked at me then tipped his head down and looked at his handcuffed hands. His body language indicated that he was pretty sure that it was over.

"Okay. I'll talk."

"Do you give up your right to talk to an attorney and agree to talk to us freely without an attorney present?" Detective Rushmore asked after he turned on the recorder.

"Yes."

"Yes, what?" Rushmore said.

"Yes. I give up my right to an attorney, and I freely agree to talk to you without an attorney present." Butler said, his voice showing that he had given up.

"I have a question for you," I said. "Did you or Steuben hire the hit men that shot me and killed my friend?"

"I had nothing to do with that. You can't pin that on me. That was all Jeff's doing."

"Jeff Slocomb?"

"Yeah."

"Why?"

"Because he was running a drug operation right under his father's nose. He got his drugs out of Detroit. He was afraid that you were getting too close and would cause him problems. He hired the hit men from Detroit to 'dispose of you' as he liked to put it," Butler said. "I was just a street dealer for him. I had nothing else to do with him."

I looked over at Mac, then at Rushmore. I didn't know what to say for several minutes.

"I'm going after Jeff," I said then turned and left the room.

As I started down the hall to the rear elevator, I could hear the sound of street shoes on the hard floor behind me. There was little doubt in my mind that Mac was hot on my heels. He wasn't about to let me go after Jeff alone.

We rode the elevator to the ground floor without saying a word. I didn't run because of my leg, but I walked as fast as I could to my SUV. I was in it and behind the wheel ready to start it when Mac got in. He didn't say a word. He knew where I was going, and he was going to be there to make sure that I didn't do anything stupid. I headed for DeeDee's town house.

I PULLED UP IN FRONT of DeeDee's town house and saw Jeff's car parked out front. I got out of my car and started up the walk. Mac reached out and grabbed my arm. I turned and looked at him.

"Don't do anything stupid. Let the law deal with him," Mac said.

The tone of his voice and the look in his eyes told me that he knew what I was thinking. I wanted Jeff in the worst way. He had taken Jennifer away from me, and I wanted him to pay dearly for what he had done. But it was the way Mac had said 'don't do anything stupid' that made me stop and take a breath. I began to think about what he said. I really didn't want anything to happen that would keep Jeff from facing the punishment he had coming under the law.

"I'm okay, Mac," I said as I took another deep breath.

Mac looked at me for a second, then nodded his head.

"Let's go arrest Jeff," he said as if it was just another day at the office.

We walked side by side to the front door of DeeDee's town house. When we were standing in front of the door, I looked at Mac to see if he was ready. I noticed that he had drawn his gun and held it at his side. He nodded that he was ready.

I drew my gun and held it at my side where it would not be seen, but was ready for anything. I then reached up and knocked on the door. It seemed to take forever for someone to open the door. I knocked again, but just seconds before the door opened. Gathering my best manners, I smiled politely.

"Hi, DeeDee. Does Jeff happen to be here? I've got a question I would like to ask him."

"Sure," she replied with a smile then turned around. "Jeff, Mr. Blackstone is here. He would like to talk to you."

DeeDee stepped aside. I could see Jeff coming toward the door. When he saw Mac, he stopped, then quickly turned and ran. It was obvious that he was going for the back door.

Mac took out after him toward the back of the house. While Mac chased him out the back, I turned, went out the front to the corner of the house. Jeff made the mistake of running around the house in an attempt to get to his car. He must have hoped that both of us would chase him through the house. With my leg still not completely back to normal, running was still a little hard for me.

As he came running around the corner, he saw me. He looked like he was going to try to run over me, that was until I lifted my gun up and pointed it right at him. At that point, he came to an abrupt stop and put his hands up. I could see that he was afraid that I would shoot him.

I walked up to him, still holding my gun so it was pointed right at his face. I wanted so much to pull the trigger. Instead, I threw a punch with my left hand that hit him on the chin. I hit him so hard that his head suddenly twisted around and he went to the ground with a thud.

Mac came around the corner just as I hit Jeff. He walked up to Jeff and looked down at him. He was out cold.

"It looks like he was trying to resist arrest to me," he said as he looked up at me and smiled.

"Yeah. I never thought that hitting someone could feel so good."

Mac smiled at me then knelt down and turned Jeff over. He put handcuffs on him then stood up.

"I'll call for a patrol car to take him in," Mac said as he looked at me. "Are you all right?"

"I am now."

"I guess all that's left for us is to pick up Steuben. I'll call Rushmore and have him come and get me. Then we'll get some backup and go arrest Steuben. You want to come along?" Mac asked.

"No. I think I'll go home. I'll talk to you later. My leg is beginning to bother me a little."

"Okay. You take care of that leg. You might want to take care of those bruised knuckles, too," Mac said with a smile.

"Oh, I'll need you to sign a report on what happened here," Mac added. "Stop in sometime tomorrow. I'll have it all typed up and ready for you."

"Sure. You want me to wait until the patrol car gets here?"

"No. He's not going anywhere," Mac said as he looked down at Jeff lying on the ground.

I nodded, then walked over to my SUV. As I got in, I saw DeeDee standing in the door watching me. She smiled, then turned and shut the door. I wondered what was going through her mind. I knew her type. She would have a new man to keep her company by this time tomorrow.

I drove to my apartment. I didn't see anyone following me. After I parked the SUV in the garage, I went into my apartment. My leg was very sore and I was tired. I took a warm shower which helped relieve some of the discomfort in my leg.

After my shower, I fixed myself something to eat. After I finished eating, I turned in for the night. My mind was clear for the first time in a long time. I was ready for a little rest. It didn't take me long to fall asleep.

CHAPTER EIGHTEEN

I WOKE THE NEXT MORNING feeling a lot better. The pressure of looking for who had murdered Emily and Jennifer was no longer occupying my mind. I felt that I could start the day as if it was a fresh new beginning.

After my usual morning shower, I went to the kitchen. I stood there looking around. For the first time in ages I believed things were going to be different, even if it was just for a day. I turned around and left the kitchen. I grabbed my keys and walked out of my apartment. I headed for the garage.

Just as I was about ready to open the garage door, a clean and shiny dark blue Tahoe came around the corner into the parking lot. It stopped right next to my garage and the driver got out. It was Les. He was returning the original Tahoe I had rented.

"Here you go. Good as new. The rental company will never know that you wrinkled it, and neither will the police."

"Thanks, Les. Send me a bill."

"You can count on it," he said with a smile. "I'll take the other one back for you."

"Thanks."

Les opened the garage door and drove the other Tahoe out. I watched him as he drove away. I had to smile. We had gone to all the trouble of switching SUVs, and I never even got asked if my Tahoe had been in an accident.

I got in the Tahoe and headed out to a restaurant that I had been to a good number of times over the years. I ordered ham and eggs for breakfast with a side of blueberry pancakes. It was not a meal I ate very often, but this morning I wanted something different. Maybe it was because I felt different.

When I finished breakfast, I drove to the police station where Mac had his office. I arrived about ten in the morning. Mac was ready and waiting for me.

"Good to see you," Mac said when I entered his office. "How are you feeling?

"Better. Did you get Steuben?"

"Yeah. We got Steuben."

"Did you have any trouble with Mrs. Dunberger?"

"We had no trouble with her at all. She turned him over to us the minute we asked for him. She said that she was not going to cover for him on a murder charge."

"What about you? Did they put you back on active duty?"

"Yeah. I got a call from the commissioner. He told me to arrest every one involved and press all charges."

"I take it you're questioning Steuben."

"Yeah, and he is talking. We can't shut him up. Butler is talking, too. The way it turned out, is Steuben strangled Emily after Butler gave her the cocaine, just like you suspected. Jeff had hired the hit men that killed Jennifer, just like Butler said. Even the hit men are talking their heads off. Thanks to you we got them all. We even got Albertson for selling drugs for Butler as a bonus."

"Great. I feel much better," I said. "By the way, you said you would have a statement about what happened with the arrest of Jeff last night for me to sign."

"Right. I have it right here. All you have to do is read it and sign it."

I took the paper and read it. It was pretty much what happened except for my hitting Jeff. It had been written so it looked like he was injured when he fell while resisting arrest.

"Looks pretty good to me," I said as I picked up a pen and signed the statement.

"Well, I guess that's it. You are free to go. What are you going to do now?"

"I'm going to make a call and see if a certain lady will go to dinner with me tonight."

"It sounds like a good idea," Mac said with a smile. "I'll talk to you later."

I nodded then left Mac's office. I left the police station feeling a little better knowing that this case was finally over, at least for me. I drove back to my office.

WHEN I ARRIVED AT MY OFFICE, I found Ralph Slocomb standing outside my office waiting for me. He had one of his enforcers with him. I reached inside my coat and put my hand on my gun since I had no idea why he was there.

"You want something, Ralph?"

"I want to talk to you."

"Thought I told you to leave the ape at home."

Ralph looked at his enforcer, then looked at me. He then turned to his enforcer.

"Go wait in the car. I won't be very long."

As soon as the enforcer turned and left, I unlocked the door and went inside. Ralph followed me into my office. I walked around behind my desk and sat down.

"What is it you want, Ralph?"

"I just want to know something. Did my son have anything to do with Emily's murder?"

"No. He did not. However, he was responsible for the death of Jennifer Taylor. For that he will have to pay."

"I understand. I want you to know that I didn't have anything to do with either of them."

"I know you didn't."

"Do I owe you anything?"

"I don't know. I will figure it out and send you a bill if there's a balance."

"That'll work. I am sorry about your friend."

"Thanks," I said as he stood up.

Ralph didn't say anything more. He simply nodded, turned and left my office.

As I watched him leave, I wondered what he was going through. It had to be hard to see your only son facing the rest of his life in jail.

I leaned back and took a deep breath. After taking a minute to relax, I reached out and picked up the phone. I called George at his home. He answered the phone almost immediately. I gave him a brief run down on what had happened and that we were all done. It was all in the hands of the police and the District Attorney now.

"We got 'um?" he asked.

"We got 'um," I replied. "George, is Julie working today?"

"No, I don't think so. She might be home. Are you going to give her a call?"

"I thought I would."

"She'd like that. I'll talk to you later," he said then hung up.

I smiled to myself then placed a call to Julie.